WEST OF NOWHERE

KG MacGregor

Lambda Literary Award Winner

Bella
BOOKS

2013

Bella Books, Inc.
P.O. Box 10543
Tallahassee, FL 32302

Printed in the United States of America on acid-free paper
First published 2013

Editor: Katherine V. Forrest
Cover Designer: Kiaro Creative

ISBN 13: 978-1-59493-345-5

Acknowledgment

For those who've been asking: no, the books don't get easier to write. This page in particular always proves a challenge because the people who have a hand in making my work the best it can be deserve special recognition, and it grows harder and harder to come up with words of gratitude that don't sound rote. Their jobs don't get easier either. I still forget the visuals, stilt the dialogue and flat-line the tension when I'm supposed to be building to a climax. I also drop, add, confuse, misspell and repeat words. It is my great fortune to be surrounded by people who know better and save me from myself. Heartfelt thanks to my editor Katherine V. Forrest, my partner Jenny, my friend Karen Appleby, and all the professionals at Bella Books.

Thanks also to Commander Chris May, US Navy, Retired, for sharing her expertise on some of the technical aspects of Navy careers and advancement. And thank you also for your service. Though I was raised in a US Marine Corps household, I discovered in my research for this book a fascination for the navy. If I were thirty years younger…okay, forty.

Please know that, despite all the assistance I receive in my writing and research, the editorial decisions are mine alone, along with each and every error you might find.

About the Author

A former teacher and market research consultant, KG MacGregor holds a PhD in journalism from UNC-Chapel Hill. Infatuation with *Xena: Warrior Princess* fan fiction prompted her to try her own hand at storytelling in 2002. In 2005, she signed with Bella Books, which published the Golden Crown finalist *Just This Once*. Her sixth Bella novel, *Out of Love*, won the Lambda Literary Award for Women's Romance and the Golden Crown Award in Lesbian Romance. She picked up Goldies also for *Without Warning, Worth Every Step* and *Photographs of Claudia* (Contemporary Romance), and *Secrets So Deep* (Romantic Suspense).

Other honors include the Lifetime Achievement Award from the Royal Academy of Bards, the Alice B. Readers Appreciation Medal, and several Readers Choice Awards.

An avid supporter of queer literature, KG currently serves on the Board of Trustees for the Lambda Literary Foundation. She divides her time between Palm Springs and her native North Carolina mountains.

Contact KG through her website at *www.kgmacgregor.com*.

CHAPTER ONE

Amber Halliday scooted her chair back from the long, boisterous table as the harried waitress cleared their breakfast dishes. Holding her cell phone high above her head, she twisted back and forth. "This is so weird. I can't get a signal at all. Is anybody else having trouble?"

She'd noticed the No Service message last night but didn't have time to worry about it, since all anyone had cared about for the past three days was packing up and loading the bus for their five a.m. departure this morning. Gus Holley and his band were kicking off a thirty-four-city tour in the US and Canada, and for the first time ever, she was going along to help sell merchandise. Most of the band had slept the first three hours from Nashville to Louisville, but they were gearing up now to make some music tonight at the Ohio State Fair in Columbus.

Her boyfriend of the past three years, Corey Dobbins, played bass for Gus, and had used his influence to have her join the tour. He even talked Gus into letting her bring along

Skippy, her one-year-old Chihuahua-spaniel mix, so she wouldn't have to turn him in to the animal shelter. Since the tour was scheduled to last five months, they'd whittled down their possessions and given up their apartment lease, hoping to find a nicer place when they returned to Nashville.

Amber and Corey were part of the second bus, mostly musicians and instrument techs. The other roadies—the stage, sound and lighting crew—traveled a day ahead and were already setting up at the fair.

"Don't worry about your phone," Corey said. "Mine's working. Who would you call anyway? Practically everybody you know is right here at this table."

"That's not true. I text with Harmony all the time," she answered, looking over at the band's drummer, Wayne. His wife ran the daycare where Amber had worked off and on for the past couple of years.

Wayne turned his phone toward her. "I just got a text from her a few minutes ago. She's bitching about some woman that always drops her kid off with a loaded diaper."

"I know exactly who she's talking about. I told her to save it and put it back on him just before his mother came to pick him up, but Harmony's like 'I can't do that,' and I'm like, 'Well, you're going to get a shitty diaper every day.' You can't let people get away with that kind of shit."

Corey snorted. "Pun intended. Hey, Amber, aren't we pretty close to where you grew up?"

Amber made a face and shuddered. She'd seen the sign for Shelbyville when they pulled off the interstate to the truck stop. "I guess that explains why the hair's standing up on the back of my neck. Gives me the creeps just to think about it."

Several of the guys in their party suddenly stood, dropped a few dollars on the table for the waitress and made their way back out to the bus, but Corey held out his coffee cup for a refill, in no apparent hurry. "Don't you ever wonder what your folks are up to these days? I get that you had it rough growing up but you don't even know if they're still alive."

"I know all I want to know."

He handed her his phone. "Seriously, you ought to call since you're so close."

She batted his hand away.

"You're too stubborn for your own good sometimes, Amber."

"What, you think I should just run over there all smiles with Skippy and say it's all okay now? I'm sure Mama would just break down and cry, and Daddy would fall all over himself to say how sorry he was."

"How do you know what they'll do if you never give them a chance? You haven't even called home a single time since you left. Not once, Amber. They could be worried sick for all you know."

"Trust me, they aren't."

Corey sighed and pulled his wallet from his hip pocket, drawing a five-dollar bill out for the waitress. He then handed Amber five twenties. "Here, take some of this money. It's not a good idea for me to carry all of it in one place."

Her boyfriend had a lot of faults—drinking to excess and a wandering eye chief among them—but he was generous, paying all the rent and household bills, and even giving her a little spending money whenever she was out of work. His propensity to sleep with other women from time to time was something she'd learned to accept, because he always came home to her. Theirs wasn't the greatest love story of all time—it was probably more habit than love for both of them—but it was dependable.

Through the restaurant's broad window she saw Wayne tipping his head toward the bus to signal it was time to head out.

"Looks like everybody's ready to go," she said.

Corey held his cup as if warming his hands. "I'm going to finish this last cup of coffee. You should go to the bathroom here before we get back on the road because we probably won't stop between here and Columbus. I'll meet you back on the bus."

A full-sized ladies' room was definitely preferable to the tiny compartment that passed as a lavatory on the bus, especially since she couldn't put her makeup on while the bus was jiggling down the road.

Amber leaned over the sink to the mirror, careful not to soak up the water she had splashed all over the counter when washing her hands. With a stiff brush, she untangled the wiry blond curls that cascaded almost to her shoulders and pulled them tight into a bushy ponytail. Her practiced hand then methodically lined her eyes with a slate-gray pencil, giving life to her face for the first time since she'd rolled out of bed at four a.m. Blue eye shadow, creamy blush and red lipstick finished the look and she stepped back to take in her overall appearance.

Her denim miniskirt, stretched out from three days since its last laundering, sagged from her hips. A pair of ribbed tank tops—one red, one black—hugged her slender frame snugly, not quite hiding the outline of her breasts and stiff nipples. Corey teased her about having a chest like a teenage boy, but she always thought a B-cup was plenty. She appreciated the trade-off of not usually having to wear a bra.

Corey made no secret of his preference for voluptuous women. Three or four times a month he slept with Rachelle, who was closer to his age at thirty-two and full-figured. Amber had never really been jealous, but she was relieved when Corey had chosen her and not Rachelle to join the tour.

A woman entered the restroom and, before going into the stall, stopped to pick up several stray paper towels off the floor and stuff them into the wastebasket. By her dress—dark green cargo shorts, a bright yellow T-shirt and sturdy hiking shoes—she wasn't a truck stop employee straightening up, just a neat freak.

Feeling guilty over the fact that a couple of those errant towels had been hers, Amber took a moment to wipe the excess water off the counter and carefully dispose of the waste. Then she stashed her makeup in her purse and fished out a pack of Marlboro Lights, knowing she'd have time for only a couple of quick puffs before getting back on the bus. It was a nasty habit, one she could barely afford even when she was working, but she'd found it impossible to quit when surrounded by so many others in the band who smoked.

When she exited the ladies' room, the first thing she noticed was a busboy separating the tables they had pushed together. Corey was already gone and the bus had moved to the front of the restaurant, which meant her cigarette would have to wait because these guys were obviously itching to get back on the road. As she stepped outside, the bus pulled into traffic and made an immediate right turn down the interstate ramp.

"Oh, very funny!" she yelled. All the guys were probably howling over the sight of her standing in the parking lot. Their trip down to the next exit to turnaround would probably take ten minutes or more, and they'd all have another laugh at her expense when they came back to pick her up.

The August sun was already beating down on the asphalt and Amber turned to look for a shady place to wait. That's when she spotted Skippy sitting patiently at the corner of the building, his leash tied to her suitcase.

* * *

"Here you go, sweetie. Two eggs over light, hash browns and sausage patties. There's jelly on the table for your biscuits, and I'll hit your coffee cup on my next trip."

"Thank you, ma'am," Joy Shepard answered graciously, despite having ordered her eggs scrambled with bacon. That party of fourteen had run the poor waitress ragged, and Joy considered herself lucky she was served at all. Fortunately, she wasn't picky.

Apparently, the crowd at the long table was part of Gus Holley's band—at least that's what she'd gathered from the tour bus outside and the excited voices of those around her. Joy had never been much of a country music fan but she knew someone who was, and had sent a couple of photos of the bus via her smart phone. She wasn't surprised when it chimed with a request for the video chat application she and her nine-year-old goddaughter used.

"That's Gus Holley!" Madison exclaimed. "Where are you?"

"I'm in Louisville, Kentucky," she answered, keeping her voice low so she wouldn't bother those around her. "I don't think Gus Holley was here. The waitress told me it was just his backup band."

After dropping Madison at her home in Newport News, Virginia, only a day earlier, Joy was already missing her like crazy. She stood her phone up next to the napkin holder so she could keep eating, and noticed Madison was calling from a kitchen that wasn't her own.

"Where are you so early in the morning? I thought you'd sleep late on the last day before school starts."

"Syd dropped me off at Tara's. We're supposed to go to the pool." She made a face at the mention of the six-year-old who lived a couple of blocks down the street. "She wouldn't let me stay at home by myself. You would have, wouldn't you?"

"I doubt it, kiddo. I think I'd rather you be with a sitter for a few more years." Madison was growing up way too fast as it was. It hardly seemed nine years since Joy had held her good friend Carrie Larson's hand in the delivery room as she gave birth to this beautiful child. When Carrie died two years later from a reaction to anesthesia during hernia surgery, the hospital forms she'd joked about having to sign kicked in, granting Joy and her partner Sydney Koehler the right and responsibility to raise Madison.

It hadn't worked out that way. Joy had been deployed at sea for much of the next four years, coming home to Norfolk to find Syd not just seeing someone else, but already married to him. While it hadn't come as a total shock—Syd had long struggled with her sexuality and the challenges they faced as a lesbian couple—it certainly upended life as they knew it. Since the State of Virginia didn't recognize parental rights for two women, Joy had bent over backward ever since to maintain a cordial relationship in order to keep her place in Madison's life. That got a lot harder when Joy returned to Oakland, California, to help care for her mother in the last stages of COPD after a lifetime of work in a textile plant.

"I wish I was still with you, Joy. I'm going to ask Syd if she'll let me come for the whole summer next year."

It was curious that Syd had never insisted on Madison calling her Mom, not even after the formal adoption. Had it been Joy, it would have been music to her ears.

"Fine by me if you want to come back for that long, but you'll probably be stuck at home with Grandpa Shep while I'm at work. Sure you wouldn't rather be playing at the pool with Tara?" Actually, she could have enrolled Madison in a summer camp for outdoor activities and crafts if Syd had given her more notice that she was sending Madison for a whole month. Calling at the last minute left Joy scrambling to extend her vacation time so they could take a cross-country trip back to Newport News in the truck camper.

The waitress refilled Joy's coffee cup and smiled over her shoulder at the picture of Madison on the small screen. The child's long hair was kinky brown with gold streaks, as though every other strand had come from each of her parents, her fair-skinned mom from Georgia and her African-American father. Creamy brown skin set off her wide blue eyes, causing everyone to look twice at her extraordinary beauty.

"Syd has a new boyfriend...Mitch Hildebrand. She likes that he's a lieutenant, so I guess that means he's supposed to be better than Johnny."

"Have you met him?"

"Yeah, he stays with us now. All of his stuff is here."

That probably explained Syd's sudden change of heart about giving Madison up for four whole weeks instead of two. At least Johnny was out of the picture for good. That marriage had lasted only sixteen months, and he'd made no effort to adopt Madison.

"Do you like him? Is he nice?"

"He's okay. I just wish Syd had gotten a girlfriend instead of a boyfriend."

"What difference does that make?"

"Just that she gets all helpless and goofy whenever she's around guys. You never do stuff like that."

Joy had to laugh at that. For a kid, Madison had an amazing understanding of what it meant to be gay or lesbian, but the concept of butch and femme was probably too much for her to grasp. "That doesn't have anything to do with her having a boyfriend or girlfriend. She just likes to be a certain way and I like to be another way. That's what makes us all so interesting. You wouldn't want everyone to be the same, would you?"

"I guess not, but I still wish Syd would get a girlfriend...and I wish it was you."

As much as it hurt to hear Madison's wish, Joy knew deep down what it really meant was she wanted the two people she loved most to be with her all the time. She and Syd went to great lengths never to say anything negative about the other, but there wasn't even a spark of love left between them.

"I don't think that's going to happen, kiddo. But you're lucky because you always have two homes where people love you like crazy." She peeked at her check and dug a couple of ones out of her wallet for a tip. "I need to hit the road so I can get home to Grandpa Shep. Did you call him last night like I said?"

"Yeah. He was grouchy, but he wanted me to come back and push him around till his shoulder got well."

"I bet he did. The nurses are probably ready to toss him out on the street."

Her father, wheelchair-bound after losing both legs in an accident over twenty years ago, had suffered a fall from his chair the day after she and Madison left Oakland on their way back to Virginia. With his arm out of commission following surgery to pin his shoulder, he had no way to get around on his own.

"Will you be home tonight? I'll call you from Kansas."

"Yeah, but it's a school night and I have to go to bed at eight thirty."

"I pick up an hour going west so I'll be sure to stop at a rest area before it gets too late. Love you."

"I love you too, Joy."

She blinked back tears as she walked to the cash register. Madison's West Coast visit had been bliss, especially the last ten days, when they had driven across the country together, through the Grand Canyon, Monument Valley and Rocky Mountain National Park. The only thing that had dampened their trip was the knowledge it would end with dropping Madison off in Virginia, followed for Joy by a long, lonely ride home.

"Thank you, ma'am," Joy said as she collected her change. Breakfast was a lot more fun at a picnic table with Madison, but it was nice once in a while to let someone else do the cooking and cleaning. However, the luxury of a restaurant breakfast had put her an hour behind schedule, which meant a long day of driving to Abilene, where she planned to camp for the night.

The young woman she'd seen in the bathroom—from the Gus Holley group—was standing at the corner of the building, a suitcase and small dog at her side. Her eyes were trained on the overpass nearby as though she were expecting someone. Apparently, she wasn't part of the band after all, just a woman who'd hitched a ride to Louisville.

Joy had sent a text to her father asking him to call when he got up, and her phone rang as she was getting into her truck.

Before she could even say hello, his gravelly voice barked, "How soon can you get here and bust me out of this hellhole?"

"Who wants to know? You or the nurses?"

"These jokers won't let me do jack…they say I can't get out of bed without the therapist here, but when he comes in, he makes me do everything in bed. I have to piss in a plastic jug, for Christ's sake, and you don't even want to know how they make me do the other. The food is pure crap. I ate better on Big John." That said a lot, because her pop had complained as long as she could remember about the awful chow on the USS *John F Kennedy*.

"I'm in Louisville right now, Pop. Looks like I'll get in on Saturday, but that doesn't leave a lot of time to figure out how we're going to do this, because I have to be at work first thing Monday morning."

"Just get me out of here. I'll figure it out from there."

Sometimes her father was too independent for his own good. From the day he arrived home from the VA hospital in a wheelchair, he'd been determined to have a life without limits, and without people fussing over him. Only rarely did he find himself at the mercy of others, and when he did, he bucked like a wild mustang with its first rider.

"If I know you, you'll try to pull yourself around with a bad shoulder and you'll make it worse." Although there was considerable risk to the staff at the rehab center if he stayed there much longer. "I looked at a few of those home health care services online last night. I'll see if I can line up somebody, but you'll have to stay where you are till I get it all set up. And whoever I get, you can't be a jerk and run them off the first day."

"If it gets me out of this place, I promise to kiss their rosy red butt."

Her father's accident would no doubt make all of them miserable for weeks. From what his doctor had said, he'd need a full-time companion to help him around the house, plus twice-weekly visits from a physical therapist. Joy could handle all the duties during the evenings but she'd need to hire someone to cover the hours she was at work. Whatever poor creature took the job would have to put up with her father's aggravation over his loss of independence, and couldn't possibly do anything to please him.

"Has anyone been to see you? The guys from the Legion?"

"They got their own problems. Barbara comes every day, though. I probably would have killed somebody by now if she hadn't been here."

Joy chuckled at the mention of Barbara Rodgers, a longtime family friend who lived across the street. The loss of her husband Hank in an engine room explosion on the USS *Midway* had brought her close to all the Shepards, especially after the accident that disabled Joy's father. She was practically family and Joy even wondered if romance might blossom one day between Barbara and her pop now that her mother was gone. It was weird to think about him being with someone else, yet comforting that he might find happiness again.

"I'll make some calls tonight and see what I can do. Try not to drive everyone there to drink."

Joy reluctantly acknowledged she'd be tied to the house every night until her father was back to his old self. Though he'd insisted he could manage on his own, she knew that was his pride talking. He'd said the same thing when her mother got sick three years ago, but he was visibly relieved when Joy left the navy to return to Oakland to help him manage her declining health.

A silver lining—if there was such a thing—was that getting her father rehabbed might make the time pass more quickly until Madison's return for the Christmas holidays.

She turned the ignition and waited to be sure all her gauges were working correctly, a habit from her navy days, when she tested and calibrated her communications equipment before each use. On the busy deck of an aircraft carrier, there was no margin for error.

As she eased from her parking space, she was startled by the sudden appearance of the young woman with the dog waving her down.

CHAPTER TWO

"Are you okay?"

A closer look revealed the young woman had been crying. "I lost my ride. I was wondering…could I maybe use your phone to make a quick call? I promise I won't use a bunch of your minutes."

Joy was smart enough to be cautious about scams, but she also knew distress when she saw it. This woman—barely more than a girl, actually—was in trouble and was taking a risk of her own by reaching out to a stranger. Turning her down meant leaving her at the mercy of someone who might take advantage of her. She passed her phone through the window. "Whatever you need."

Before she dialed, the woman lit a cigarette, its smoke wafting through the open window. Too late, Joy realized the phone had connected automatically to the wireless device in her truck, which meant she could hear every word.

"Corey, what are you doing?"

"Go home to Shelbyville, Amber. You're only fifteen miles away. You just aren't going to make it on your own."

"I told you I didn't ever want to see them again. You always said you understood that. It gives me nightmares just to think about it. Come on back and pick me up."

"Can't do it." He sighed heavily. "It's over for us. It's not anything you did…it's just not working out anymore. I thought this would be a nice clean break."

Amber, clearly flustered, slapped her hand against the side of the camper. "Look, Corey. If this is about you and me, fine. I'll get my own place to live when we get back to Nashville, but you guys still need me to sell merchandise. I'll sleep on the bus."

"Gus already has a vendor to handle the merchandise. It's the same company he uses all the time."

"Are you telling me this whole thing was a setup?" Her voice was quivering and her cheeks red. "You couldn't just break up with me like a normal person? No, you had to haul me all the way out here and dump me on the side of the road?"

"You're not on the side of the road. Just call your folks. They're fifteen minutes away. Your mom's waiting to hear from you."

"You called her?"

"Amber, I'm not a bad guy. I wasn't going to just kick you out and make you sleep in the bus station. I wanted to be sure you—"

The line went dead.

In her side-view mirror, Joy could see Amber leaning against the camper, her arms at her sides and her face skyward with her eyes closed. She knew that feeling, the blunt realization that the faith you had in someone was poorly placed. Though eager to get back on the road, she could spare a few minutes for this girl to get her senses back and decide what she needed to do.

She was too thin, Joy thought, and wore too much color in her eye makeup, blush and lipstick. Her right shoulder blade sported a tattoo of what looked like a bass guitar.

"One more call?"

"Of course." There was no way she could avoid listening without letting on that she'd heard the entirety of the first call.

"Harmony…it's me, Amber. Look, it didn't work out for me going on the tour and I need to get back to Nashville. Is there any way I can get my job back at the daycare?"

The woman on the other end groaned. "Listen, girl. I can't take you back. Wayne says Corey wants a clean break, you know?"

"Corey doesn't have anything to do with any of this. I'm not even going to see him anymore. I just need a job…and a place to stay for a couple of weeks until I can get settled somewhere else."

"I can't do it, Amber. I wish I could, but Wayne and Corey… they're the band. You know how it is. Everything's always about what's best for the band. Sorry, kid."

Amber cut off the call and slumped again against the camper for a few seconds. As if suddenly remembering she wasn't alone, she straightened up and returned to the driver's window with the phone. "Thanks."

Joy watched as she flicked her cigarette butt to the ground and walked back to the building where her tiny dog began dancing with excitement. She drew the pup into her lap as she sat forlornly on her suitcase. If those calls were any indication, the poor girl had no choice but to call her family, who happened to live nearby. At least Corey—whoever he was—had made it seem like it would be okay.

She started to pull out and realized Amber was sobbing. Dropping her off somewhere would probably eat up an hour of her day, but Joy knew she'd never sleep tonight if she went to bed worrying about how this turned out.

"You need a lift somewhere?"

The girl shook her head. "I don't know where I'd go."

With the engine still running, Joy walked around and opened the passenger door. "Hop in. We'll figure it out."

Amber hesitated for a few seconds but stood, which enabled Joy to grab her suitcase and toss it in the crew cab behind the front seat. "Which way are you going?"

"I'm headed west on I-64, but I can drop you off wherever you need to go. I'm sure there's a bus station around here, and if you need some help with a ticket, I can spare a few bucks." Joy climbed in on her side and buckled her seat belt, signaling to Amber to do the same.

"Are you going anywhere near a place called Limon, Colorado?"

"Colorado?"

"I have a friend there. I can stay with her while I look for a job."

She hadn't figured her friendly gesture would result in a rider for the next two days. "Did I hear you say you had family near here?"

"I'm not going back there…not ever. I've got some money to help pay for gas. If it's too much trouble, I'm sure I'll find somebody else going that way." She started to unbuckle her belt.

"No…no, that's okay." A girl as desperate as this one would probably get into a car with anyone, and it might not be safe. "I'll be passing through Limon sometime tomorrow afternoon. You're welcome to ride."

The relief on Amber's face was unmistakable. "I'm Amber… Amber Halliday."

"Joy Shepard. Who's your friend?" The black and tan pup, about half the size of a typical cat, cowered in Amber's lap, terrified either of Joy or the truck.

"Skippy. He's part Chihuahua. I got him last year at the shelter in Nashville."

She reached out to give him a pet, prompting a low growl that made her pull her hand back in a hurry. It was going to be a long day.

* * *

"…I'm a ground crew chief at the airport in Oakland. You know, one of those people in the orange vests who guides the planes into the gate and makes sure they get serviced."

Amber nodded along, though she had no idea what Joy was talking about. She'd never been on a plane in her life. "And you're what, on vacation?"

"Yeah, sort of. My goddaughter Madison—she's nine—she flew out to California a few weeks ago to visit my pop and me. I took her back to her home near Norfolk and we had a nice camping trip along the way...went to Yosemite and the Grand Canyon, then through the Rockies."

"Norfolk...that's in North Carolina, right?"

"Virginia."

Amber had never been much for geography. Like most other subjects in high school, she couldn't imagine why she'd ever need it. All those lessons about map reading were unnecessary when you had a GPS on your phone telling you everywhere to turn.

Just about everyone she knew in Nashville drove a pickup truck, but none were as nice as this one, with its camper shell attached. It had tan leather seats with wood trim on the dashboard, a wide-screen navigation system, CD player and satellite radio, and touch controls for everything on the steering wheel.

"Nice truck...lots of fancy stuff."

"Thanks. Technically, it belongs to my pop, but he never drives it anymore. He bought it about four years ago when my mom got sick so they could take a few trips together. She died not long after that and...well, he and I get along just fine most of the time, but not well enough to spend time together in a pillbox like this."

California women were nothing like the ones Amber knew in Tennessee and Kentucky. In the first place, she didn't know a single one who would just pick up and drive all the way across the country by herself. Practically all her friends had boyfriends or husbands, and it was the guys who went off and did crap like that.

In the second place, she looked strong and physically fit, with muscles in her arms and legs. Her appearance was meticulous, like she'd gone out of her way to make every single detail perfect. Her bright yellow T-shirt, with a pocket logo that read Big Stick, was tucked into her shorts. Both had obviously been ironed.

Ironed! Who ironed shorts and T-shirts?

Joy's obsession with neatness extended well beyond picking up paper towels in the restroom. There wasn't a speck of dust on the dashboard or even a smudge on the windshield.

"What sort of work do you do, Amber?"

Amber sighed, wishing she could have another cigarette. "A little of this, a little of that. My last job was at a daycare. Before that I worked at the Friendly Mart...that's a convenience store in Nashville, but don't be fooled by the name. The owner's an asshole. I've flipped hamburgers, made tacos, sold vitamins over the phone...sat with old people. I would have liked doing the merchandising for Gus Holley, but that was all one big joke on me."

"That's a lousy way to treat somebody. I'm sorry they did that to you."

"You know what they say...lay down with dogs and get fleas." She was accustomed to disappointment. All those jobs she'd mentioned had ended with her being fired or quitting because she couldn't work under ridiculous conditions with bosses who yelled at her all the time for no reason. She would have done great work for Gus if only he'd given her a chance.

"So you know Gus Holley? My goddaughter tells me he's a pretty big name in country music."

"Yeah, he's a nice guy...a lot better than those jerkoffs in his band. I bet he'll be pissed when he hears what Corey did to me."

She was tired of thinking about Corey and turned her thoughts to Molly, one of the first friends she'd made in Nashville after splitting up with Archie, her boyfriend from high school. She and Molly had shared an apartment with two other girls for about a year, during which Amber discovered she liked sleeping with women a lot more than with men. Though they'd kept it casual—not to mention secret—she'd been disappointed when Molly left suddenly to take a desk clerk job at her cousin's motel in Limon. She'd even toyed with moving out there when

Molly said there was a job cleaning rooms, but by that time she'd started seeing Corey and it just seemed easier to stay put.

They passed a sign for a rest area and Amber decided she could wait no longer for a cigarette. "Can we stop here?"

She went first to the restroom and then used the time walking Skippy to smoke. From the hillside above the parking lot, she watched as Joy took a cloth and cleaned both the windshield and headlights before wiping down the truck's grill. She'd never seen someone so finicky about a stupid pickup truck.

Joy met her at the passenger door with a plastic bag. "Here, I thought you might need this to clean up after Skippy."

Amber stuffed it in her pocket. "He didn't do anything this time." Actually he had, but she had no intention of marching back up the hill to pick up dog shit. Just because Joy was obsessive-compulsive didn't mean she had to be. A few germs here and there were supposed to be good for you, helping ward off colds or the flu.

When they got back on the road, Amber passed the next hour pretending to sleep, still mired in thoughts of how she'd been duped by Corey and the band. In hindsight, there were lots of clues and she'd foolishly missed them all. Corey had moved his belongings into storage while encouraging her to sell everything she didn't absolutely need. When she'd almost backed out of the tour because she didn't want to give up Skippy, he'd come back with the great news that Gus said she could bring him along. Then her phone stopped working all of a sudden—because Corey had canceled her service—and he'd even given her a little spending money as a kiss-off.

What really hurt was realizing all her supposed friends had been in on it. Everyone had followed his cue and gotten up to go to the bus when he first mentioned calling her folks. Even Harmony knew about it and was ready when she called to let her down. It was bad enough to be betrayed by a bastard like Corey, but everybody!

On the far side of St. Louis they stopped at another rest area, where Joy went into the camper to make lunch. She'd grown quiet too, probably wondering what she'd gotten herself into by picking up a stray on the side of the road, one who sulked like a brat.

"You need any help in there, Joy?"

"I can handle it. You like mustard?"

"Sure." She didn't care what she ate—or even if she ate—but she needed to straighten up and be nice. They still had a full day to go to get to Limon, and she wasn't going to get a better ride than this, not with food and a place to sleep thrown in.

Joy emerged through the narrow door balancing two plates piled with sandwiches, chips and chunks of watermelon. "You want to get our drinks? I left two cups on the counter. There's iced tea in the fridge, but make sure you put it back in the slot on the door."

Amber wasn't surprised to find the inside of the camper as tidy as the rest of the truck. It was a teeny space but efficiently arranged. A closet-sized bathroom with a shower was on her left across from a dinette that looked just big enough for four very skinny people. Next was a sink, a cooktop with a microwave mounted above it, and a small refrigerator. Beyond the kitchen area was a step up into a sleeping compartment that extended over the truck's cab. Naturally, its sheets and blanket were perfectly trimmed. A TV was mounted on a swivel so it could be seen from either the bed or the dinette. Every cubic inch that wasn't plainly visible appeared to be storage.

Expecting to feel claustrophobic in such a cramped space, she was surprised to find it cozy and welcoming. If she had the money for a rig like this, she'd never have to worry about where to live. On a day like today, she could have parked this baby under a shade tree and chilled.

"This is really cool. How much does one of these outfits cost?"

Joy was seated at a concrete picnic table in the shade, already eating. "I think the camper was about twenty and the truck another thirty-five. You in the market?"

"Yeah, right. More than likely, I'll be sleeping on a couch by tomorrow night."

"Is that what's waiting for you in Limon?"

"Probably. My friend Molly moved there when her cousin took over one of the motels. She tried to get me to come out and work for her but I'd started seeing Asshole so I said no. I just hope she still has an opening."

"What if she doesn't have anything right now? There are a lot more people out there than jobs these days."

"We'll work it out. She's practically my best friend so at least she'll put me up until I find something."

"It's a good feeling to have friends like that."

"It would be even better if I had one of these," she said, indicating the truck camper.

"I know what you mean. Sometimes I feel like a turtle carrying my house around."

When Joy finished her lunch, she stretched her long frame upward to grab the crossbeam of their picnic shelter, and in a sudden burst, did three quick pull-ups before dusting her hands and tossing her trash in the bin.

Amber almost laughed aloud to realize the biggest difference between Joy and the other girls she'd hung out with—none of them did pull-ups on a whim. Joy was probably gay.

CHAPTER THREE

"I'm really sorry, Joy."

"It's okay. I'll have it mopped up in no time." Joy had opened the refrigerator to a mess because Amber forgot to secure the iced tea in the drink compartment.

There was still another half hour of daylight, but she liked checking into the RV park before dark. It was easier to handle the electrical and water hookups, and to get acclimated to the amenities, like the Wi-Fi network and the store. The amenity that mattered most was the shower, and she was looking forward to a hot one before bed.

Amber was sitting at the picnic table outside scrolling through Joy's laptop for a listing of motels in Limon. Skippy's leash was looped around her bench.

"Did you figure out how to get in touch with your friend?"

"Looks like they have about ten motels but I can't tell which one is hers. I don't think it's one of the chains."

"You should start calling them and asking if she works there. You're welcome to use my phone."

Joy chopped a small onion to brown with ground beef, and then stirred in a package of frozen chopped broccoli, a can of mushroom soup, water and rice. The savory dish took only twelve minutes on the stove. It was a simple recipe on the side of the rice bag, but Madison had suggested one final touch—grated cheese on top. Joy sprinkled it around and covered the pan so it would melt down through the dish.

"I need to walk over to the camp store for a couple of things. Want me to pick up some dog food?"

"I'll come with you," Amber said. She quickly untied Skippy's leash from the bench and fell into step with Joy.

"You know, I probably should set that laptop inside the camper and lock up." Even Madison, a fourth-grader, knew better than to leave valuables lying around in the open. "Might not be a bad idea to put Skippy in there too, since they don't allow dogs in the store."

At the store, she replenished her breakfast supplies, enough to last the rest of her trip, since she'd be dropping Amber in Limon the next day. Eating out of the camper instead of a restaurant would save her at least an hour a day, enough that if she pushed it, she might get into Oakland late Friday night. That would give her two full days to arrange home care for her dad.

Amber tapped her foot impatiently as the clerk, a dour-faced woman in stretch pants and mismatched floral top, took her time restocking a ChapStick display beside the cash register.

"Anything else?" the woman asked gruffly as she rang up the box of dog food.

"Pack of Marlboro Lights." Amber caught the box as it slid off the counter after the woman's careless toss. Her voice heavy with sarcasm, she added, "If it's not too much trouble."

Joy shot her a wink when she turned and rolled her eyes.

"Will that be all?" the clerk barked to Joy.

"Yes, ma'am. Thank you very much." Joy counted out exact change and helped bag her groceries. Then she joined Amber on the porch, where she'd already lit a cigarette.

"I can't believe you were so polite to that woman. What a crab!"

"When you grow up in a military household, respect for your elders gets drummed into you from the time you learn to speak."

"My folks tried that with me but it didn't take. Respect is something you have to earn."

"I usually try to give everyone the benefit of the doubt. It takes a lot less energy. Maybe I'd feel different if I had to put up with it all the time, but I figure we'll be rolling out of here about eight o'clock tomorrow morning, so it doesn't really accomplish anything to be rude."

"Too bad she doesn't see it that way." Amber flicked the last of her cigarette onto the ground, its sparks scattering. "What time do you think we'll get to Limon?"

"Around two, I think." Joy tried to keep walking but couldn't overcome the urge to grind the butt out and pick it up for proper disposal in the waste bin at their campsite. "I saw some kids walking around barefoot earlier. Wouldn't want one of them to step on this."

"You're kind of big on cleaning up, aren't you? Your folks must have been pretty strict."

"Compared to some, I guess they were. Although my real training came when I was in the navy. Believe me, you learn real fast not to leave even a wrinkle in the sand. Every last detail has to be perfect."

"Is that why you iron your T-shirts?"

Joy noted the teasing smirk and checked herself before responding defensively. "I'll have you know I don't iron my T-shirts. But if you take them out of the dryer when they're still a little warm and fold them just right, they won't get wrinkles. Any more questions?"

"So if someone wanted to torture you, all they'd have to do is wrinkle your clothes and drop cigarette butts everywhere."

"I'm sure I could handle...you're not going to do that, are you?"

Amber laughed for the first time all day. "I can see the headline now. Body dumped on Kansas roadside, clothing laundered and pressed. You'd make sure my hair was combed too, wouldn't you?"

"Maybe. But it wouldn't matter if your head was missing, would it?"

"I'll try to be neater, since you've been so nice." She smiled at Joy, showing off pretty white teeth. "I mean that, by the way. You've been really great. I don't know what I would have done if you hadn't given me a ride."

Joy decided against admitting that her conscience wouldn't have allowed her just to drive off. She didn't want Amber to test her limits.

When they returned to the camper, Skippy danced excitedly on his hind legs as Amber filled a small bowl with dry morsels. Joy dished out their dinner and set the plates on the small dinette. Though the circumstances were unusual, she had to admit she appreciated the company. Amber seemed a bit immature, but probably had seen tough times in her young life.

"Have you thought any more about what you're going to do if things don't work out in Limon?"

"They have to," Amber said glumly. "There's nothing to go home to in Nashville. No job, no place to live, not even a friend to help me out. That's the way it is with the band. You're either in or out, and once you're out, it's like you don't even exist anymore. I've seen it happen to other girls over and over. Don't know why I thought I'd be different."

Joy didn't want to let on that she'd overheard the whole conversation with Corey, but she was curious about the rift between Amber and her family. "And going back home isn't an option?"

"No way. Your dad might have been strict, being in the military and all, but mine...he's the biggest son of a bitch that ever lived." She picked up Skippy and settled him in her lap as she ate. "He yelled at me about everything...school, what I wore, who my friends were. Mama, too. I couldn't do anything right as far as they were concerned. I had this little dog, Coco. One of my friends gave her to me. She was mostly poodle, about the size of Skippy here…sweet as she could be. One night I stayed out later than I was supposed to…not much, maybe half an hour. When I got home, Coco was lying in the road, hit by a car. Mama said it was my fault…that Daddy threw her out the front door when I didn't come home on time. They weren't sorry or anything."

"Unbelievable."

"No shit. My boyfriend Archie was into electronics and a friend of his wanted him to come to Nashville and work on the sound crew with Rascal Flatts. That's a pretty good gig, so we just took off. I left a note basically telling my parents to go fuck themselves, and that's the last I ever saw of them."

"Wow, that's pretty heavy stuff." Even though Joy couldn't identify with her feelings, she understood perfectly why Amber had cut her family ties. "Do you have any brothers or sisters?"

"One brother, six years older. Last I heard he was in jail for cooking meth. That was about three years ago."

"Sounds like getting out of there was a good idea."

"It was for me." Amber pushed her plate away despite having eaten only half of what Joy had served. With a smirk that was now familiar, she asked, "So what's your story? I'm guessing you don't have a boyfriend."

"Not exactly my thing."

"That's because they're all scared to death about what'll happen if they accidentally drop a crumb on the floor. Maybe if you'd loosen up a little, they wouldn't be so afraid."

Apparently, Amber hadn't grasped her message. "I don't have a boyfriend because I don't want a boyfriend. I've never wanted one and I never will. Now a girlfriend…that's different. I wouldn't mind having one of those."

"Yeah, I figured that when I saw you doing those pull-ups. Not many of my straight girlfriends do that." Again, she said it teasingly.

"Sounds like you need to get out more. You ought to see some of those women in the navy doing pull-ups. Some lesbian…some straight, but they all like proving they can do it."

"I'd never be able to pull my chin up over a bar like that. I can hardly pull myself into your pickup truck." Amber flexed her bicep, which barely registered.

"I bet you'd pass out on the obstacle course at boot camp. All the smokers were puking their guts out."

Amber twirled the pack of cigarettes around on the table. "I'm going to quit one of these days. That might come sooner rather than later if I don't get a job right away. These suckers are getting expensive."

Joy was pleased at Amber's reaction to the news about her being a lesbian, or rather, her nonreaction. One aspect of the navy she didn't miss was the oppressive Don't Ask, Don't Tell rule, especially when she found herself working around people who would turn her in if she gave them the slightest bit of ammunition by talking about her girlfriend back home. The policy's repeal had come too late for her, but at least she could now proudly proclaim her status as a gay veteran.

"I'm going to hit the bath house and then I have to make a few calls to the West Coast. I'll leave my phone in case you want to call those motels in Limon."

She removed her tidy toiletry bag, a towel and a change of clothes. Her wallet and keys were in her pocket, so the laptop and phone were the only items of value not locked up or stored where they would be hard to find. It wasn't that she didn't trust Amber, but there was no reason to tempt her.

Though she'd had misgivings at first, having Amber along for the ride had made the day pass more quickly. Her fascination with the countryside was a lot like Madison's, and they were halfway through Missouri when Amber confessed she'd never been west of Kentucky. She'd been looking forward to seeing the country on tour with Gus Holley. Now she was headed for a culture shock in Limon.

* * *

"...Right, Molly Jackson, from Tennessee."

It had taken her six calls, but she finally found a motel owned by a family named Jackson—the Gateway Lodge. The clerk said Molly worked on the day shift.

"No, there's no message. I might be passing through tomorrow, but I want to surprise her."

She'd been thinking about Joy's observation that jobs weren't easy to come by, and thought it best to show up out of the blue. She didn't want to risk having Molly tell her not to come. This way Molly would be so glad to see her that she'd find a way to let her stay, especially when she found out Amber had left Nashville for good and had nowhere else to go.

She lifted Skippy onto the picnic table and lit another cigarette, her third since Joy had gone to the shower. Before long, they'd turn in for the night and she'd have to do without until morning, even if she couldn't get to sleep.

Sleeping arrangements tonight looked interesting. One bed, two people. And Joy was gay. Amber had already made up her mind it didn't matter. If Joy had something in mind to make up for giving her a ride, she was okay with it. It wasn't as if she had a problem sleeping with girls.

On the other hand, with the lousy day she'd had, Joy would probably expect her to sleep in the truck or on the floor by the kitchen sink. Whatever...it was only for one night. Maybe this time tomorrow, she'd be climbing into bed with Molly again. As far as she was concerned, they could pick up right where they left off as long as she got a place to stay. That was the story of her life—figuring out who could help her and how she could give them whatever they needed to keep her place secure. She wasn't proud of it, but there weren't many opportunities for women who didn't have training and skills.

Harmony said the best thing about getting married to Wayne was not feeling like a prostitute anymore. Amber never thought of her situation with Corey as prostitution. To her, it was survival. She didn't have sex with people who disgusted her. Corey was all right when he wasn't drunk, and Archie had treated her fine until that whole fiasco with the baby.

If she had it to do over again, she would have followed Harmony's lead and opened a business of her own. With the daycare, Harmony had a way to provide for herself and their son if her marriage to Wayne didn't work out, and because she ran the business in her home, she always said she'd get to keep the house if they got a divorce. Amber should have taken advantage of her time with Corey and started her own pet-sitting or grocery delivery service. Then she would have had a job to go back to instead of climbing into a truck with a total stranger and heading out west to the middle of nowhere.

Joy returned, her dark wet hair slicked back behind her ears and her towel folded neatly over her arm. Wearing gray knit shorts and an Oakland A's T-shirt—obviously what she slept in because her shirt wasn't tucked in—she was a lot less intimidating. "Any luck?"

"Yeah, I think I found her. She works days so she should be there tomorrow afternoon."

Amber studied her from behind as she entered the truck camper, thinking again about how she'd react if Joy expected something in return for the ride. She was the kind of person Amber normally found herself drawn to. It wasn't her physical characteristics, though there was nothing about her that was a turnoff. It was her strength and independence. She looked like she could take care of herself...and maybe even someone else if she had a mind to. Except Joy would drive her crazy with all those persnickety habits.

When she went into the camper to get clean clothes and toiletries for the shower, she found the dinette folded down and the back cushions laid flat to make a second bed. Fresh sheets and a pillow were stacked neatly in the middle.

Joy was putting away the last of the dishes.

"I'm sorry. I could have done that."

"No big deal. Finding your friend was more important."

"I bet you're ready to get rid of me tomorrow."

"I wouldn't say that, but I think you'll be happier once you're back with people you know."

"I hope I like Colorado. I've always loved the mountains."

If Molly couldn't get her hired as a housekeeper, she'd try to get shift work somewhere in the evening, maybe at a restaurant. That would free her up to go hiking and exploring in the daytime. After all her years in a city like Nashville, it would be nice to be close to nature for a change.

"I don't think Limon has any mountains," Joy said. "I drove through there when I moved back to California three years ago. If I remember correctly, it's a lot like Kansas…really flat with thunderstorms and tornadoes. An old railroad town, I think."

"You must be thinking of a different place. Molly said there were a bunch of motels there so it has to be some kind of tourist town."

"I doubt it. Several highways intersect there. That's probably why they have so many motels. You should look it up on my laptop while I finish."

"It's okay. I'm going to hit the shower and get ready for bed." If Limon turned out to be a hellhole, she'd rather not know about it tonight.

CHAPTER FOUR

Joy hated to disturb Amber, who was sleeping peacefully with Skippy tucked under her arm, but it was seven a.m.—time to eat breakfast and roll out. Limon was nearly six hours down the road under the best of conditions, but they were driving into a massive thunderstorm that would slow traffic and have Joy wrestling with crosswinds.

Fearing Skippy would snap at her, she opted to wake Amber with her voice instead of jostling her. It took several shouts before she finally stirred.

"God, this bed...that was the best night's sleep I've had in years. Maybe it's because I didn't have to sleep with Corey. I hope he got bedbugs at his hotel last night."

When she rolled back the covers and swung her bare legs to the floor, Joy whirled away on impulse, realizing Amber was wearing only a long T-shirt with nothing underneath. She was practiced in such avoidance from her years in the navy, where a lingering gaze could lead to a dishonorable discharge.

"Do you drink coffee?"

"Gallons," Amber replied groggily. She pulled on the faded denim skirt she had worn the day before and clipped Skippy's leash to his collar.

Joy had gone to bed the night before trying to think who Amber reminded her of and was startled when it came to her— her ex-partner Syd. It wasn't anything to do with the way she looked, since they couldn't have been more different. Syd was a large woman, not fat but big-boned, and she had straight black hair. Amber looked like a shopworn Tinkerbell.

No, the main similarity was the way they both sought to hitch their wagons to whoever could take them along. Syd was overtly sexual in her quest, turning on her sad brown eyes and pouty lips whenever she wanted something, an act that had usually resulted in Joy falling all over herself to please her. Amber's look was genuine desperation, but it triggered the same sort of emotional reaction in Joy—the urge to come to the rescue.

Knowing her tendency to respond to women in distress was not the same as accepting it. For the last four years she'd berated herself for being Syd's patsy, especially since she'd practically rolled over and given up all claim to Madison. Syd had her over a barrel because she couldn't fight for custody without her personal details coming to light, a move that would have ended her navy career. Had she known she'd be leaving only a few months later to help take care of her mother, she would have put up more of a fight. To this day, she felt guilty for putting the navy ahead of Madison.

Breakfast was simple fare, cereal with bananas and coffee. Joy wanted to get on the road quickly. After dropping Amber in Limon, she hoped to push herself for eight more hours all the way to Evanston, Wyoming, which would put her in striking distance of getting home late Friday night.

To shorten her long day, she set the cruise control at eighty, five miles above the limit. That would get her into the RV park around eight o'clock, thanks to the extra hour she'd pick up crossing into Mountain Time.

Amber kicked off her shoes and rested her feet on the dashboard, causing Skippy to stand, twirl twice, and settle back into the same position in her lap. "You know, my friend Molly is gay too. In fact...well, when we lived together, we shared a room...and a bed. So you might not be the only gay person in this truck. How about that?"

"Hmm." That explained Amber's live-and-let-live attitude, but Joy doubted someone who had lived mostly in relationships with men was ambivalent about her sexuality. "Most of the lesbians I know tend not to have boyfriends."

"I don't know about that, but I bet I'd have been a lot happier if they'd been women. Corey had this other girlfriend, a woman named Rachelle. Sometimes she'd stay over too and one time we all—"

"Oh, no! Too much information." Joy started singing "Home on the Range" loudly when it became obvious Amber was enjoying the torturous effect her personal details were having.

"What? You never did a three-way?" Amber was practically giddy.

"I did not. One at a time, thank you, and never, ever with a man. That is the definition of a lesbian."

"If you say so. But I bet there are a lot of lesbians out there who end up with guys just because it's easier. Or maybe they never felt like they had a choice. Doesn't mean they aren't lesbians."

Joy knew that firsthand, thanks to Syd, who couldn't deal with the stress of secrecy and yearned to fit in with everyone else. She had never learned to define her life with her own identity, choosing instead to be a reflection of whomever she was with. "Being a lesbian isn't just who you decide to sleep with. It's who you are."

"Isn't that what I just said?"

Joy silently conceded it was, but gave Amber a skeptical look just the same. A journey of self-discovery was one thing. Dabbling in both worlds when it suited you was another.

"Did you get that problem with your dad worked out last night? Sounded like you were going at it with somebody."

Joy groaned. "I can't believe these people. I found four different agencies that do home health care but all of them say they don't allow their workers to lift. Something about their insurance not covering back injuries. I told them my pop didn't need to be lifted. He just needs someone to provide a little leverage so he can lift himself without having to use his bum shoulder."

"What happened to him?"

"He's been in a wheelchair for twenty-some years, but he's got good upper body strength, so he can do just about everything on his own. In fact, he absolutely hates it when he has to ask for help." She didn't add that he'd grown even more stubborn about it since her mother died, and was getting worse every year. "Last week he went for his poker night at the American Legion and took a header when his chair caught a bump on the ramp. Broke his shoulder and had to have surgery. It happened the day after I left with Madison, but he didn't even tell me about it for three days because he knew I'd turn around and come back."

"How long is he going to be like that?"

"The doctor said he had to let it heal for eight weeks and keep getting physical therapy for a couple of months after that. If I know Pop, he'll try to cut that in half, and he'll hurt himself even worse. Right now, he's stuck at the rehab center until I can get somebody lined up to come to the house while I'm at work. And that's the other thing. I have to be at work at five o'clock in the morning and they say it's hard to schedule someone to come that early. The only way they can guarantee it is if we hire two shifts—midnight to eight, and eight to four."

"That's freaking ridiculous."

"No kidding. That's twice as much money just to cover three measly hours."

"No, I meant you having to be at work at five o'clock. That's insane."

Joy gave Amber a sidelong look and was only half surprised to realize she wasn't kidding.

Amber said, "The best I ever managed was eight thirty at the Friendly Mart and half the time I was late."

"You were lucky you weren't fired."

"I was." With that, she laughed. "Seriously, how do you go to work at five o'clock in the morning? Are you a vampire or something?"

"Our first plane rolls out at six. I have to get it loaded and fueled."

"In your little orange vest."

"Now you're making fun of me." Joy had no problem being teased as long as she was sure that's what it was. "You wouldn't want me to get crushed by a 737, would you?"

"You wouldn't believe the getup they made me wear when I worked at Taco Loco...it was one of those Mexican ponchos. It looked like a rug with a hole in it for my head. And at the Friendly Mart, they gave me this blue smock with half the snaps broken off. It had coffee and grease stains all over it that wouldn't come out. So nasty."

"My orange vest is sounding better all the time."

"How did you end up working at an airport? That actually sounds kind of fun, except for the five o'clock part."

Joy's hand crept over to pet Skippy, who eyed her nervously but for the first time didn't growl. "I was a plane handler in the navy. I spent nine years working on the deck of an aircraft carrier, the USS *Theodore Roosevelt*. We called it the Big Stick, because that was TR's motto. 'Walk softly and carry a big stick.' It was my job to get all the planes in position to launch and then put them back in the hangar."

"You lived on a boat for nine years?"

She cringed at what most in the navy considered an epithet. "The *TR* was not a boat. It was a *Nimitz*-class nuclear powered supercarrier. But yes, we were deployed at least six months a year the whole time I was in the navy. Over five thousand of us on board. It was like a floating city."

"I don't know how you did that." Amber shook her head vehemently. "I'd go crazy looking out at nothing all the time."

"That's only if you were lucky enough to look out. Some of those guys in the ship's company stayed below deck for weeks at a time. They lost all sense of day and night. At least those of us in the air wing got outside nearly every day."

"Yeah, I'd probably kill myself if I never got to go outside."

"There were a lot of days going out on deck wasn't much fun. We'd have rough seas and winds so strong we had to wear tethers on our belts to keep us from getting blown off the deck. Man, it was something else."

"More power to you, but there's no way they'd ever get my ass on one of those things. I like my feet dry, thank you very much." Amber wiggled her toes, which sported dark red nail polish.

"It's not for everyone." She shuddered to think how fast someone like Amber would wash out in boot camp at Great Lakes. She'd barely make it off the bus before they sent her home.

Conversation died as the sky darkened and heavy rain began to pound the windshield. For more than an hour they crept along the highway with everyone else, barely keeping up with the taillights in front. All the time Joy had banked doing eighty was lost, and then some, putting Evanston out of reach for the night. As the storm finally broke, they found themselves crossing the Colorado state line.

Joy resumed her chatter but Amber had lost interest in conversation. By the worried look on her face, she was coming to grips with the reality of life in the middle of nowhere. When they stopped for lunch at the Colorado Welcome Center in Burlington, she stood in front of the truck with Skippy, staring into the horizon. Only seventy-nine miles to Limon and still not a mountain in sight. And hardly a tree, for that matter.

"You getting excited about seeing your friend?"

"I reckon," she said, without a trace of enthusiasm. "You really think Limon's as flat as this? It's like one gigantic vacant lot out there."

"There might be a rolling hill or two, but mostly...yeah, it's a lot like this."

"I guess beggars can't be choosers. I just need to hang out long enough to get back on my feet...get some money saved. Maybe then I'll buy me one of these and see the whole country."

Joy felt a pang of sympathy but nodded along just the same. Amber probably knew such dreams were a long shot for someone in her position. Then again, that's what made them dreams.

* * *

"There it is, the Gateway Lodge," Amber said, her voice quiet with apprehension.

The motor lodge, a single-story L-shaped building painted pale green with white trim, sat barely fifty yards from the interstate off-ramp. Around the corner from the office was a rusted singlewide mobile home, and parked between the two structures in a patch of gravel and dust was a faded red pickup truck, its front fender a dull gray.

It was, without question, the most miserable place Amber had ever seen.

Joy pulled into the parking lot, turned around and backed into a space opposite the office. Though she put the vehicle in Park, she left the engine running, and with it, the low whir of the air conditioner. "Welcome to Limon, Colorado."

Amber couldn't will herself to move. The thought of working here—and perhaps even living in the trailer out back with the Jackson family—was almost as depressing as going back to Shelbyville. No matter how happy Molly was to see her, it wouldn't be enough to make this place bearable.

The minutes ticked by while she summoned the courage to open the door, but Joy sat patiently, neither moving nor speaking.

Amber's whole life was littered with reckless decisions like the one that had brought her here. Leaving Shelbyville without a plan for her future had made her dependent on Archie, two years of her life that had come to nothing. Then there was the taco job she'd quit because she couldn't get the day off to go to a party. And she'd paid almost a thousand dollars to a vitamin marketing company on the promise she could earn it back four times over through phone sales that never materialized. Gullible, and with zero impulse control.

This one took the cake, and the moment she stepped out of this truck, she needed to start making a real plan for getting her life back on track, which wasn't going to happen in Limon. Joy had refused her offer to help pay for gas, so she still had about two hundred dollars in her purse. That might get her home on a bus, but she probably wouldn't be able to take Skippy, so that was out. More than likely, she'd have to find someone on their way back east and hope they were as nice as Joy.

But where was home? Corey had gone to great lengths to make sure she wasn't welcome back in Nashville. There wasn't a soul there who would take her in until she got on her feet, and she couldn't just sleep in the park. His whole plan had been to box her into going back to her parents in Shelbyville, probably the only people in the world who would put a roof over her head.

Except maybe Molly, whom she hadn't seen or spoken to in over three years. Limon sucked, but it wasn't Shelbyville, and if those were her only choices...

Then without a word Joy slid the gearshift into Drive and eased out of the parking lot. At the intersection she turned onto the highway and merged with westbound traffic, setting her cruise control at seventy.

Amber didn't care if Joy strapped her on top in a crate, as long as she didn't leave her in Limon.

* * *

Joy had never done anything so crazy in her whole life. It was one thing to pick up strays on the side of the road, but quite another to bring one home.

"Okay, Amber, I have this idea." For reasons she couldn't fathom, she was nervous. It was presumptuous to think Amber would go for her plan, but it had to be a better alternative than staying behind in a place that made the Bates Motel look like a five-star resort. "My pop needs some help for the next three or four months. Suppose you come with me to Oakland…try it out for a week or two. If it works out, you've got a place to live while you get back on your feet and figure out what you want to do next. If it doesn't, I'll get you a plane ticket for wherever you want to go. Skippy too."

Amber didn't miss a beat. "First of all, yes. Second of all, what exactly do I have to do?"

"Just be there to help him. He won't be able to get in or out of his chair by himself, and he can't push himself around with just one arm."

"Do you think I'll be able to lift him? I'm pretty strong. I used to help Corey haul his amplifiers all over the place, and believe me, that shit's heavy."

Her voice had come alive with excitement, Joy noted, a dramatic contrast to the gloom she had shown only moments ago at the Gateway Lodge. In the next couple of days, Joy would have to work on dialing back that eagerness because her father wouldn't be able to stand it.

"You shouldn't have to lift him at all. Just help stabilize him so he can swing himself in and out of his chair."

"I get it. You're saying he can stand on his own if I just stabilize him."

The question jarred her and she mentally played back everything she'd told Amber about her father's condition. "No, he's a bilateral above-knee amputee…he doesn't have any legs."

"Oh."

Joy was accustomed to dealing with people's initial discomfort about her father. Her childhood friends had stared with curiosity at his pinned-up pants, and a couple of potential girlfriends had vanished after their first meeting, no doubt put off by the prospect of someday having an invalid father-in-law. What none of them realized was how utterly normal his life was, with only the smallest of limitations.

"Does that bother you?"

"No, I just…I've never been around anyone like that. But I'll do whatever he needs—cook, clean…I can even give him a bath. All you have to do is show me how. I learn fast."

Joy was glad she hadn't been drinking anything because it would have been spewed on her dashboard. "I wouldn't mention the bath if I were you. He might like that idea for all the wrong reasons. But he'll be glad to have somebody clean the house for him. That doesn't mean he won't look over your shoulder and yell at you for doing it wrong."

"And I thought you got all that neat-freak stuff in the navy."

"I did, but before that, I got it from him, and he got it from the navy. I've been yelled at so much, I finally decided it was just easier to do it right the first time."

Amber groaned. "Great, he's probably going to rip my head off every time I turn around. But like I said, I'll learn."

"Don't worry about it. Just do your best. He'd be more annoyed if you were perfect and he didn't have anything to complain about."

"Sounds like a piece of work. But I can handle him."

Joy had her doubts about both of them. Her pop would probably take one look at Amber and ask whose bratty kid she was. And Amber…after one of her father's tirades, she'd either dissolve in tears or erupt in swear words.

At least Joy wouldn't have to be there while they worked out their differences. Too bad the airline didn't allow overtime.

CHAPTER FIVE

With her eyes open barely a slit, Amber studied Joy's profile as she drove westward in the waning light. From this angle, she looked a lot softer than she had chinning the crossbeam, but was still a far cry from anything Amber would call feminine. Tiny gold post earrings peeked out from under her dark hair, which was cut even with the top of her collar, and what she had first thought was a smooth complexion was actually a light coat of perfectly applied makeup, barely enough to notice.

"You're wearing makeup!"

"I am not."

Amber swiped a finger down Joy's cheek and checked it, finding a beige smear. "You most certainly are. You wouldn't let me put any on because we were in such an all-fire hurry to leave."

"It's not makeup. It's sunscreen." She opened the mirror on the underside of her sun visor and rubbed the smudge off her cheek. "I wear it everywhere I go. You should too."

"I should have known."

"What's that supposed to mean? I have no problem wearing a little makeup when the situation calls for it, but that doesn't include riding in a truck across Wyoming."

"No need to get so defensive. I wasn't trying to imply that you never dressed up or anything like that." Though it was hard to imagine Joy going out of her way to look "pretty" in the normal sense, no matter what the situation. "I'm just not surprised that you always wear sunscreen...and your seat belt, and sensible shoes. Because you never even get in the truck without walking all the way around it to check the tires."

"What's wrong with that? You ever have a flat tire on a truck this size? It's a pain in the butt."

"All flat tires are a pain in the butt. Believe me, I've had my share."

"Maybe if you checked them before you took off down the road, you wouldn't have so many." Her voice wasn't particularly scolding, and she even wore a little smirk in the corner of her mouth.

Joy was regimented about practically everything, and it began to dawn on Amber that her new job with Joy's father might be tougher than she'd first thought. Corey always said the only thing worse than her cooking was her housekeeping, and there was some truth to that. Of course, he was a slob who expected hamburger to taste like steak, so she couldn't have pleased him if she'd tried. But she didn't want to blow this chance in California, and she especially didn't want to let Joy down, not after she'd done so much for her.

"So you're a military brat. I'm guessing that gay thing didn't go over well."

Joy huffed...almost a chuckle but not quite. "Could have been better, but it turned out okay. They were hoping for lots of grandkids."

"Kids are overrated. I think the best parents are the ones that have to adopt. They appreciate their kids more because they have to jump through so many hoops to get them. It's not like you can skip a few pills and accidentally adopt one."

"I don't know about that. Getting Madison was kind of an accident, but I couldn't love her more than I do. I'd give anything to adopt her though."

As Joy described her relationship with her goddaughter, Amber tried to imagine one of her friends designating her as a guardian for a child. That would never happen in a million years, not only because no one in their right mind would trust her with a child, but also because she'd never agree. Raising kids took something special. At the very least, you needed a stable home life and a good job, to say nothing of a halfway decent role model from your own parents.

"I had a baby once," Amber announced flatly. "A boy. Five years ago, when I was nineteen. I gave him up for adoption and I've never had the urge to see him again."

Joy didn't reply, but her wide eyes suggested she was somewhat taken aback. Little wonder, since Amber's choice of words probably made her sound cold and uncaring. Nothing could be further from the truth.

"See, I got pregnant back when I was with Archie and it totally freaked him out. Me too, for that matter. I wasn't ready for a baby any more than he was, but I figured we screwed up so it was time for us to start acting responsible. His idea of being responsible was for me to have an abortion. I kept putting it off because I thought he'd change his mind when it started kicking and stuff. Instead, he took off, and after feeling it move around inside me…well, I decided it was alive and I couldn't just kill it. My friend, Molly, the one who moved to Limon…she hooked me up with a lawyer who found this couple in Arkansas to pay all of my medical expenses if I gave them the baby as soon as it was born."

She recalled the meeting in the lawyer's office. The woman had been through some kind of cancer scare that left her unable to have children, and it seemed like a baby was what she and her husband wanted most in the world. It was the first time Amber could remember people being so nice to her, asking about her health and well-being, and if she needed anything to be comfortable. She knew from the get-go they were more concerned about the baby, and with staying on her good side so she wouldn't change her mind. It gave her comfort to know he would be going to a family that would love him and provide for him in a way she couldn't.

"They offered to do one of those open adoptions, where I could send birthday cards and presents and they'd send me pictures as he grew up, but all that stuff sounded like it was for me, not him. I thought we'd all be better off if I just got out of the picture."

"Hmmm."

Still no reaction, but at least she wasn't being critical, Amber thought.

"What, you think that was bad? Harmony did. She was like, 'How could you abandon your own child?' It's not like I left him on a doorstep. I made sure he was going to a good home."

"It's never bad when you put a child's well-being first. That's what responsible adults are supposed to do. You're lucky you felt good about where he ended up. I thought leaving Madison with Syd was best for her, but I'm not so sure anymore."

"How come she ended up with you guys? Didn't she have any grandparents?"

"Not really. Her father was African-American and that didn't go over very well with Carrie's folks. She quit having anything to do with them and they never even came around looking for Madison after she died."

"Sounds like something my folks would have done."

"That's what I meant about you doing right by your baby. I don't always trust Syd to put Madison's needs first."

"And that's the main reason I don't want to see my kid anymore. I want to think of him as happy and healthy…because there's nothing I can do about it now if he isn't. It's not like I could turn into a great mother all of a sudden and get him back. It's all I can do to take care of Skippy, and let's face it—I couldn't even do that if you hadn't picked us up. What if I'd been left in a parking lot with a five-year-old?"

Joy shook her head. "I don't think that would have happened. Having a kid makes you more sensible whether you're ready for it or not."

"I'll have to take your word for it."

* * *

Joy positioned her laptop so she was directly in front of the webcam and cracked her knuckles.

"I hate when you do that!" Madison squealed from the screen, covering her ears. "I can't believe you always do that to me."

"Because I know it drives you crazy," she said with a mischievous grin. "How was your first day of school? You like your teacher?"

Amber had volunteered to do their laundry, giving Joy a small window to catch Madison before she went to bed. She'd been careful not to tell her goddaughter about how she'd picked up someone on the side of the road, since it wasn't in keeping with the lessons about being cautious about strangers.

"I'm in Cheyenne, Wyoming…a little over halfway home. My butt's going to feel weird next week when it doesn't have that truck seat attached to it."

"I know. I close my eyes and it still feels like I'm riding. I wish I was."

"Nah, it's better for you to be in school with your friends. I bet Syd's glad to have you back home."

"If you say so."

Joy couldn't tell if that was a typical response to having homework, chores and bedtime rules again, or something in particular related to Syd and perhaps her new boyfriend. Whatever the cause, it made Joy want to turn around and go back for her, especially after her conversation with Amber today. It didn't seem right to leave Madison floundering where she clearly wasn't happy.

"Are you getting to know Mitch?"

"I guess. He goes upstairs after dinner and shuts the door. Syd goes too but then she comes back after a while…to make sure I go to bed." The last words she muttered drearily. "She'd be mad at me for telling you though. She told me last night that what we do at home is private, and I'm not supposed to talk about it at school and stuff."

It wasn't surprising Syd would want to keep her new living situation on the down low, especially since Mitch—like all the others—would probably be history in a few months. But Joy didn't like the idea of making Madison feel ashamed about her home life.

"All families are like that, sweetie. We like to keep certain things private, but you don't have to worry about what you say to me. I'm family too, you know."

"I'm not even supposed to tell people about you anymore, or even Grandpa Shep. Our teacher wants us to write a story about what we did over the summer, and I'll have to say stupid stuff like going to the pool with Tara." Madison must have known her words would be hurtful because she delivered them with genuine scorn.

Joy managed a thin smile for the benefit of the video, which was all that kept her from erupting in anger. Syd's sole reason for telling Madison to keep their visits secret was because she was a lesbian, and it was a clear breach of their agreement to stay positive when they talked about one another.

"You're a smart girl. I bet you can figure out how to write about the fun stuff."

Footsteps outside the camper door announced Amber's return from the laundry room.

"Okay, sweetie. I've got to go and so do you. It might be late tomorrow when I get to camp, so what if I wait to call when I get home? Is that okay?"

"Don't forget."

"Not a chance. Love you."

She had barely disconnected the call when Amber came in with the laundry basket.

"I...uh, I ran into sort of a problem with some of our stuff. I think it might have been that red tank top I had on yesterday. I forgot it had never been washed before."

Joy looked dismally upon a small pile of pink-tinted underwear. She reached into the basket—hoping against hope—and withdrew her beloved yellow T-shirt from the USS *Theodore Roosevelt*, now streaked with red. Not that the color mattered... since it was now two sizes too small.

"Looks like you washed everything together...in hot water."

"Yeah, I didn't think there was enough for two loads, and I wanted to be sure it all got clean."

"Looks like it did," she said quietly. Her pink bras ought to still fit, since they were polyester, but the cotton panties were a lost cause.

"I'm really sorry. Maybe it'll wash out next time."

"Hmmm." Joy hoped the really small people who frequented Goodwill liked pink.

* * *

"Are you as cold as I am, Skippy boy?" Amber drew her knees to her chest on the bench of the picnic table and rubbed her bare legs briskly. The guy at the RV park store who sold her a pack of cigarettes said the temperature in Cheyenne dropped at night because the altitude was almost six thousand feet. There was a hoodie in her suitcase, but she didn't want to go inside until it was time for bed. Staying out of Joy's way seemed like a good idea on account of the laundry mishap.

This wasn't the brand of silent treatment she was used to, where Corey would bang drawers and turn up the volume on the TV every time she tried to talk to him. Joy was talking to her but her voice was glum. Understandably, she was disappointed over having her favorite shirt ruined by carelessness. Amber had even offered to buy her another, but apparently they were available only in the ship's store.

Perhaps all would be forgiven if she and Skippy froze to death.

Joy suddenly opened the door of the camper and called out, "Hey, we probably ought to turn in. Tomorrow's another long day."

She hustled inside to find her bed already set up, and with an extra blanket. "Thanks for doing this. I would have come sooner if…I figured you were still kind of mad at me."

"I wasn't mad," Joy said. "Just kind of bummed about the shirt because it was special. But I shot off an email to a buddy of mine who's still on the ship and she's going to send me a couple of new ones. It'll be okay."

"Aw, that's great. I'll pay for both of them. I promise."

"Don't worry about it." Joy was already dressed for bed and wasted no time climbing up into her loft, where she rolled onto her side and pulled the covers to her chin. "But I should warn you…if you turn my pop's skivvies pink, he might decide not to wear any, and that'll be bad news for everyone at breakfast."

It took a moment for Joy's words to register, and then Amber got a vision of an old naked guy in a wheelchair. "Ewww."

It was only when Joy chuckled that Amber finally let go of the tension that had strained their interactions all evening. Walking on eggshells wasn't usually her style, but she didn't like her chances in a head-on conflict with Joy. Someone so regimented wasn't going to give an inch anyway, and it wasn't worth the risk of ticking her off. Besides, she liked Joy. More than that, she respected any woman who took care of herself the way she did and called her own shots.

Amber turned on the tiny reading lamp over her bed and turned off the overhead light, casting the rest of the small space into darkness. As she bent to retrieve her nightshirt from the drawer below the seat, she wondered if Joy might be watching her from the shadows. Unlikely for someone so honorable. Still…it was kind of exciting to think so, and Amber took her time getting dressed, purposely stretching her nude body as she dropped the nightshirt over her form.

It could be fun to have sex with someone like Joy, she thought, smiling to herself as she spread the blanket over her feet and settled Skippy into the crook of her arm. Thanks to Molly and Rachelle, she'd had lots of practice satisfying women—enough that she could show Joy a thing or two.

* * *

Joy squeezed her eyes tightly shut, but not before getting an eyeful of Amber as she stripped to nothing and readied for bed.

She needed a girlfriend—tonight if at all possible—and anyone but Amber. For most of her tenure in the navy she'd been involved with Syd, and that had worked like an off-switch when it came to sexual interest in other women. The closest she'd come to dating someone since returning to California was Danielle Hatcher, her sometimes fling whenever she got depressed about not having female company. Though Joy found Dani interesting and attractive, they weren't well suited for a serious relationship since Dani was set in her ways—ways that didn't include being around kids like Madison or cranky old guys in wheelchairs. A social worker schooled at the University of California at Berkeley, she was a proud feminist who regularly organized women for one political cause or another, and she seemed to know every lesbian in the East Bay.

As soon as Joy got back home and got Amber settled in with her household duties, she'd call Dani for dinner. Or Jeannie, or Cassie or whoever that girl was she met at Dani's potluck where they all had to donate to the women's center.

Anyone but Amber.

There were dozens of reasons to steer clear of her passenger, not the least of which was the sleaze factor. Amber was desperate, and probably willing to do almost anything just to get by, including bartering sex. Only a creep would take advantage of a situation like that, and the fact that Amber gave it so freely meant she didn't value intimacy in the same way Joy did.

Then there was the matter of Amber's youth. Though she was twenty-four—only five years younger than Joy—she was hardly a mature adult. From her self-absorbed and impulsive behavior, it was almost as if she'd been raised by teenagers in a home where no one was left in charge. By contrast, Joy had been as responsible as any adult at sixteen, even before the navy got hold of her. She wasn't interested in becoming a parent to someone who was old enough to take care of herself and had given away a child of her own.

And if all that wasn't enough, there was the fact that Amber, though she'd hinted at the possibility of being a lesbian herself, was likely just an opportunist, seeking shelter wherever she found it. In other words, she was Syd all over again.

Joy shuddered and drew the sheet up over her head, wishing her eyes had a backspace button. If she could just survive one more night of sharing close quarters, at least she'd get her privacy back…and with it, a chance to release her sexual frustrations.

CHAPTER SIX

"I'm thinking of a person," Amber said.

Joy groaned. "Not again. I don't know any of those country music people. Tug This, Yank That."

"Who said it was a country music person?"

"Is it?"

Amber smirked. "Yes."

Joy beeped the horn twice. "Welcome to Utah."

The Rocky Mountains had faded behind them, giving way to a rolling brown landscape, a featureless mix of dirt, rock and dry grass. Too much like Limon for Amber's taste.

"I just can't imagine what kind of people live in a place like this," she said, answering her own query with the realization that there wasn't a dwelling in sight. "By the way, I haven't thanked you today for not leaving me at the Gateway Lodge. I don't think I ever felt so hopeless in my whole life."

"Yeah, I sort of figured that when you wouldn't get out of the truck."

"You think they allow smoking in Utah? I could do with a cigarette, and Skippy could probably do with a bush...if they had any."

Joy flipped on her blinker and exited at the Welcome Center. "Pop's going to start harassing you the minute he gets his first whiff of cigarette smoke on your clothes. Sure you wouldn't rather be smoke-free when you get there? You said you had to quit anyway."

"I've been harassed by the best of them. I figure I can wait until he rags on me, and then he'll get to take credit for it when I quit." She lit a cigarette the second she hopped out of the truck. "Besides, I still have cigarettes. A smoker can't quit until they're all gone."

"I can fix that," Joy said, suddenly snatching the pack from her hand.

"You wouldn't."

"I might."

Skippy growled menacingly at Joy.

"Sic her, boy."

Joy handed them back. "Here, keep your stinky old cancer sticks. And call off your attack dog." She took the leash and led Skippy to the pet walk area.

"Everybody has vices," Amber called loudly before shuffling to catch up.

"Not me. I like a cold beer every now and then, but that's about it."

"I bet your ex-girlfriend could come up with a better list than that." Amber had spent much of the morning wondering what sort of girlfriend Joy had been. "Did you starch her underwear? Kick her tires every time she went somewhere?"

"Very funny. She was navy too so I didn't have to deal with her sloppy habits. You may not know this—of course you don't—but responsible people clean up after themselves."

"God, I bet a crumb never hit the floor in your house."

Amber enjoyed the effect of her teasing on Joy, who played along as if she were indulging a naughty child. It was tempting to terrorize her with more trashy stories about her sexual adventures just for the shock value, but it bothered her a little to think Joy might not have been exaggerating her disgust over the idea that she'd freely slept with both Corey and Rachelle. If she had it to do over again, she'd have kept the details to herself, but thinking before speaking had never been one of her strong suits. She couldn't count the times her mouth had gotten her in trouble.

* * *

Joy leaned against the hood of her truck and smiled at the look of childlike amazement on Amber's face. The Great Salt Lake, with its white streaks, sandbars and distant peaks, stretched out for miles before them.

"Man, I wish my phone worked. I'd take a picture of this."

"Mine does," Joy answered, snapping a shot of the lake with Amber in the foreground.

Amber took one last look over her shoulder and climbed back into the truck. "Thanks. Save it for me, will you? Maybe one of these days I'll be able to get phone service again and you can send that to me."

"With you taking care of Pop, I definitely want you to have a phone. That's one of the details we have to work out."

Joy had spent an hour the night before researching guidelines for live-in health care workers, which she'd found to be a lot more complicated than she'd first thought. Now that she'd offered the job to Amber, it seemed silly to bother with a background check, something most of the websites advised. But there was still the matter of filling out all the appropriate tax forms and negotiating an appropriate salary and work schedule.

"I talked with Pop again last night. He's ready to bust out of rehab, so we want to make sure everything's set for him to come home day after tomorrow."

"Whatever you need, just tell me."

Amber's eyes glazed over as Joy went through the ins and outs of which services her father needed and who paid for what.

The bottom line was in-home assistance wasn't covered, so they'd have to pay out of pocket.

"What would you say to room and board, and five hundred bucks a week for the next three months? We'd have to hold back some for taxes, but you wouldn't have any expenses of your own…especially since you're going to quit smoking."

Her offer was met with silence, not altogether surprising, since the salary was on the low end of what was recommended. Joy had thought that reasonable since her father didn't require a lot of personal care, but now she wasn't so sure.

"What do you think?"

Amber managed to shake her head and nod at the same time, a gesture that Joy took to mean she'd probably have to start negotiating.

"It's good…in fact, it's more than I've ever made in my life. I've got some friends that do this home health care kind of stuff and they don't make that much, so…great."

No doubt Amber's friends worked hourly jobs with agencies that provided benefits and bonding, along with administrative support. Joy hoped this twelve-week gig would help Amber on a path to stable employment. All that depended, of course, on her doing a good job.

"You know, there are a lot of jobs out there for people who do this kind of work. Most of the people I talked to at the agencies said all their techs were certified, so maybe you could look into getting a certificate. If they have classes at night or on the weekends, you can sign up right away. I can sit with Pop while you're gone."

"That would be cool, and then—" She huffed and shook her head. "Except how would I get there? I don't have a car, and you don't trust me to drive this one, even with you sitting beside me."

"That's because you've never driven anything this heavy. It's dangerous if you don't know how to handle it. But you'd be able to drive Pop's car."

"Your father has a car?"

"I told you. He can do practically everything but walk. That's why he's going crazy at the rehab center, because he's used to taking care of himself."

"Yeah, well he better get used to being taken care of at home. I'm going to cook. I'll clean. I'll do all his laundry...on second thought, maybe he ought to handle the laundry."

It was good to hear Amber laugh, and especially to hear the eagerness in her voice when she talked about going to work. In the long run, this would probably turn out to be not only the best-paying job she'd ever had, but also the easiest. And if it started her down the road toward gainful long-term employment, so much the better. Getting dumped at a truck stop in Louisville, Kentucky, might end up being the luckiest break she ever had.

* * *

After a dismal start, Utah had turned out to be the most interesting state so far. The drab rolling hills had become winding canyons leading into Salt Lake City, and the blinding salt flats had given way to a deep red sunset over rugged westward peaks. Seven states in three days, with only Nevada and California left.

Amber waited in the truck with Skippy while Joy checked in at the campground office. "One more day, boy. Then we've got to go to work."

Though she'd tried to appear confident about taking care of Joy's father, she wasn't all that sure she could pull it off. It had always been a point of personal pride that she didn't take shit from anybody. Anytime one of her bosses gave her attitude, she usually gave it right back and then some. But that was when she still had a roof over her head in case she got fired.

From the way Joy talked about her father, he might well be a flaming asshole, and she had no choice but to suck it up. Even more than that, she was worried about screwing up and getting fired again, only this time, she'd be two thousand miles from everyone she knew.

Joy returned to the truck and placed a permit on the dashboard. "Anywhere on Row Three, he said."

They crept slowly down the pavement through a canyon of campers and motorhomes, all parked diagonally and separated by a picnic table, outdoor grill and trash can.

"There's a spot," Amber said.

No sooner had the words left her lips than the door opened at the adjacent motorhome. One man practically fell outside laughing at another who appeared shirtless behind them, flipping him off and screaming that he was a motherfucker. Each man held a beer can, and several more were stacked in a pyramid on the picnic table.

"On second thought…"

Joy parked at the end of the row and, after hooking up the water and electricity, went to work preparing dinner, which was pasta shells with peas, tomatoes and tuna.

"This is really good," Amber said. "Where did you learn to cook?"

"This isn't cooking. This is called making dinner. I'm sure people who actually cook understand the difference."

"Maybe to you, but this would be gourmet at my house."

Joy set the pasta box on the table and turned it toward her. "Nearly everything I make has the recipe on the side of the box, or the bag or the can. If I want something more complicated than that, I go out to eat."

Amber slipped a forkful of tuna to Skippy, who had been watching every bite with anticipation. "I thought for sure you were going to tell me they taught you to cook in the navy. They taught you everything else."

"One of the girls I went to boot camp with studied cooking…culinary specialist, she was called. Guess what she's doing now."

"Wearing a poncho at Taco Loco?"

Joy chuckled. "She's working in the kitchen at the White House."

"Now there's a job I'd like."

"She had to work her way up to that, including about six years cooking below decks on an aircraft carrier."

"Screw that. You and your crazy boats."

"Ships."

"That's what I said." Amber collected their dishes and twisted in her seat to set them in the sink. "I'll clean up if you want to get a shower."

"Good deal. We probably should turn in early. Ten hours on the road tomorrow gets us home."

By the time Amber got the dishes washed, dried and stowed where they wouldn't bounce around, Joy was back.

"You might want to skip over to Row Four to walk to the bathhouse. Those two guys we saw on the way in are smashed, and they're getting into it with the old couple next to them. I won't be surprised if the cops show up soon."

"Wonder why the owner doesn't just kick them out?"

"He should but someone that drunk doesn't need to be driving out of here, especially in a vehicle as big as a motorhome."

"Good point."

Joy and her father were technically her bosses now, and she needed to get used to taking their orders. Still, she couldn't resist checking out the raucous excitement and she walked down the row hoping to hear the fight between the two drunks and their neighbors. Whatever had gotten stirred up was over. The campground was relatively quiet and most campers seemed to be turning in. Two others were leaving the bathhouse, an older woman and a toddler who might have been her granddaughter.

Amber took her time, savoring the steam of the shower as she shaved her legs and conditioned her thick, curly hair. Just because she didn't iron her tank tops didn't mean she couldn't make herself presentable. A good first impression on the old guy would probably make her job a lot easier.

It was almost eleven when she finally exited the bathhouse, her dirty clothes rolled up inside her wet towel, and she felt bad for taking so long. Joy was probably waiting up, since she'd never go to sleep without locking the camper door.

"Look what we got here, Jerry." The shirtless drunk was right outside the door taking a leak against the side of the bathhouse. "This one's not as ugly as all the others around here."

"Not as fat, either," Jerry said as he stepped around the corner into view.

After seven years of hanging out with bands, Amber had been around her share of drunks, enough that she could tell which ones were simply hopeless, and which ones were trouble. The fact that these guys had already tangled with the neighbors suggested they were in the latter group, and she decided to ignore them.

"Come have a beer with us. We've got some hooch too. You like hooch?"

Jerry sidestepped until he was blocking her path. "I bet she likes hooch, Ray."

"No thanks, guys. Time to go to bed…sleep it off."

"I've got a nice big bed back at my place," Ray said, slipping his arm around Amber's waist, and his fingers inside the back of her waistband. "You'd like my bed. I'd make sure of that."

As she whirled out of his reach, Jerry caught her and slapped a hand over her mouth from behind. She responded with several backward kicks to his shins, ineffective with only rubber flip-flops. His massive arm pinned both of her elbows to her sides while Ray wrapped her legs in a bear hug. Together, they carried her past two motorhomes to theirs.

Amber kicked violently as Ray loosened his grip to open the door, and she saw his head snap back as her heel landed a lucky blow against his jaw.

"You bitch!" With blood spurting from his split lip, he drew back his fist.

"Let her go." Joy's trembling voice rang out from behind them, followed by a metallic click.

Ray, his eyes wide with fear, wiped his bloody chin. "Jerry, she's pointing a gun right at your head."

Jerry released Amber's arms immediately, causing her to fall on her backside with a thud. Then he lunged toward Joy, swinging an elbow hard into her chest.

The blow caused her to stagger backward and she momentarily lost her grip on the gun.

Lucky for them, Jerry was too drunk to take advantage of the opening. The sideways lurch made him lose his balance and tumble over the bench of the picnic table.

From her sitting position, Amber kicked again at Ray, this time catching his kneecap squarely so that he howled in pain.

Joy recovered and swung the pistol from one man to the other. "Amber, get back to the truck."

"Fucking dyke," Jerry muttered, still crumpled on the ground.

Amber followed Joy back to their camper, checking over her shoulder to be sure the two drunks weren't in pursuit. "That was the most awesome thing I've ever seen in my whole fucking life. You were fucking amazing!"

"Pack up. We're getting out of here."

"Why? You had those guys pissing in their pants. They know better than to mess with us now."

"Are you insane? I nearly got both of us killed. If that guy hadn't been so drunk, I would have been sitting on the wrong end of my own gun."

Amber secured the loose items inside the camper while Joy unhooked the water and power. In less than five minutes they were pulling out the front gate and back onto Interstate 80.

"I didn't even know you had a gun. Where do you keep it?"

"Locked up. That's the first time in my life I've ever pointed it at a real person." Joy's voice still shook, and her hands fidgeted all about the steering wheel. "I can't believe I just did that."

"Not only did you do it, you were fucking amazing. Believe me, if I had one of those, no one would ever fuck with me again."

"Do you have to say fuck all the time?"

Amber was startled by the sharpness of her voice. Clearly, Joy was shaken by the experience. "Sorry. Are you okay?"

Her first answer was a deep sigh and a trembling hand through her hair. "I'm just freaked out because of what could have happened if I hadn't come looking for you. You could have been..."

Amber finished the sentence in her head. She would have been raped. Even though both men had been stinking drunk, she'd been totally defenseless when they picked her up and carried her to their camper. And who knows what they might have done afterward to cover their crime?

But they hadn't, and she had more than enough bad memories that were real without torturing herself over something that hadn't happened.

A sign on the otherwise barren road said Elko, Nevada, was ninety-eight miles away, and Joy methodically located three different campgrounds on her navigation system. Though it was nearly midnight, Amber was too hyper to worry about dozing off, and from the nervous way Joy's fingers kept tapping the steering wheel, she too was wired. They'd probably get a later start than usual tomorrow, but at least they'd be a couple of hours closer to Oakland.

She studied Joy in the bluish glow from the dashboard. To the list of traits she'd already compiled to describe her—responsible, orderly, independent, capable—she'd add brave. And no matter what she'd said about nearly getting both of them killed, Amber still thought she was fucking awesome.

CHAPTER SEVEN

After a long quiet day on the road, Amber welcomed the growing cheer in Joy's voice as they got closer to home. Both of them had been positively morose when they first awakened at the campground in Nevada, most likely still hung over from the events of the night before.

"I always tell everyone I live in Oakland because no one knows where Alameda is," Joy explained animatedly as she drove through the residential grid.

Several of the streets were named for presidents, Amber noted, but not in an order that would help anyone find their way. They turned onto Garfield Avenue, where small, modest homes sat only ten or twelve feet from the sidewalk. No two looked alike, and yet all were similar, single-story with long narrow driveways that disappeared through a fence or ran all the way to a guesthouse in the back.

Joy pulled to the curb in front of a tidy bungalow, light gray with white trim, and charcoal steps and shutters. The front porch was covered and enclosed by a half-wall with two pillars on each side.

"Welcome to your new home…for a while, at least."

Eager for a cigarette, Amber hopped out of the truck and lit up before Joy could remind her that she'd promised to quit when they got here. She still had three left and planned to savor each one.

"Looks like Rocky mowed the grass," Joy said, nodding toward the front yard, which was no larger than an average living room. "He's the kid next door."

Amber furiously puffed her cigarette while she led Skippy around the yard, and then ground it out on the concrete sidewalk. On the steps, she caught Joy's stern look and hustled back to pick up the butt.

"How many more?"

"Two." She followed Joy onto the porch, noticing only a tiny beveled incline at the front door. "Where's the wheelchair ramp?"

"Around back. Pop thought it might invite thieves."

"You could always shoot them." The hard-faced look Joy gave her made Amber wish she'd swallowed that quip instead of blurting it out. Thinking first wasn't her strong suit.

Joy led her inside. On the right side of the house, the living room, dining area and kitchen were open all the way to the back porch. It was immediately obvious from the scuffed wood floors, the open space at the dining table and hip-high countertops that a handicapped person lived there.

"Pop's room is here."

They walked through a wide doorway on the left side of the house to a room that held an adjustable single bed, nightstand and dresser. There was no door on the adjacent bathroom, where the toilet, sink and shower stall had been custom-made for wheelchair access.

In the hallway outside were wide doorways leading to a smaller bathroom, and then a second bedroom.

"And this is your room?" Amber asked. There was a double bed pushed all the way up to the window, a chest of drawers, and a small desk and chair.

"Actually, it's yours."

Amber walked back out to the main living area and looked around. No more doors. She could see the whole backyard through the kitchen windows, and there wasn't a guesthouse—only a carport that covered a white Ford sedan and a dark green Jeep with a canvas top.

"Okay, I give up. You do live here, right?"

"Yes, but my room is still parked out front. I need to open the gate so I can pull it around back and hook up the water and electricity."

"You live in that fu—I mean that freaking camper all the time?" No wonder Joy was so quirky.

"I like my space."

"And you call that space."

Joy laughed as she drew a couple of beers from the refrigerator. "Someday I'll show you a few pictures of life on an aircraft carrier. You'll see why that camper feels like a palace. The best part is I don't have to share it with seven others."

Amber took a welcome swig of cold brew from the bottle. "Beer goes with cigarettes, you know. I might have to go get another pack just to get me through this bottle." She jerked it away when Joy tried to grab it. "Seriously, can I smoke outside if I promise not to throw my butts on the ground? And I'll shut the windows so it won't blow back in."

"I'm not your mother," Joy answered, not hiding her disappointment. "You're the one who said you wanted to quit because it was expensive. They're five dollars a pack in California, so a pack a day is going to cost you more than a thousand bucks a year."

Put another way, it meant two weeks at this job paid for her nicotine habit for a whole year.

"You can put your things away in the drawers and closet." She started outside but stopped at the back door. "Oh, and we have to share that bathroom, but I'll keep my gear outside so it won't be in your way. Make yourself at home."

Amber wandered back through all the rooms, trying to imagine it as home. It was nothing like any of the other places she'd lived since leaving her parents' house. All of them had been apartments, not houses with yards, and they'd been in varying stages of disrepair. On top of that, each and every one had been a mess from top to bottom because Amber refused to pick up after others, and saw no need to pick up after herself if no one else did. She and Corey had forfeited the security deposit on their last place because of the grime they left behind, especially in the kitchen and bathroom.

To call this house neat would be an understatement. Inside the kitchen cabinets, dishes and groceries were lined up like soldiers, and there wasn't a crumb to be found anywhere. Even the contents of the refrigerator were perfectly placed.

In the living room was a worn leather recliner, the father's presumably. Also a couch with two end tables, and a wall-mounted flat-screen TV. It took her a moment to realize what was missing—a coffee table, which would have taken up too much space and made it tricky to navigate in a wheelchair.

A credenza behind the recliner held several framed photos. Her eyes were drawn immediately to one of Joy, a headshot taken in her navy uniform—a dark jacket with a white shirt and small tie, and a black-and-white cap. Her look was captivating, enough to make Amber admit she had a thing for women in uniform. Judging from Joy's age in the photo, it was taken soon after she entered the navy over a decade ago. Her hair looked exactly the same as today, tucked behind her ears to her collar, but the thin face in the photo had filled out since then.

Right beside it was a similar photo of a young man, its faded colors suggesting it was taken many years ago. Joy's father, no doubt, since they had the same sharp blue eyes. Next was what looked like a relatively recent family photo, with Joy's father and mother seated, and Joy standing behind, again looking sharp in her uniform, this time with rows of ribbons on her chest.

"Look at this, Skippy," she mumbled mockingly. "This is what a happy family looks like."

The rest appeared to be sequential school photos of a child, a beautiful mixed-race girl, obviously the goddaughter, Madison.

Joy delivered her suitcase to the back door and Amber went to work organizing the contents in the bureau. Any other day, that might have meant stuffing things wherever they'd fit, but she found herself folding and stacking her belongings in neat piles, and arranging them perfectly straight in the drawers, afraid someone would come in and check.

When that was done, she explored a little more, flipping through the magazine rack by the recliner in the living room. *The American Legion,* TV listings from two weeks ago and a book on Operation Desert Storm. On the credenza by the photos was a coffee table book on aircraft carriers. Only a military veteran would find such trivia interesting.

The power button for the TV remote control did nothing— no picture, no sound. Why were they always so complicated? You always had to push this first then that, and only if you also had another remote for the cable or satellite dish.

She was officially bored, and coincidentally, nearly out of cigarettes. If Joy could point her in the direction of a convenience store, she could take Skippy for a walk. That would kill an hour or so. The problem with that was she didn't want to disturb Joy, who probably was relishing her solitude out back, or possibly even sleeping after the long drive.

"Silly me...of course she's not sleeping," she told Skippy as she looked out the kitchen window to see Joy power washing the camper. "She'd never rest as long as there was a speck of dirt somewhere."

The truck camper was parked on a concrete pad next to the back of the house, its door only a few steps away from the back deck, which had a long ramp leading to the concrete driveway that ran all the way back to the carport.

"You need any help with that?"

"Nah, I'm almost done."

"I thought you'd be out here resting. I should have known better."

Joy turned off the water and coiled the hose around its caddy. "I need to go see Pop at the rehab center and let him know what we've got worked out."

Amber followed her into the house. "I was thinking about taking a walk with Skippy. You know…checking out the neighborhood. Is there a store I can walk to?"

"Cigarettes?"

"Dog food…and yeah, cigarettes."

Joy's only response was a soft chuckle, for which Amber was relieved. The last thing she needed on top of all the stress of a new home, a new job and getting dumped by her boyfriend of three years was grief over smoking. There were only so many problems a person could deal with at the same time.

"Here's a key to the front door," Joy said, scribbling directions to a market a few blocks away. Suddenly she crossed the living room and lifted the beer bottle Amber had left on the credenza. "You can't set drinks on wooden furniture, Amber. It leaves a ring."

All she could do was watch as Joy vigorously wiped the damaged spot. With her luck, the credenza was her father's favorite piece of furniture…probably made it himself in woodshop as a teenager. "I'm sorry."

Joy sighed and gave up her efforts. "Don't forget to lock up when you leave."

Amber clipped Skippy's leash into place and carefully checked the front door to make sure it latched. "How about that, boy? We've been here less than an hour and already ruined something. I better start looking at the want ads."

CHAPTER EIGHT

"I didn't just pick her up off the side of the road. It's more complicated than that." Joy knew she'd get nothing but grief over bringing a total stranger to their house, especially one with zero training in home health care. Wait until he found out she had even less in housekeeping.

"Ah, what the hell…I don't give a shit if she's Lizzie Borden as long as I get out of here."

Getting her father home was as much a matter of his health as his sanity. In just the week since his accident, weight loss was noticeable in his face, neck and chest. It was important he not lose muscle mass, since his strength was what enabled him to maintain his independence.

"What's taking them so long? Why can't I just leave?" he groused.

"You know how these places are about rules. They insist on pushing everyone out in a wheelchair." She ducked a flying box of tissues.

"Smartass."

Her father, reclining on the bed, was already dressed in khaki shorts and a loose-fitting white oxford shirt, which Barbara had brought from home. Beneath his shirt was a Velcro-strapped shoulder brace, and on the outside, a sling. His only other personal effects were the clothes he'd been wearing when he slipped on the ramp at the American Legion hall. He was clean-shaven, and his short gray hair had been parted neatly, but on the wrong side.

She couldn't believe he'd sat still for someone to do that. He'd already ranted to her about the bathroom indignities, but now that she'd seen his surgical incision, it was clear why they were being careful not to let him do too much.

"Your physical therapist is supposed to meet us at the house to go through all the exercises."

"He's a putz. He has me balling up towels in my hand and twisting my neck from side to side. I keep telling him my hands and neck are just fine. All I need is a way to get in and out of my chair, and roll myself around. He says that's not on his orders."

Joy sifted through the pages of exercises on the bedside table. "I guess I should take all these home so Amber can study them."

"So what's this Amber person like? I figure she has to be cute or you wouldn't have picked her up."

By his teasing tone, he was convinced there was something going on between the two of them, but Joy was sure that would change once he got his first look at her. He'd know better than to think she would go for someone so immature and irresponsible, and with a tattoo, no less. And then he'd give her hell for bringing home someone like that to take care of him.

"She's twenty-four, but still basically a kid who's down on her luck, Pop. Her parents overdid it on the discipline end and she left home a few years ago without much of a plan." She shared her idea about Amber getting health care certification in her off hours. "A little experience and responsibility under her belt could be just what she needs."

"How do you know she's not going to run off with the silver?"

"Well, first there's the fact that we don't have any silver. But honestly, she doesn't strike me as someone who would do that." What Joy saw was a vulnerable young woman, but telling her father that would prompt him to tease her about how her favorite make-believe scenario as a child was rescuing damsels in distress. "I was clear about what we expected. If she doesn't work out, she's on a plane back to Nashville, but that goes for her too...which means if you're a jerk, she'll leave and you'll have to come back here. I can't take care of you and go to work too."

A tall brunette wearing a colorful nurse's smock swished past the door, and he yelled loudly, "If she can cook better than a one-eyed sailor on crack, it'll be an improvement over this hellhole!"

Nonplussed, the woman flipped him off behind her back and continued down the hall.

"Your new girlfriend?"

"She's not so bad," he answered smugly. "At least that one has a sense of humor. That's more than I can say about the rest of these asshats."

A burly African-American with a nametag that read Roderick appeared in the doorway with a wheelchair. He checked his paperwork and asked, "Oliver Shepard?"

"Call me Shep, and I brought my own wheels. Custom V-8 under the hood."

Joy chucked his good arm. "Behave yourself. It would be a shame if Roderick forgot to set the brake."

Roderick hesitated, clearly uncertain as to what sort of help he should render.

"Let me," Joy said. She rolled her father's chair beside him, locked the wheels and lowered the electric bed so it was even with the chair. While he grasped the arm of the chair with his good arm, she clutched his belt on the injured side and gave him just enough lift to allow him to spin into the seat. "Okay, he's all yours."

Her father glanced up at the orderly as they rolled out the door. "Hey, Roderick...help me with this footrest, will you?"

* * *

Amber dropped her cigarette in a soda can the moment she heard the car in the driveway on the side of the house. As Joy backed into the carport next to the Jeep, she contemplated whether to walk out and meet them or wait on the porch out of their way. Deciding it was best to show she was eager to get to work, she met Joy on the passenger side as she opened the door for her father.

"Nice to meet you, Mr. Shepard."

"Please help me, little girl," he pleaded. "I need to be in a hospital but my daughter won't pay."

Startled, Amber looked suspiciously at Joy.

"Knock it off, Pop, or I'll take you right back there and dump you on the doorstep."

He looked anxiously at Amber and clasped his hands as if begging. "You won't beat me like she does, will you?"

Joy sighed and shoved his chair against the seat of the car. "Ignore him, Amber. I need to show you how to do a transfer. You ready?"

Amber stepped closer, observing the strong muscles of the man's forearm as he gripped the chair arm.

"Grab his belt and pants right here at the hip and tug upward." As she demonstrated, he swung himself into the chair.

"Make sure you grab the side and not the back," he said. "Otherwise you'll give me a wedgie."

"You can feel free to do that if he gives you any trouble," Joy went on, picking up a stack of laundry from the backseat. "Why don't you go ahead and push him in?"

Amber nearly tossed him out of the chair when she thrust him forward without first releasing the brake. "Sorry."

Joy walked ahead into the house.

Halfway across the backyard, he said, "Hey, toots. I think Joy left my shoes in the backseat. Will you grab them for me?"

"Sure."

She set the brake again and returned to the car, searching all about. "I don't see them," she called.

"Maybe they're in the trunk. There's a button by the driver's seat."

After accidentally releasing the hood, Amber finally located the proper latch and checked the contents of the trunk. There was a strongbox labeled Earthquake Kit, jumper cables, a toolbox and a spare wheelchair, but no shoes. "Nothing in here. Joy must have picked them up."

"No, I'm sure she didn't. Did you look under the seat?"

She went back and scoured the car. "Nope."

"Maybe she dropped them under the car."

She was on her belly on the ground when Joy appeared at the back door.

"Did he ask you to look for his shoes?"

"Yeah, do you have them?"

"Amber...he doesn't have any feet."

As it dawned on her what that meant, Joy's father roared with laughter.

She returned to the chair and shoved it forward, again without releasing the brake. He'd been laughing so hard that he nearly slid off the seat. She would have apologized except she wasn't the least bit sorry.

"Get in here, you two. The physical therapist is here."

"I'll give you twenty bucks to wheel me around front and down the block."

This guy was turning out to be worse than all the three-year-olds at Harmony's daycare put together. "I'm starting to realize why Joy offered me so much money for this job."

"How much?"

"Five hundred a week."

"Holy crap! I'd get up and walk for that."

* * *

Joy closed the door behind the therapist and turned back to her father, who rolled his eyes. "You heard him, Pop. Three times a day every day."

"Such a load of crap. I get more exercise wiping my—"

"Please don't—"

"—countertops," he said, smirking. "Speaking of that, any chance I could get some lunch? Anything edible will do."

Joy noticed Amber had been keeping her distance, clearly intimidated by her father's surly disposition. "Amber, maybe you and Pop could practice moving him from his wheelchair to the recliner and back. If you drop him a couple of times, that'll be okay. That's why we call it practice."

She watched the first two attempts and was glad to hear her father had dialed back his attitude for Amber's sake. He was quite easy to manage when he wasn't acting like a two-year-old. The funny thing about him—and the reason he was behaving himself right now—was that he wasn't a jerk at all, just a joker who sometimes went too far. It wasn't in his nature to be genuinely cruel.

Coming up with an edible lunch proved harder than she thought, since she'd thrown out most of the contents of the refrigerator last night. There was bacon but no eggs, and hot dogs but no buns. Peering through the canned goods, she remembered one of her mother's recipes. Twenty minutes later, she called the others to lunch.

"Hawaiian stew!" her father proclaimed as Amber rolled him to the head of the table. "Now that's what I call edible."

"It looks like beanie weenies to me," Amber said.

"But it has pineapple and bacon," Joy explained. "This was my favorite meal as a kid. I never outgrew it."

Her mother's Hawaiian stew always made her nostalgic for her childhood. It wasn't just the memory of her mom in the kitchen. It was realizing as she grew up how her mother always dressed up such a simple meal to make it seem like a feast. Such was life on her mother's factory salary and her father's disability pension, but Joy had learned to get by with less, a habit that had served her well in the navy.

In typical fashion, her father wolfed down his meal, but then sat patiently while she and Amber finished. Amber pushed the food around on her plate, eating a few of the hot dogs, some bacon and finally the pineapple, but not the beans.

Joy couldn't be bothered with a picky eater. If Amber wanted to turn her nose up at dinner, she could do without.

"Joy tells me you're from Nashville," her father said, his voice pleasantly polite for the first time all day. "I had a machinist's mate from there...Wally something or other. He ate beans like it was caviar."

Amber fidgeted and glumly ate a forkful of beans, looking very much like Madison when she was encouraged to eat vegetables.

"You play backgammon?"

"I don't even know what that is."

He rubbed his hands together and grinned. "Don't worry, kiddo. I'll teach you everything you need to know."

"And then he'll take your money," Joy added.

"We'll play for Goobers. Grab me some, will you? There's a whole box in the door of the refrigerator."

"He's addicted to Goobers," Joy explained as she got up from the table.

"It's all I could think about for the last two weeks. If I closed my eyes I could almost taste them."

"Where did you say they were?"

"Right there in the door."

"Goobers...you don't mean those chocolate covered peanuts?" Amber asked, her eyes growing wide.

He was practically smacking his lips. "Damn things are worse than potato chips. You eat one, you have to eat the whole box."

Joy got a sinking feeling when she heard Amber's questioning tone, and she casually lifted the lid on the trash can. Sure enough, there was the empty Goober box. No wonder Amber hadn't been hungry.

"You know, Pop…I think I might've tossed those out accidentally last night. I'll get some more at the grocery store. Why don't I go now and let Amber clean up?"

Leaving the pair alone together would force them to get to know each other. More important, it would give Joy a break from both of them.

* * *

Amber had vague childhood memories of being left with a babysitter who scared her half to death. Miss Hodges was from the neighborhood, the kind of woman who yelled when kids walked across her lawn, or when anyone parked in front of her house. She was old, her house was old and all the trinkets inside it were old. Amber had been terrified to move, afraid she would break something and be subjected to her wrath.

Fifteen merciful years had passed since she last thought of Miss Hodges. If the old hag had ever raised a son, he would have grown into someone like Shep Shepard.

She was sure he knew she'd eaten his Goobers, even though he hadn't come out and said so. It was in his eyes, the way he stared at her from his recliner while pretending to watch a baseball game.

A teensy, tiny part of her actually wished she'd gotten out of the truck in Limon. By now she would have been on her way back to Nashville with—

"Skippy!" She bolted from the couch for her bedroom, where she had closed him up hours ago so he'd be out of the way when Shep's wheelchair rolled in. So much excitement would have set him off on a barking frenzy and he might even have gotten caught under one of the wheels.

"Who's Skippy?" Shep called after her.

She was too late. The foul odor of his accident hit her the second she opened the door, and instantly spread throughout the small house.

"Jesus, you got an elephant in there?"

No, but there was dog diarrhea in several places, including the rug in front of the bed.

Skippy was curled up on the bed, quivering in obvious fear, his ears flat as though he knew he'd done something wrong.

"It's okay, boy." She probably shouldn't have fed him those Goobers. Corey had told her once that chocolate was like poison for dogs, but he was always exaggerating. At least she had given him only three or four.

She shuttled back and forth between her bedroom and the bathroom cleaning up the mess, noticing Shep's interest. With the worst of it cleaned up, she finally emerged with Skippy in her arms.

"This is Skippy. I shut him up in the room so he wouldn't make a fuss when you got here, but then I forgot."

"I don't much like dogs."

"He won't be any trouble. I promise."

"Yeah, I can tell…no trouble at all. Good thing I don't have any plants or they'd have keeled over by now."

Most people got one look at Skippy and melted. He was small, fluffy and cute. There was nothing not to love.

And yet Shep didn't love him. But then Shep didn't seem to love anything except his precious Goobers. He was turning out to be every bit the jerk she'd feared.

She dropped Skippy back on the bed, but before she even got to the door, he'd run past her back into the living room. His toenails clicked on the hardwood floor as he sprang back and forth in front of Shep, barking sharply as if demanding attention.

"What the hell?" Shep grabbed his long-handled grippers, the pinchers he used to pick up things on the floor. "You want a piece of me?"

"Skippy, no!" She scrambled to catch him, stopping to give Shep a threatening look. "You son of a bitch…don't you dare hurt my dog."

Amber was in the bedroom with the door closed before she realized what she'd done. She'd be fired the moment Joy got home. Back to Nashville with nothing, not even a place to stay for a few nights.

Her mouth had gotten her in trouble again. Every time something like this happened, she always made sure to get the last word before storming out, even just a parting shot she yelled over her shoulder after being fired. Her last words to Shep were to call him a son of a bitch.

At least she and Skippy would be safe, and she wouldn't have to deal with that asshole anymore. It bothered her, though, how much this would disappoint Joy, who was just about the only person who'd ever shown any faith in her—based on practically nothing.

What bothered her more—now that it was too late to take back what she said—was that this gig was her only shot at making it on her own. No matter how she felt about Shep Shepard, she had to go out there and apologize, and hope to hell he accepted.

"Wish me luck, boy."

Careful this time to keep Skippy closed up in the bedroom, she returned to the living room, her head hanging with shame. "I'm sorry I called you a name."

"I've been called worse," Shep said, without his usual trace of sardonic humor. "I wouldn't have hurt your dog, you know. It's just that dogs never liked me, not since I was a kid. And now with this chair, I feel kind of…I don't know, helpless. I figure if I scare them off, they'll leave me alone."

"Skippy isn't like that. He'd never hurt anybody."

"People always say that about their dog…right before it eats the baby."

"Does Skippy look like he'd eat a baby?"

"I guess not. At least I don't have any ankles to bite." His morbid sense of humor had returned. "Go get him. Let's see if we can be friends."

* * *

If Joy hadn't seen it with her own eyes, she'd never have believed her father would be sharing his recliner with a dog. Skippy was stretched out alongside him, his head tucked under her father's hand.

Less surprising was the fact that the lunch dishes were still unwashed, stacked in the sink. For a moment, she toyed with the idea of washing them, but the errands of the day—on the heels of a long drive yesterday—had worn her out. As much as she hated leaving a mess, dealing with it was as simple as walking out the back door to her camper, climbing up into her loft and closing her eyes.

CHAPTER NINE

Maintenance crews at Oakland International Airport conducted regular sweeps of the gate areas, tarmac and runways for articles and debris that might puncture tires or get swept up in a plane's engine. Foreign Object Damage, it was called. Joy did her own FOD walk several times a day over the four-gate area she supervised, and expected the same from her crew. She'd seen how easily small objects like zipper pulls from luggage and plastics from food service trucks could fall onto the tarmac, and knew that even the tiniest scrap could cripple a plane.

She was excited to be back at work—until she found an incident report, the first by a StarWest ground crew in Oakland since she'd joined the airline three years ago. One of the airline's recent hires, a baggage handler named Thomas Epley, had turned a train of carts too close to an aircraft, clipping its engine. Mechanics eventually cleared the aircraft for departure, but not before ruining the travel plans of 132 passengers.

Thomas, a twenty-year-old aviation technology student at Alameda College, had seemed a natural for the job. Like all the others on her crew, he was strong, hardworking and dependable, but there was something else she'd liked about him—he always wore his uniform polo shirt tucked in. It was a minor detail to others, one she never bothered to mention in evaluations because even the other crew chiefs wore their shirttails out most of the time. To her, one's appearance was a point of personal pride and she liked that Thomas cared how he looked when he came to work.

Too bad he hadn't taken as much care in how he drove. Clipping an engine was a big deal, and he'd have thirty days of unpaid suspension to improve his concentration. She hoped he wouldn't use that time to find a new job. Persevering when the job got tough showed character and dedication.

Joy was taking a rare breather, a small window before the midday rush that happened only on days when all their flights were running on schedule. All four StarWest gates were clear but ST 413 was on approach from Chicago, while ST 644 from San Diego was in range. That would kick off a flurry that would last until her shift ended at one thirty.

Angie Low, an Asian-American ramp agent who also served in the National Guard, climbed up on the tug beside her, licking her fingers from the sticky bun she'd just finished. "I'm so glad you're back, Joy. Punch had everybody ready to quit last week after that dustup with Thomas. He ran out to supervise all the belts, the baggage carts, the tugs...everything. He treated all of us like it was our first day on the job."

"I probably would have done the same thing," Joy said. She liked to think the incident wouldn't have happened on her watch, but she couldn't be everywhere all at once. Whatever lapse Thomas had suffered likely would have occurred with her on the clock as crew chief. "I'm just glad I wasn't here when it happened."

"How was your trip?"

"Madison was a blast." She related the highlights of their cross-country adventure, but offered nothing about the return trip, nor her father's accident. Bringing Amber Halliday home was probably one of the stupidest, most impulsive things she'd ever done, and she didn't want anyone else to know about it.

"I bet that ride back by yourself was a long one," Angie replied.

The radio on Joy's belt crackled and she took her position atop the tug to signal the aircraft into the gate. "Show's on, people! Four-One-Three is on the ground."

* * *

Amber closed her eyes and luxuriated in the feel of the morning sun on her skin. Northern California was plenty hot in August, but without the humidity it wasn't nearly as oppressive as Nashville.

She loved that Joy and Shep's backyard was fenced in with a gate on the side. That meant Skippy could run free in the grass and she didn't have to keep an eye on him. Not that she would have had to, anyway. Shep, whose wheelchair was parked beneath an umbrella on the deck, nibbled on Goobers and watched his every move.

"I suppose I should go in and do my exercises again," he said. "Wouldn't want to lose all the muscle control in my pinky. How would I drink my tea?"

Amber had led him through an early-morning regimen using the notes from the physical therapist. The whole drill seemed like a silly waste of time, since Shep could do all the exercises easily and without pain. The only reason she bothered at all was because Joy had pretty much ordered her to make sure he did them three times a day, whether he wanted to or not.

She wheeled him back to the dining table and spread out the towel he was supposed to roll up with one hand. "Ten times, and then the neck twists." There wasn't much to supervise, but she felt she ought to sit with him while he did the repetitions.

"Any ideas about lunch?" he asked. "Grilled cheese would taste pretty good about now."

The thought of lunch hadn't even crossed her mind. Her usual fare was a bag of chips and a candy bar, and today's version of that was leftover popcorn from last night and two handfuls of Shep's Goobers.

Harmony made grilled cheese sandwiches for the kids at daycare at least once a week, but Amber had never watched to see exactly how she did it. It couldn't be that hard...bread and cheese, cooked in a frying pan instead of a toaster.

Her first clue that it was trickier than she thought was the piercing sound of the smoke alarm, which went off while she was counting reps for Shep.

"Let me guess," he said. "You've never made one of these before, have you?"

She scrunched her nose and shook her head, examining the charred remains of her first effort.

"I'm going to give you a grilled cheese lesson. Wash that pan."

She assembled all the ingredients and utensils he asked for—she'd had no idea a grilled cheese sandwich was supposed to have butter on it—and perched on a stool in the corner of the kitchen, feeling like a three-year-old in time-out. Clumsily, he demonstrated with his good arm the basics of grilling without burning. Low heat was the key, he said, which struck her as an idiotic oxymoron. Heat was supposed to be hot. Besides, it was grilled cheese, not prime rib. But when she watched how it worked, it made sense.

Twelve weeks of cooking lessons from a one-armed guy in a wheelchair. She could stand it. At least she wasn't scrubbing toilets in Limon.

* * *

Joy nearly barreled into the gate, not expecting it to be closed. It made sense, she realized, that Amber would want to let Skippy out to roam in the backyard, but they needed a signal for when she was on her way home. It would be devastating for all of them if the dog got under her wheels when she drove through.

It drove her half-crazy that Amber never seemed to think about how her actions—or inactions—affected others. She didn't take hints very well, certainly not the one Joy had dropped about keeping her toiletries out of Amber's way. She'd hoped for the same courtesy, but instead had found the bathroom a wreck this morning. Amber's cosmetics, with some of the bottles and tubes still open, lined the sink, and towels hung haphazardly over the shower bar. Joy wondered what part of "share the bathroom" she hadn't understood.

She collected her shopping bags and entered through the front door, waking both Skippy and her father from a nap in the recliner. The back of Amber's head—surrounded by a swirl of cigarette smoke—was visible through the kitchen window.

"Hiya, Pop."

"You're late."

It was nearly four o'clock, two hours past the usual time she arrived home.

"I had a few things to pick up." She held up one of the bags. "Including Chinese food for supper. Did you and Amber have a good day?"

He twisted his head to make sure Amber was out of earshot. "Are you sure she's twenty-four? Madison's got more common sense than this one."

Joy wasn't at all surprised to hear about the burnt sandwich because she'd smelled it the moment she walked in the door.

"If I hadn't asked her about lunch, I think she would have let me starve. Didn't you say she was going to handle all the cooking and cleaning? She left all that crap piled up in the sink. It would still be there if Barbara hadn't come over and cleaned up."

It was painfully clear Joy had done a poor job of communicating her expectations. Amber wasn't the sort of person who could take the initiative to do whatever needed to be done. Joy would have to spell out every single task. It was little wonder the girl hadn't been able to hold a job.

"I'll talk to her. Anything else?"

He sighed. "Don't be too hard on her, but jeez…five hundred bucks a week to tug on my shorts a few times a day, and that's only if I can get her attention."

When Joy stepped out onto the deck, Amber quickly stood and closed her *Country Update* magazine, a ragged one she'd been reading off and on since they'd met.

"I didn't know you were home."

"Yeah, the gate was closed. I got you something." Joy presented her with a small shopping bag. "Your own cell phone. For now, you're on my plan…unlimited talk and text."

"Wow!" Her excitement was tempered when she saw it was a basic flip phone, not a fancy one with games, pictures and web surfing.

"I figured you might be out running errands for Pop and need a phone for emergencies. I had the guy at the store program the house phone and my cell, and I put in a few other numbers you might need, like the therapist and Pop's doctor at the VA."

"Okay…cool."

Joy asked, "So how did it go today?"

"Kind of sucky, if you want to know the truth." She slumped back in her chair and gazed grimly out at the backyard. "I don't know if I'm cut out for this."

Joy wasn't so sure either, but at least the two of them had survived the first day together. She'd wanted this to be a good experience for Amber, a chance to learn responsibility and prepare for a steady job that would allow her to take care of herself. But what mattered most was taking care of her father. If Amber wasn't up to it, Joy needed to find someone else right away.

"Why do you say that?"

"I feel like I can't do anything right. I'm not saying your pop's being critical or anything like that…just that I'm not very good at stuff…like cooking. And I think I get on his nerves. I've been out here almost all day trying to stay out of his way."

So that was it. Amber was feeling intimidated, and instead of sticking close to her father and helping him, she was avoiding him.

"Look, I know Pop can be difficult. That's mostly the navy talking. He was always sort of a tough guy, and Mom said his accident made him act even tougher. But that's just it. Most of it is an act." When he cared about someone, he was one of the softest, gentlest people she knew. "You should see him with Madison. Those two—gosh, they worship each other. You shouldn't be afraid of him, not as long as you're working hard and doing what needs to be done. He'll respect that."

She nodded. "At least he likes Skippy."

"That reminds me." Joy reached into her other bag and produced a roll of blue plastic bags, specifically designed for pet waste. "I'd appreciate it if you kept the yard cleaned up. I got a rude surprise this morning when I walked out."

"Sorry."

As much as she hated to pile on, she took the opportunity to ask Amber to keep the bathroom and kitchen clean, and to check on her father regularly. Breakfast at eight, lunch at noon.

"I worry that Pop will try to do things by himself, and he'll hurt his shoulder. I don't want him to look around and see little jobs that need to be done. You think you can stay in front of all that?"

"Sure." Amber leaned over the rail of the deck to drop her makeshift ashtray into the trash can. "I'll clean up the yard and the dishes. Would it be all right if I walked over to the store after that?"

More smokes. Amber sounded just like Madison, bargaining for privileges in exchange for doing chores and homework. How on earth she'd gotten by for the last few years was a mystery. Thank goodness she'd been smart enough to realize she wasn't ready to be a parent. Pity the poor child she might have raised.

* * *

Amber washed the last of the dishes after supper, careful not to make too much noise. Joy and Shep were a few feet away at the dining table using the laptop to video chat with Madison before she went to bed. From the story Joy had told about knowing her since she was born, it was easy to understand her affection. Shep was the one who fascinated her—no relation at all and yet it was obvious he loved the little girl like a granddaughter.

It was rare that she thought of the baby she'd given up, but when she did, it was to imagine his adoptive family loving him the way Joy and Shep loved Madison. If she'd had a sympathetic grandparent or aunt and uncle, she might have been able to get away from her parents before their relationship got so bad. Maybe she could have weathered the storm.

But then she wouldn't be here, and while "here" wasn't exactly paradise, it was interesting. There was something mystical about California, a whole other world from places like Kentucky and Tennessee. Here they didn't wave the Bible in your face like it was a razor strap, or make you feel like an outcast if you didn't think like everybody else. At least Joy and Shep didn't do that.

When they finished their call, she brought the towel to the table and spread it out. "One more time, Shep."

"Oh, Christ," he grumbled.

"Sounds like she's got your number, Pop."

Amber counted off the repetitions and helped Shep back into his recliner so he could watch the baseball game. The moment he got settled, Skippy was in the chair with him.

"You've stolen my dog."

"He's my little buddy," he answered, petting Skippy as he curled up in his lap. "I think he likes that I don't move around much, and I don't blow smoke in his face."

She huffed. "I don't blow smoke in his face either. Besides, I'm going to quit soon."

"I smoked for about twenty years...started when I was a punk teenager because I thought it made me look cool. Cindy—

that was my wife—she didn't like it much, but she put up with me."

"How'd you quit?" Not that Amber was planning to quit anytime soon, but one of these days, she would.

"Stupid old VA had a No Smoking policy. I spent eight weeks there after I lost my legs."

Both Joy and Shep talked about his injury in an offhanded way, almost as if it weren't that big a deal. She couldn't imagine having to deal with such a trauma day in and day out. At the very least, she'd be bitter—certainly toward the navy, if not everyone else.

"Can I ask what happened?"

"Joy didn't tell you?"

She shook her head, glad she'd finally gotten the nerve to bring it up. It was curious that Joy hadn't told her any details. Maybe it was too awful to talk about.

"You know anything about aircraft carriers?"

"Just that they're really big and flat on top so planes can land on them. Oh, and I'm not supposed to call them boats."

"Joy pinned your ears back on that one, didn't she?" He laughed. "I was a green shirt on the *Carl Vinson*. That means I worked on the catapult and arresting gear. Hand me that book over there."

She fetched the coffee table book on aircraft carriers and followed along with the pictures of planes being launched by the catapult and then caught by cables when they landed.

"See, there we are—the green shirts. Purple shirts did the fuel...red shirts were bombs and bullets. The yellow shirts were the plane handlers."

"Joy was a plane handler." Now it made sense why she was so attached to her yellow T-shirt.

"That's right. Our homeport used to be right here in Alameda at the Naval Air Station, but they shut it down back in ninety-seven." He closed the book and managed a weak smile. "I remember the day it happened like it was yesterday, but only up to the accident. Everything after that's a big blur, and I hope it stays that way. Some of the guys who were there say it still gives them nightmares."

Amber had already heard the story of how Barbara's husband Hank had burned to death in a fire in the engine room. It was hard to imagine anything more horrible than that.

"We were on training maneuvers with the Marine Corps off San Diego. It was after sunset and the last man out was an F-14 Tomcat. He came in hot and caught the third cable, first time all day. It pulled taut and slowed him down but then all of a sudden it snapped. He took a nosedive right off the end of the deck."

From the pictures he'd shown her and the way his hand glided along the arm of his chair, she could picture it as though it were happening before her eyes.

"The pilot's seat blew before he ever hit the water, so everybody knew he was okay. But we were staring out at the bow when that broken cable all of a sudden whipped back on all of us there on the deck…like a steel snake coming at you at a hundred miles an hour. And it was nearly dark, so we could hear it better than we could see it. Believe it or not, I was the lucky one. Two of the yellow shirts were killed."

Amber was stunned, not only at the horror of Shep's accident, but at the realization the same thing could have happened to Joy. No wonder she was so regimented. On the ship, it was a matter of life and death.

"How could you stand having your daughter join the navy and then take a dangerous job like that? Weren't you scared?"

"Sure, but I was proud too. I always knew what kind of person Joy was, and that's who I'd want out there if I was bringing one of those planes in."

She knew what kind of person Joy was too. For the first time since arriving in California, she thought of the night Joy had confronted her attackers with a gun. Though it had nearly ended in disaster, at least she had known what to do and had the courage to do it.

When Shep closed the book and turned his attention to the ballgame, Amber slipped out for another cigarette. Seeing the light on in the camper, she was tempted to knock on the door to see if Joy wanted a beer, or maybe just some company.

Her opinion of Joy—and in fact, all her thoughts about Joy—had come full circle since the moment almost a week ago when she picked her up in Louisville. She'd been grateful at first, then increasingly wary as she took in all the meticulous habits and routines. She'd secretly laughed at her quirks, even tossing cigarette butts on the ground to watch how it bothered her. It all began to shift when Joy pulled out of the parking lot at Limon, her compassion outshining her eccentricities. From there, she'd become a gallant protector, and then the dashing figure of her photo in uniform.

A woman like that had to be a powerful lover.

—

CHAPTER TEN

Joy released the latch beneath the 737's cockpit and fastened the power cable, allowing the jet to power down its engines. Then she uncoiled the air conditioner tube from its caddy and dragged it along the underbelly of the plane to its socket. With each step, she counted under her breath to calm her flaring temper.

Robbie Pascal, who hired on at StarWest two years before she did, parked the baggage conveyor at the rear compartment and swung the heavy door upward. Though he'd bristled a bit last year when she got promoted to crew chief over him, he was a conscientious worker and proud to be part of the team that got the highest performance marks nearly every quarter. He also was fun to work with.

Too much fun today, Joy thought. Since they had only twenty-five minutes to turn this plane around, she climbed up into the cargo hold instead of calling him out onto the tarmac.

"Look, Robbie. I don't know what you and Freddie were playing today, but a wing-walker has one job, and that's to see the plane in and out of the gate without clipping something. You can't do that when you're horsing around."

By his look of astonishment, her scolding was unexpected. "Joy…we were just—"

"I don't care what you were doing. I care what you *weren't* doing. These planes cost millions of dollars and these passengers have better ways to spend their time than sit around and wait on us to fix a mess that shouldn't have happened in the first place."

She didn't wait for a comeback, jumping out onto the tarmac to load the bags Robbie had already sent down the belt. When the other baggage handler arrived, she returned to the front of the plane to ready the tow bar for pushback.

Freddie worked under another crew chief at the next gate, and it was all she could do to hold back from reporting him. Even after a week, she was still smarting from learning about Thomas's incident. Reports like that drew attention from upstairs, which meant her whole crew would be under heightened scrutiny by StarWest brass and airport authorities until they were satisfied she had a handle on discipline.

The ridiculous part was that she trusted Robbie to do his job, even as he joked around from time to time with his co-workers. Every single member of her crew was careful, efficient and dependable. They had all the discipline of the *TR* air wing.

The person she'd lost confidence in was Joy Shepard and it had nothing to do with her ground crew, or her job at StarWest for that matter. It was that her mind wandered all day long.

Amber Halliday was the one who couldn't handle her job, no matter how many times Joy had tried to train her. It took daily reminders to get her to scoop up Skippy's business in the yard, keep the kitchen clean and hang up her towels in the bathroom. If that weren't enough, she'd bleached her father's dark blue sheets and set another ice-cold drink on the credenza to leave a ruinous ring.

Taken together, the mishaps and jobs undone were so frustrating that she even wondered if Amber was intentionally trying to push her buttons. Joy didn't want to think she'd do that, but she'd all but admitted to a history of intentionally riling her bosses. Her saving grace was that she seemed to genuinely like her father, and the feeling was clearly mutual. He'd taught her to play backgammon and she'd introduced him to a couple of her favorite soap operas. As silly as that was, at least they were diligent about the physical therapy and he was distracted from actions that might injure his shoulder.

Joy considered the irony that she'd just chewed out Robbie for not concentrating on his job, and here she was mired in thoughts of Amber. She needed to knock it off and focus.

And she needed to apologize to Robbie for coming down so hard.

* * *

Amber craned her neck to see the front bumper of the big sedan as it cleared the parking space. She wasn't used to driving a vehicle this size, since Corey hardly ever let anyone else behind the wheel of his "baby," a black and chrome Chevy Silverado.

She still had the schedule Gus Holley's road manager had handed out. The band was working its way down the East Coast, playing in Baltimore tonight and Raleigh two nights later. They weren't due in California until mid-November. Shep told her she ought to get tickets in the front row so she could hold up a sign telling Corey to kiss her ass.

After a week of worrying the whole time about getting fired, she was finally feeling comfortable and secure in her new job. If only she got along with Joy as well as she did with Shep. Shep didn't nag her over trivial stuff the way Joy did. He actually treated her like a person instead of just the hired help, taking the time to tell stories about the navy and what Joy was like growing up, as well as asking about her life back in Kentucky and Nashville. Joy came into the house for a couple of hours around dinner, but then disappeared into her cave for the rest of the night. Practically the only time she said anything to her was to point out something Amber hadn't done right.

This was Amber's third trip out in Shep's car. The other two had been for groceries and dog food, but this was a special errand to the sporting goods store to pick up the dumbbells and stretch bands Shep needed for his next phase of physical therapy.

She'd had no trouble finding the place, since it was on the opposite end of the shopping center from the Safeway where she went for groceries. The tricky part was getting out of the parking lot. She found herself in a Right Turn Only lane, knowing she needed to be going the other direction. A swarm of traffic kept her from getting over to where she could turn around, and before she knew it she was on a road called the Nimitz Freeway heading toward Oakland International Airport and San Jose.

"Crap!"

She wasn't that far from home, because Joy said it took her only ten minutes to get home from the airport. But then the airport exit looped her all the way through baggage claim and back out to the freeway, where she had no idea which ramp to take to get back to the neighborhood.

When she saw the big arena in her rearview mirror—the one where Gus Holley would play in November—she realized she had guessed wrong. At the next exit, she asked a gas station owner to direct her toward the Safeway.

"Which one?"

"Alameda."

He didn't know about the Alameda Safeway but he got her back on the freeway in what she hoped was the right direction. An exit sign pointed her to Alameda, but when the exit forked, there was no indication as to which way she should turn. Nothing looked familiar, or even remotely like a residential area.

A horn blasted behind her and she inched forward, turning right because it seemed the less seedy of the two. She'd gone only a few yards when the car began to sputter. It was the first time all day she'd noticed the gas gauge. It was on WWPE, as Molly used to say—way, way past empty.

There wasn't a gas station in sight, only industrial buildings and warehouses covered with graffiti. Cars were parked on both sides of the street but the only way to get to any of the buildings was through gates that were locked.

It was no use to call Shep. Even if he could help her find her way home, she couldn't get there without gas, and there was nothing he could do about that.

She got out and waved down a passing car, two men who appeared to be Mexican and didn't speak English.

She dreaded calling Joy, but she was out of options.

"Is everything okay?" Joy asked, her voice anxious.

"Yes." Except it wasn't. "No, not really. Your pop's fine, but I went to pick up some stuff he needed for his exercises and now I'm lost...and out of gas."

Amber could practically hear her seething as she went through a series of questions to determine where she was. Then Joy gave explicit directions to what she thought was the nearest gas station—about half a mile away.

That's when Amber let the other shoe drop. "I don't think I can walk that far. I was just going out on this one little errand and I...I didn't wear any shoes."

"Oh, for God's sakes!" Joy sighed heavily and went stone quiet for several seconds. "Just stay where you are. I have to find somebody to cover for me."

Amber had no choice. It could be twenty minutes or two hours, but one thing was certain—Joy would be hopping mad when she got there.

* * *

Joy trudged through the back door, later than usual because she'd stayed to help Punch with his lost baggage logs. That was her payback for him giving up his lunch break to supervise her crew while she ran out to deliver a gallon of gas to Amber. What kind of idiot drove past a half dozen gas stations on her way to running out of gas? Apparently, it was the same kind who went to the store without shoes.

Amber was in her room with the door closed. That was the safest place for everyone concerned, Joy thought. She'd been so angry when she got to the car that she spoke only to give Amber directions home—left at High Street all the way to Garfield. A blind mouse could find it.

"Heard you had a little adventure," her father said, not bothering to hide his amusement.

"It wasn't funny. My whole crew's under the microscope and instead of being there to supervise them, I have to play babysitter to somebody who wouldn't even have enough sense to come in out of the rain."

Joy shuddered to realize her father, his eyes wide and his forehead wrinkled, was looking past her in the direction of Amber's door. Sure enough, footsteps crossed the room behind her into the kitchen, and she turned to see Amber rinse a glass and put it in the dishwasher.

Exasperated, Joy stalked out to the back deck, where she planted both hands on the rail and drew a deep breath. An apology was in order, but it would only be for saying something insensitive, not for thinking it. Amber would see through it, and it would probably make matters worse.

She'd already wasted enough time today worrying about Amber. There was no amount of instructing, demonstrating or reminding that could train someone to do even the most basic of tasks when she was just too lazy or careless to follow through.

Joy wanted to like her. Clearly her pop did, and he had to find her ineptitude just as annoying as she did. That probably meant it was up to Joy to change her attitude, not Amber to change her behavior.

Not yet ready to go back inside and apologize, Joy went into the camper and changed from her work clothes to gray sweatpants and a black tank top. A good workout at the gym was just what she needed to dump her frustration. She left through the back gate, yelling to no one in particular that she'd pick up dinner…something that wouldn't dirty any more dishes.

* * *

Amber leaned against the bathroom door, staring up at the towel she'd thrown over the shower rod this morning. There was only one bar in the tiny bathroom and that was for a hand towel she shared with Joy, so it wasn't as if she had any choice but to hang it up there. That said, it was dry now so she took it down and folded it along with her washcloth.

Back in the bedroom, she cleared a drawer in the bureau for all her bathroom items, and neatly lined them up. Next she returned to the kitchen and wiped down all the counters and swept the floor. Then she carried out the trash, making a special effort to police the yard for anything Skippy might have left.

"Hey, kid. Come in here and sit down a minute," Shep said. He muted the TV, picked up one of the dumbbells and began a series of slow bicep curls with his injured arm.

Forgoing her usual seat on the couch, Amber dragged a stool beside Shep's recliner so she could support his arm like the therapist had shown her as he raised the weight.

"Joy's dealing with some trouble at work right now. One of her crew had an accident while she was gone and they wrote him up. That's a pretty big deal in her line of work, and she feels responsible because it was her guy. That's what's under her skin right now, not you."

"Do you really believe all that bullshit that comes out of your mouth?"

Shep laughed and, with his good hand, tousled her hair until it came loose and fell from its tie all around her face. "Let me put it this way," he said. "You're only part of the problem, and right now she's off somewhere feeling bad about what she said. I know her. She's gone to take it out on a bunch of weight machines, and by the time she gets back, it'll all be over."

Until next time, Amber thought. She had only herself to blame. Joy had made it clear from the first day they met that she was a perfectionist, and while Amber had sort of tried to keep the house and yard neat, she hadn't tried hard enough. It was always clear her primary job was taking care of Shep, and she focused on that while sloughing off the rest. That was how she operated in every job—doing the very least that would get her by.

"No, she's right, Shep. If I'd done what she asked me to do, she wouldn't have gotten so pissed over what happened today. I don't blame her. She gave me a chance and I let her down. All that's going to change...starting right now."

* * *

Sweat-soaked and rank from her workout, Joy entered through the back door and deposited chicken, potato salad, coleslaw and biscuits on the pristine counter. Her father was watching TV with Skippy in his lap, and she could hear the water running back in his bathroom.

"Dinner's here. I'm going to grab a shower. You and Amber go ahead and start without me if you're hungry."

She collected fresh clothes and toiletries from the camper, and returned to find the bathroom scrubbed from top to bottom, and Amber's personal items gone. A toothbrush hanging in the caddy was the only sign she hadn't packed up to move.

Joy wasn't unhappy at all to find the bathroom clean for a change, but she regretted how it had come about. She never meant for Amber to feel like a house slave.

When she emerged, two places were set at the table—hers and her father's. Amber's bedroom door was closed.

"What's going on, Pop?"

"Looks like somebody's trying not to poke the bear."

She'd hoped to sweep the day's events under the rug just by being polite and upbeat at dinner, but apparently it would take a full-fledged apology to mend this fence. After a few seconds of dancing from one foot to the other outside Amber's door, she knocked and waited for a response.

"Hey...I got enough chicken for everybody. Come on and join us."

Amber was on her bed with a magazine, and her room was as clean and neat as the rest of the house. "Thanks, but I thought I'd give your pop a break. He has to put up with me all day."

A full-fledged apology. "Amber, I'm really sorry. I could make excuses about having a lousy day, but that wouldn't make what I said okay. It was rude...and it was wrong."

"I don't know, Joy. It's true I've been caught standing out in the rain before."

Joy laughed softly, grateful to get a lighthearted response, but still unsure if her apology was accepted. "I bet if you asked around among my navy buddies, you'd probably find out I have too."

Amber finally smiled but made no move to get up.

"Please come join us. Pop really wants you there." That was her stupid, stubborn pride talking, and it was unraveling her intended apology. "And I want you there too."

It was a wrenching few seconds before Amber finally answered. "Okay."

Joy set another place at the table while Amber helped her pop into his wheelchair and rolled him to the table.

"Did you two kiss and make up?"

Of all the words he might have chosen, that was at the bottom of Joy's wish list, and she answered it with a vicious glare.

"It was just a figure of speech," he said, smirking like a mischievous imp.

CHAPTER ELEVEN

A wet kiss took Amber by surprise as she stretched out on her bedroom floor.

"What's up with you, Skippy? I was beginning to think you didn't love me anymore." She knew better, since he still slept with her every night, but this time of day he was usually out sharing Shep's recliner.

She was experimenting with the dark cherry bureau, on the lower part of the leg near the wall, which she'd intentionally wet with a damp cloth until a small white spot appeared. Using a soft dry T-shirt as a buffer to the wood, she pressed a warm iron against it for several minutes until the stain vanished. Then she tiptoed into the living room past a napping Shep and applied the same technique to the two marks she'd made on the credenza.

Enormously proud of herself, she rewarded her good deeds with a cigarette while Skippy wandered around the backyard. The last three days had been the most industrious of her life.

In addition to her normal routine of helping Shep in and out of his wheelchair, and with his therapy, she'd taken on the monumental tasks of washing all the windows in the house and cleaning his car inside and out. She'd have done the same for Joy, except Joy never let things get dirty in the first place. Besides, even though she'd ridden across the country in the camper, that was Joy's bedroom now, and it felt wrong to go in there when she wasn't home.

What fascinated Amber most about her transformation was the feeling of satisfaction she got from seeing the fruits of her labor, and from knowing Joy and Shep were impressed. It wasn't as if she'd never worked hard before, but she'd usually done so grudgingly under the watchful eye of a demanding boss. Once she started taking responsibility for the duties Joy had assigned, the urge to go above and beyond was all hers. For that, she couldn't help but feel proud.

Her cell phone, which she hardly used, rang from her back pocket. It could only be one person on the other end, but she double-checked just to be sure. Joy normally called on the house phone, but since their blowup the other day she had started sending friendly text messages just to check in and see if there was anything she could pick up on her way home. Amber appreciated the gesture, particularly because it eased the anxiety she felt about having screwed up so much.

"Hey, Joy. Everything okay?"

"Yeah, I was just calling to let you guys know I'd be a little late today. I have a union meeting after work and then I have to take my Jeep in for service. I ought to be home by six. You want me to pick up dinner?"

"Nah, we have stuff here. I can throw something together."

Joy made a sound that was almost a chuckle, but then seemed to think better of it. "I guess I'll see you then. What's Pop doing? You guys watching your soaps?"

"He's snoring like a chain saw right now but I'm taping them for later. He'll be upset if he misses any good dirt."

"You guys crack me up." There was a garbled noise in the background, like an intercom announcement. "Okay, got to go. Text me if you change your mind about dinner."

Amber smiled to herself as she tucked her phone back into her hip pocket. As bad as she had felt the other day when she overheard Joy's cruel words to her father, the result was worth it. For the first time since leaving Kentucky, the air between them was clear, and she actually began to think they could be friends.

* * *

Joy drummed her fingers on the steering wheel, waiting for her chance to slide over into the exit lane. If there was one advantage to starting her workday at five a.m., it was missing all this crazy rush-hour traffic. She was glad Amber had declined her offer to pick up dinner since it would have meant waiting in another line.

Still, she smiled to think of Amber's offer to fix dinner. According to her pop, she'd finally mastered the art of the grilled cheese sandwich but had shown little aptitude for much else. Regardless, Joy would go out of her way to show her appreciation for whatever she fixed if only for the fact that Amber had tried.

The last couple of days had been interesting, to say the least. Still feeling guilty about the hurtful words Amber had overheard, she'd gone out of her way to be friendlier. As a result, there was a lot less tension in the house, so much that she'd hung out with everyone the night before to watch a talent show on TV and cheer for Amber's favorite, the country music singer.

Amber also had responded to the shift, or so it seemed. Not only had she stepped up and taken charge of all the household duties, she'd done it with a dose of humor, berating them during last night's show for spilling popcorn on her floor after she'd worked her fingers to the bone to clean it. The whole incident had led to a hilarious popcorn fight, after which Joy had graciously swept up.

Traffic thinned out when she pulled off the freeway, and she was glad to find the gate open so she could drive all the way through to the carport. The next thing she noticed was the shine on her father's sedan. A peek inside revealed that it had been vacuumed and wiped down as well. She didn't know whether to feel grateful or guilty. It was nice that Amber was doing a few jobs that needed to be done, but Joy had never meant to make her feel that all those extras were expected.

At the kitchen door, she was greeted by the savory smell of dinner, and she caught herself hoping Barbara had brought pot roast over for everyone. The table was set for three but there was no one in sight.

"Anyone home?"

Her father's wheels thumped along the wooden floor as he emerged from his room with Amber pushing his chair. "Madison called," he said gruffly. "She's in some kind of trouble at school."

"What?" Joy looked at her watch—a quarter after six, which was nine fifteen on the East Coast, past Madison's bedtime. "Why didn't she call me on my cell phone?"

"Wouldn't have made any difference. You were in that union meeting."

"What kind of trouble is it?"

"Homework. She says it's too hard and her teacher's mean."

Madison had grumbled last week that Syd hardly ever helped her with her homework anymore now that Mitch was there all the time. "God, I wish I could talk to Syd about this. She needs to give Madison more help at home."

"Why can't you?" Amber asked.

Joy sighed. "Because I have to walk on eggshells around her. If I make waves, she might not let Madison come out to visit."

"What a bitch!"

That summed it up perfectly as far as Joy was concerned, but she didn't have the luxury of getting worked up like that. The last time she'd called Syd out—over letting Madison watch an R-rated movie that gave her nightmares—the poor girl had lost her phone privileges for two weeks. Syd never said it was because of Joy complaining, but she knew it had to be more than coincidence.

"I'll call her in the morning. If she's having trouble with her schoolwork, maybe I can help her in the afternoons when I get home."

"Wow, look at this!" her pop said, licking his lips as Amber set a steaming bowl on the table.

Joy lunged toward the kitchen counter for a trivet and slid it underneath the hot dish, which appeared to be a concoction of ground beef, rice and peas. "Looks great! What is it?"

"I did what you said," Amber answered proudly. "Took the recipe right off the side of the mushroom soup can. It was easy."

"Good for you." Joy bit down on something crunchy…the rice, unfortunately. On her second bite, she realized the peas were still cold, and looked up to find her father eyeing her warily from across the table.

"What do you think?" Amber asked. She had yet to taste it.

"These ingredients…they go together really well."

"Yep, tasty," her pop said, setting down his fork to take a gulp of water.

Amber took a bite, paused mid-chew and pronounced, "It's not done. My peas are still frozen."

Joy guessed she missed the part where it said thaw before cooking. She may also have overlooked the line that instructed her to cook the rice before stirring it into the pot. She sprang to her feet and collected her father's plate. "I know how to fix this."

By stirring in water and zapping the mixture in the microwave, she made dinner edible.

"I probably should be barred from future dinner details," Amber said sullenly.

Joy bit her tongue, and so did her pop, which caused all three to burst out laughing.

"You should have seen Joy the first time she made pancakes."

"Oh, give me a break. I was ten years old!"

He held up his hand in the shape of a C. "They were like giant round sponges, burned to a crisp but soupy on the inside. And this one"—he pointed to Joy—"was covered with flour from head to toe, and she tracked it all through the house."

Joy huffed with feigned annoyance. "That's what you get for leaving a ten-year-old unsupervised."

"Like it would have made any difference. You always did whatever the hell you wanted. Your mother too. I've been at the mercy of one or the other for almost forty years."

Joy looked at Amber and rolled her eyes. "Do you believe any of that?"

"Not a word."

Her pop had a treasure trove of stories, mostly lies and exaggerations about how she and her mother had persecuted him his whole life, and he launched into one after another while she cleaned up the kitchen and Amber listened. The laughter and silliness was reminiscent of their times with Madison, so much that it made her wish she were there too. Tonight, Amber's laugh was the one that was infectious.

* * *

Amber held the screen door so that it closed quietly behind her and whispered to Skippy to be still while she fastened his leash. It was almost ten o'clock, which meant Joy was probably sound asleep.

"You don't need the leash. I closed the gate." The voice from the dark startled her.

"I thought you'd be asleep."

"Tomorrow's Saturday. I plan to sleep late, probably till seven thirty."

"I don't know how you do it, getting up at four in the morning." As her eyes adjusted to the darkness, she made out Joy lying in a lawn chair beside the camper. "You look relaxed. Can I bring you a beer?"

"I've got some out here in the fridge. You want one?"

"Sure."

Joy fetched a bottle and reached under the deck for another lounge chair like hers. "Is Pop watching the A's game?"

"Yeah, from bed. He thought all those stories at dinner would make me forget about his exercises but he was wrong. Now he's complaining that I wore him out."

"That's Pop. He always has to complain about something." She clinked her bottle to Amber's. "Cheers."

"Back atcha." Amber lit a cigarette and shifted her chair so the smoke wouldn't blow toward Joy. "It's pretty quiet out here. Back in Tennessee, all you ever hear at night are crickets and frogs."

"We usually hear the freeway." Joy chuckled. "Speaking of freeways…now that you've been out here a couple of weeks, what do you think of California?"

"Well, I'm not too crazy about the lack of road signs." Amber hugged herself and rubbed her arms briskly. "Or the fact that it gets so cold after the sun goes down. It's just September and I'm freezing already."

"Maybe you should think about wearing more clothes." Joy, who had on jeans and a fleece pullover, disappeared inside the camper. When she returned, she draped a fuzzy blanket over Amber in her chair. "Sweaters are a lot like shoes. Around here, you should never go anywhere without them."

"Thanks, I learned my lesson on the shoes. You know, I didn't say it at the time—mostly because I was too scared to speak—but I really appreciate that you didn't just leave me hanging out there all afternoon until you got off work. I was already getting freaked out about that neighborhood. The buildings all had iron gates around them and most of the cars had those steering wheel locks." She almost said she'd never been so glad to see someone, but then she thought of the night the two guys had grabbed her in the campground. "Just curious…what would you have done that day if you'd been me?"

"Under those circumstances, probably the same thing you did—call for help."

"But the difference is you wouldn't have run out of gas in the first place."

"Probably not, but I could have broken down or had a flat tire. We all get jammed up sometimes."

"Yeah, right. When was the last time you did?"

"Let's see, Pop already told you the pancakes story."

"You were ten freaking years old. Are you telling me you haven't screwed up since then?"

Joy laughed evilly and finally confessed, "Well, there was one time at Dulles Airport in Washington where I made a little boo-boo."

"Go on." Skippy climbed into Amber's lap and nosed his way under the blanket.

"Syd and I managed to get leave at the same time around Thanksgiving one year and I talked her into flying out here to meet Mom and Pop. She didn't really want to, to put it mildly. Her way of punishing me was not to lift a finger to help, and when we went to get on the plane, I accidentally grabbed somebody else's bag instead of hers. She got out here with nothing to wear but some guy's neckties and boxer shorts."

Amber loved hearing Joy laugh, especially since it was coming at Syd's expense. "You know, from everything you've said about that woman, I have a hard time picturing you with a crab like that."

Joy shrugged. "I find it kind of hard to picture too, but there were some good times. We met in boot camp at Great Lakes and got to be friends. Then I went to aviation A-school down in Pensacola and she went to Georgia for supply corps. Both of us ended up in Norfolk a few months later, me on the *TR* and her at the base. We started hanging out because we didn't know anybody else. I think if we'd both waited a while, we might have met people we liked better. Syd told me right up front she wasn't even sure she was gay. That should have been a big red flag, but I was sure I could sway her with my charm."

"And with your ironed T-shirts." She grinned, even though she doubted Joy could see her in the dark. "Funny how we fall into relationships just because they're convenient. I never would have run off with Archie if he hadn't been my only way out of town. As for Corey…let's just call that a three-year mistake…or maybe a three-year lesson, because I won't ever do that again."

Not long ago, she'd written off as necessity her habit of hooking up with people just because they put a roof over her head. There was even a moment on her first night with Joy when she'd considered falling in bed with her if she'd asked. Now the idea was a shameful reminder that she needed to start taking responsibility for herself so she wouldn't have to take on relationships she didn't really want.

"I probably haven't said it enough, but I really appreciate you giving me this chance. I don't mean just picking me up off the side of the road. I feel like I'm finally doing something worthwhile and I have a chance to stand on my own two feet."

"You're doing a good job, Amber." Left unsaid was the fact that she'd been doing a lousy job before their blowup. "Have you thought about what kind of work you want to do after this?"

"A little." Up until a few days ago, she'd been looking for a job to replace this one, either when she got fired or quit in a huff. "I get on Shep's computer sometimes when he's asleep and look at what kinds of jobs are out there for somebody like me. There's not a whole lot. The best part of this gig is it comes with room and board, and I don't need a car to get to work. I found a couple of those live-in companion jobs, but they all say certified only. I don't even know what kind of certification they're talking about."

"Probably CNA, Certified Nursing Assistant. One of the guys on my crew says his wife needed that for her job. I think she works at a nursing home."

The problem with working at nursing homes or places like that was they didn't pay enough to get by, at least not if you lived by yourself. She'd looked for apartments too, and there was hardly anything out there for under a thousand bucks a month, certainly nothing that would let her bring Skippy.

"I can't believe how much people around here want for just a studio apartment."

"Yeah, welcome to California. Property's outrageous, and so are the taxes."

"And if you look for a job in a place you can afford to live… hell, they don't pay you as much, so you're screwed either way."

"There's always school, you know. Alameda College is just right up the street."

"What would I even study?"

"That's up to you," Joy said. "We talked about this on the road, remember? You're going to be here for at least ten more weeks with Pop, probably till December. That's more than enough time to sign up for a program you can finish at night or on the weekend. You can use Pop's car, and I'll sit with him on Saturday if you have to be there."

The more Amber thought about it, the more the idea of taking classes piqued her interest. Getting specialized training meant she'd have a chance to work for smart people instead of the usual dolts who managed taco stands or convenience stores—and for better money.

"I suppose I could look at their website. I wonder how much something like that would cost?"

"I don't know, but think of it as an investment. You have to put money into it if you want to get money out." Joy stood and stretched, a sign she was ready to call it a night. "And just think of all the extra money you'd have if you—" She slapped a hand over her mouth.

"I heard that." Amber scooted Skippy out of her lap and folded the blanket. "Better watch your step tomorrow morning. I didn't see where Skippy went."

"Oh, don't worry. If he left me any presents, I'm sure I'll find them."

Amber chuckled at the mental image, which was easier to do now that she was fairly sure Joy stepping in dog shit wouldn't turn her into a raging maniac. Their interactions had changed and were definitely more relaxed. Part of that was because Joy felt bad about losing her temper and basically calling her an idiot. The other part, she admitted, was because she had finally gotten off her ass.

CHAPTER TWELVE

Joy returned the thumbs-up sign to Robbie, who had just disengaged the tow bar from the 737. When he hopped onto the back of her tug, she reversed to get a visual with the jet's captain and told him through her radio headset that he was ready for departure. With that signoff, ST 1114 to Dallas now officially belonged to the tower.

Things were back to normal with her crew, who had aced a surprise safety inspection by the airline brass this morning.

"Man, I can't believe it," Robbie said as they coasted back to the gate. "Did you get a look at that flight attendant that brought out the oversized bags? Candace...wowza!"

"Can't say as I did," Joy said.

"You should have, because she was sure looking at you."

"I wish you had poked me. I would have gotten her number." A little flirting would feel pretty good right now, particularly if it got her mind off a certain houseguest.

Right there was part of the problem. Amber wasn't a houseguest. She was an employee, and there were all sorts of reasons thinking about her so much was wrong. Joy's instincts always called for her to save the damsel in distress, but saving Amber meant helping her learn to be independent, not taking advantage of her vulnerability. It was already showing in the changes she'd made just in the last week, which—coincidentally—just happened to be when Joy had begun to find her more interesting.

Joy's pocket had vibrated while she was out on the tarmac and she expected to find a text message from Amber. Instead, it was a voice mail from Dani Hatcher, an invitation to meet for coffee the following week at the airport. She confirmed their date with a text, smiling to imagine the grief Dani would give her for picking up a stray on her way home from Virginia.

Speaking of that stray, Amber was taking her pop to the doctor today. With all four of her gates clear, Joy ducked into the break room to call for an update.

"They took his stitches out," Amber said. "He wailed like a four-year-old with a scraped knee."

"That's his sympathy move. Must have been a pretty nurse nearby."

"No, she was the doctor. Wish you could have seen her face. She looked at his shoulder, then his legs, and said, 'Seriously?' Then he told me to shut my piehole because I couldn't stop laughing. Who says piehole anyway?"

Joy wished she had been a fly on the wall for that. "What about his shoulder?"

"Coming along, she said. No more sling, but he has to keep the brace on. And of course, when she was finished, he asked if it was okay to use his hand now to tie his shoes. She went for it, so I was glad to see I wasn't the only idiot to fall for that."

"You're a good sport." She giggled at the memory of Amber down on her stomach looking under the car. "Look, I'm going to be a little late. I have to pick up something. See you guys around four."

She walked out to the tug, where Robbie handed her a pair of orange signal cones. "Sea-Tac's coming in twelve minutes early and LAX is on time for a change," he said.

"Great. Let's hope they don't fight over a parking spot."

"I've got dibs on the flight attendant," he yelled as he walked to his position on the wing. "With my luck, it'll be Martin."

Joy howled with laughter as she recalled Robbie going into hiding to avoid the gay flight attendant's flirtations. "You could do a lot worse than a nice guy like Martin!"

It was a huge relief to have workdays back to normal with her crew. With things going smoothly at home also, that left only Madison to worry about. It wasn't like her to do poorly in school, and Joy hoped the problem would straighten itself out when she got used to her new teacher.

At least Syd had stepped up as a parent when she got the teacher's note. According to Madison, she'd set up time every night to go over homework. Syd usually did right by Madison when push came to shove, but Joy couldn't fathom why things had to come off the rails before she paid attention to what the girl needed. A good parent was supposed to stay on top of the situation and anticipate when it was time to step in.

She groaned loudly, knowing no one could hear her given the rumble of the jet's engines as it taxied toward the gate. Here she was again, letting her mind wander to something other than her job. If one of her crew had done that, she'd be all over them.

* * *

The yelling started the moment Joy walked through the back door.

"Will you tell this woman they're my Goobers and I can eat them whenever the hell I want?" Her pop was sitting in his wheelchair with a barbell in his lap.

"You can have your stupid Goobers when you finish your stupid exercises," Amber said indignantly.

"You hear that? She's doling them out to me like I'm some kind of trained seal." His usual crotchety voice was tinged with humor, making Joy wonder if the whole game had actually been his idea.

"Hurry up and finish, Pop. I need to talk to Amber about something."

"You heard the woman," Amber said. "Ten more reps and you're done."

With his elbow tucked against his side to immobilize his shoulder, he curled the dumbbell ten times, grunting the numbers as if in agony. When he finished, she dutifully counted out ten Goobers and put the others inside the refrigerator.

"Pop, are you okay by yourself if we go out to the camper for a little while? I'll have my cell phone if you need anything."

"Get me a clean shirt and a comb before you leave. Barbara's coming over to watch the A's game."

Amber helped him get settled and teased him with the TV's remote control before turning it over and following Joy out onto the deck. "Do I have time to grab a smoke?"

"Sure. Is he like that all day?"

"All day, every day. Fortunately, I have experience with three-year-olds in daycare."

"He likes you. He wouldn't kid around like that if he didn't."

"I like him too, and I wouldn't either." She lit a cigarette and turned her head to blow the smoke away. "What's up? You wanted to show me something?"

"Yeah." Joy held up a stack of booklets. "I went by the community college and picked up some catalogs and brochures. I thought you might want to look over the programs."

"Ooh, let me see." She took the thickest one and started thumbing through it.

"Come inside when you're finished with that nasty—I mean, with your cigarette—and we'll look at a few others on the web."

While she was waiting for Amber, she pulled off her khaki uniform slacks and replaced them with jeans. Then she opened the package that had arrived in today's mail, two yellow T-shirts with Big Stick stamped on the pocket. She was about to put one of them on when Amber stepped up inside the camper.

"Sorry. I didn't know you were getting dressed."

For nine years, Joy had shared showers and more with hundreds of women, so it made no sense at all that she suddenly felt modest about being seen by Amber in her bra. It also triggered her memory of the night in Wyoming when she'd secretly watched Amber undress as she readied for bed.

She slipped the shirt over her head and slid onto the bench behind the dinette, motioning for Amber to sit beside her. "No big deal."

"I see you got your new shirt. I promised to pay for that, remember?"

"And I told you to forget it, remember?"

"Okay, but the least you can do is let me wash it for you. I think I have a cheap blue tank top from Malaysia that hasn't been washed yet."

"You've been hanging around Pop too long." Joy spread the brochures on the table. "A couple of these schools offer vocational training and certification classes, and they aren't that far away. The College of Alameda has a whole bunch of two-year programs, but that's a big-time commitment. Not saying you shouldn't do it, but it's hard to go to school full-time and work a job on top of it."

"I don't think I've ever lasted for two years at anything." From her tone, it seemed more that she was voicing doubts than dismissing the idea completely. "Do they have a class I could do in a few weeks while I'm here? You know, some kind of certification like we talked about."

"A few. There's the CNA program—certified nursing assistant. Ten weeks, three hours every night and all day Saturday. That's perfect for your schedule here."

Amber studied the brochure, her face alight with interest. "It says CNAs are qualified for in-home care. That means I'd be qualified for another job just like this one, maybe even one with benefits."

"That's right. And the average salary in Alameda County for CNAs is thirty-six thousand. You probably wouldn't make that much at first…more like in the twenties, but the longer you work, the more money you'll make."

"I could do this." As she turned to the last page, her face fell. "But maybe not. What else do they have?"

Amber's sudden lack of interest was puzzling, especially given her enthusiasm only a moment earlier.

"Well, they have a program for administrative assistants."

"That's like a secretary, isn't it? I don't think I'm very good at that sort of thing."

"But the whole idea of going to school is learning how to be good at something."

This time Amber flipped all the way to the back page of the brochure and began shaking her head. "No, they want people who are organized and I'm just not like that. I'd get fired the first day."

Joy had more faith in Amber than that, especially after seeing what she was capable of when she set her mind to it.

"Okay, how about food service? There's this food safety course you can take to be a certified food handler. Every single business in California that serves food needs to have at least one person with this kind of certification."

"What would I have to do?"

"Looks like it's just twenty hours of class and then you take a test. And then after you work for a few years, you can go higher than that and get certified as a food safety inspector."

Amber scooped up all the brochures into a pile in the center of the table. "I can't do any of these courses, Joy. All of them say you need a high school diploma. I didn't finish. I ran away in February my senior year, and I never got my GED." As she talked, her voice began to quiver, and her eyes misted with tears. "I'm never going to get a decent job."

That explained her sudden lack of interest as she leafed through each brochure. All of it was out of reach without a diploma.

Joy typed a few words into the search engine on her laptop and spun the results toward Amber. "Here you go—adult education. GED classes twice a week at the library, plus online instruction."

"For how long?"

"It's up to you. You take the test whenever you feel ready." She scrolled through the overview. "It says the instructors treat everyone as an individual and work with you until you're prepared."

"I bet that wouldn't take long. I got mostly Bs in school… and some Cs. But I got an A in history once, and we had a really hard teacher."

Joy had a feeling those Cs were the norm. It was easy to imagine Amber struggling in school, but it was more a matter of lack of self-discipline than her intelligence. She and Madison could probably share plenty of tales of homework that never got done.

"You should do this GED, Amber. Get it out of the way while you can so you can start planning for whatever's next."

"But even if I get it, I won't have enough time to go for anything else."

"You don't know that. You might get lucky and find another job like this. Pop knows a lot of veterans. Now that you've got some experience, he might be able to help you find another job right away. Or maybe the physical therapist knows somebody." Joy did something she hadn't done before—she took Amber's hand and squeezed it. "The important thing is to be ready. You can even make Pop help you study."

Amber laughed, and squeezed Joy's hand in return. It was clear the idea was taking hold. "Yeah, and whenever I get a question right, he tosses me a Goober."

"Sounds perfect. Let's go tell him."

Joy started to get up but Amber, still holding her hand, pulled her back.

"Thank you. Again. A million times."

"You're welcome," Joy answered, smiling as she noticed tears about to fall.

"Seriously, I don't know what I did to deserve all this, but I'm going to do whatever it takes to pay you back."

"You don't have to pay us back. Just keep doing a good job. We're both pulling for you."

For a fleeting moment, Joy wanted to draw her into a hug. All that stopped her was another flashback of Amber standing nude at the foot of her bed.

* * *

Amber needed many things in her life, but a big sister wasn't on her list. Yet that's what Joy seemed determined to be, imparting her grownup wisdom to the youngster not yet out of the nest. She'd probably be mortified to know where Amber's thoughts strayed each night after she went to bed—to imagined visions of Joy's powerful physique dripping wet from the shower or stretched out naked across fresh sheets in her private lair. Definitely not sisterly thoughts.

Only one person had ever triggered Amber's sexual fantasies like that—Gus Holley's wife Michelle. Practically everyone had those dreams about her. She was sweet and charming, like the girl next door, but only if you lived next to a modeling agency.

Joy wasn't drop-dead gorgeous like Michelle Holley, but she had an aura of strength and self-assurance that Amber found mesmerizing. That fascination was further fueled by proximity, knowing Joy was only a few feet outside her window, separated by two wispy screens. If she strained to listen, she could almost imagine Joy's deep steady breaths as she slept, a sensation that made her roll onto her side and clutch her pillow.

That moment in the camper when Joy had taken her hand, she'd almost felt a spark between them. But Joy hadn't been expressing feelings of romantic or sexual attraction. She'd been giving advice and encouragement…like a big sister.

Even if there had been a hint of more—which was almost laughable given Joy's distant and businesslike demeanor—acting on it wouldn't be a good idea. It didn't take a genius to know the quickest way to screw up your job was to sleep with the boss. Besides, Amber had more at stake than just a job. Joy had laid an opportunity in front of her that she'd never had before, a chance to get some training that could land her a giant step forward on the job front. She wasn't used to putting off the here and now for the future, but Joy helped her see what was possible if she invested the effort.

As far back as she could remember, there had never been anyone—not a teacher, not a friend and definitely not a family member—who had made her feel like she could do whatever she set her mind to. No wonder she was falling for Joy. She was the first person who ever believed in her.

CHAPTER THIRTEEN

Joy ripped open three packets of sugar and dropped them into her steaming latte, smiling to realize this could have been the vice to which she confessed when she tweaked Amber about her smoking. Coffee wasn't drinkable without sugar—loads of it—and life wasn't worth living without coffee.

From a small table in the corner of the coffee bar she watched for Dani, who was flying out to a conference in Denver. Since members of the ground crew were out of place on the concourse, she disguised her uniform with a black pullover sweater, though the lanyard that hung around her neck identified her as an airport employee.

Her last meeting with Dani had been a couple of months ago—dinner at a sports bar, followed by a lecture on feminist politics in modern literature. Dani was always pulling her toward causes and philosophies that stretched her brain, and while Joy would often ponder the takeaway for several days, she didn't exactly hunger for more. What made Dani so interesting was how she took those theories and applied them to the everyday lives of her friends. She was a pied piper when it came to rallying women to her various causes because no one had figured out how to say no.

Dani bustled into the small seating area and parked her suitcase by the table. At four eleven and a half, she still managed to fill every room with her buoyant personality and high-pitched, enthusiastic voice. A friendly peck on the lips passed for a greeting as she grumbled about her experience going through security. "It galls me to know they can actually see my tampon on that stupid x-ray machine. Watch my stuff while I grab some coffee."

Joy bore the brunt of everyone's air travel complaints once they learned she worked for an airline. She didn't dare mention that she wasn't subjected to the same intrusive security procedures despite having unfettered access to the planes.

"So what's happening in Denver?" she asked when Dani returned to the table. "Is there a special variation of feminist theory that applies only at ten thousand feet?"

At thirty-nine, Dani wore her short, prematurely gray hair and bifocals like badges of honor. "Laugh all you want, fly girl. It so happens I'm off to a networking conference. We're setting up a national resource bank for lesbians who need professional services—doctors, therapists, attorneys, financial planners—the whole shebang."

Joy nodded her approval. "If anyone can pull off organizing that many people, it's you."

"It's not as easy as you might think, but we've got some smart gals on the steering committee. Everyone we've approached wants to be listed because they all think they're experts. But working with lesbians takes special skill and know-how. Our issues aren't like everyone else's." Dani leafed through the condiments for a packet of artificial sweetener. "Good thing I don't like sugar. So, enough about the conference...I wanted to share some news with you. It appears I have a girlfriend."

"Appears?"

"Seems that way. I've been trying to convince myself otherwise, but our relationship's starting to walk a lot like a duck. Her name's Clara Lewis and it so happens she lives in Denver."

"Imagine that." The prospect thrilled Joy, not only because she wanted her friend to be happy, but also because it meant the end of all their friends' speculation that she and Dani would end up together when both of them knew it would never happen. "When do I get to meet her?"

"She was out here last weekend but I was still in denial. And now I'm going to visit her."

"I'm really happy for you, Dani. It's going to be tough keeping a stiff upper lip in front of all our friends. They're going to assume I'm heartbroken."

"Yeah, but I've got a fix for that. How about you and I get married so I can use your employee discount to fly back and forth to Denver?" She took a sip of coffee and looked at Joy over the top of her bifocals. "I'm kidding, of course...unless you're willing to go for it."

"No problem. You free Tuesday?"

Dani had half an hour more to kill, so Joy caught her up on what was going on with her pop. Her effort to gloss over the story of how she'd come to hire Amber was met with a screech.

"You did what?"

"It just happened."

"Is she cute?"

Joy hesitated. "Yeah."

"Then it didn't just happen. You were trolling."

"I was not! She was in a jam and it just worked out for both of us."

Dani gave her a wink. "You're sleeping with her, aren't you?"

Joy slapped the tabletop, which caught the attention of nearby customers. "That's it. The wedding's off. If we can't trust each other, we have no business getting married."

"You kill me."

Lowering her voice, Joy said, "We're not sleeping together, but I admit the idea might be a little intriguing if she weren't twenty-four going on sixteen."

There was also the matter of Amber's sexuality, but Joy didn't want to discuss that with Dani. She had her own thoughts. The fact that Amber was open to women, or even that she liked them in some ways better than men, didn't make her a lesbian. It didn't even make her bisexual. Joy had learned from Syd that women who felt they had a choice generally chose the path of least resistance. Amber added a different twist, choosing whichever offered the best opportunity.

"Don't hold your breath for anything to happen on that front," Joy told her. "But if she decides to stick around Oakland when her time's up with Pop, I'll bring her to one of your events so she can have her awareness raised."

"That's right, humor me." Dani stood at her boarding announcement. "Now wish me a safe trip."

"I don't have to. I inspected your plane personally."

"That's even better."

They shared another peck on the lips and Joy walked her to the gate. "Tell Clara that I'm looking forward to meeting her."

"Ha! Tell Amber the same."

* * *

Smoking used to be a lot more fun, Amber thought. Now every cigarette was tainted with the specter of how much she wanted to quit. It wasn't only the expense, or even the health reasons, which everyone who didn't smoke drummed into her at every opportunity. It was the fact that this nicotine addiction owned her, invading her thoughts at predictable intervals and demanding she feed it.

Other people's opinions about smoking had never bothered her much, but she cared what Joy and Shep thought. Even though neither gave her too hard a time about it, their disapproval was unmistakable. The way they saw it, it was a matter of self-discipline. It wasn't like either of them to surrender control of their body. It was why Shep had never given in to the ease of a motorized wheelchair, and why Joy kept herself in top physical condition.

Amber would love to feel that kind of self-confidence about her physical self, but the reality of that was so far away it felt out of reach. Working out in the gym seemed like such a waste of time. For those she knew who did it, it was every bit as addictive as nicotine. If it were only a matter of trading one vice for another, she might as well smoke.

Joy's Jeep crackled down the driveway and eased into the carport, sending a swell of excitement through her. It was silly to feel so eager about something so ordinary, but she looked forward every day to Joy coming home from work. The fact that she was later than usual created even more anticipation to know where she'd been.

Like a cowboy at the end of a long trail ride, Joy sauntered lazily up the stairs and collapsed into a deck chair, where she immediately propped her feet on the top rail.

"You're late, missy. You'd better have a note from your boss."

Joy chuckled. "Don't tell my boss, but I left work a couple of minutes early. I met a friend of mine for coffee."

"Nice." Except nice wasn't exactly what Amber was feeling. Of course Joy had friends, but she'd never even mentioned any of them before. Could it be this was actually a date? "I was starting to wonder if you had any friends."

"So happens I thought about that when we were riding back from Kentucky. If I were to find myself homeless tomorrow, I might be hard-pressed to find a couch to sleep on for more than a night or two. Once in a while I can get someone to show up for coffee."

"I don't get that. You've been back in town for what, three years? You ought to have a girlfriend by now." She could imagine several reasons, not the least of which was Joy's stiff military demeanor, but still...Joy was nice to look at, had a job and treated women with respect. Amber knew dozens of girls back in Tennessee who were looking for a husband with all that, and most of them would settle for one out of three. Surely there were lesbians who wanted that in a lover too.

"I went out with Dani a few times—that's the woman I met today—but it just didn't click. I like her though. She's just too much of a whirlwind for me…always going to lectures or meetings, raising money for this or that. I like to get out every now and then, but I like to sleep once in a while too."

"Yeah, you do have a brutal work schedule. It's hard to date when you have to be home at seven thirty to go to bed."

"Eight thirty, but close enough."

Amber's cell phone rang, and with Joy sitting right next to her, the only other person it could be was Shep. "I told you never to call me here."

"What's a guy got to do to get a taco in this joint?"

She looked over at Joy. "Tacos?"

"Great idea…Juanita's," she said, slapping her thighs as she stood. "Tell him he's buying."

* * *

Bypassing the handicapped space near the door, Joy selected a spot at the far end of the parking lot at Juanita's. Though her father had a special permit, he always chose to leave the blue-lined spaces to those who had trouble walking. All he needed was enough room on the side to maneuver his chair in and out of the car. If he could do that, it didn't matter how far he had to roll it.

Joy opened the back door for Barbara, who had eagerly joined them. Amber pulled the wheelchair from the trunk, and in seconds, had it put together and waiting by the passenger door.

"I hope I get to stick around long enough to see you do this by yourself, Shep," she said, "especially the driving part. I can't wait to see you do all that with just your hands."

Her pop swung into his chair as Amber tugged on his shorts. "I wish I could drive with voice commands. That way I'd have my hands free for obscene gestures."

Joy traded eye rolls with Barbara, who said, "I remember your mother telling me he tried to get her to do that for him."

"Can you just imagine my mom—Cindy Shepard, of all people—flipping off a stranger on the highway? The pope would do that before she would." She yelled ahead to Amber, "I wish you could've been there the time he got pulled over and the officer told him to step out of the car."

"I asked the guy if he was pulling my leg. He didn't think that was funny either."

Though her mother was gone, Joy still felt warm feelings of family among the four of them tonight. Barbara had been a mainstay in their lives for decades, and in only a few short weeks Amber had inserted herself as well. She may have landed in Oakland totally unprepared for this job, but she'd caught on to the work aspects fairly well and had made up for her shortcomings with a cheerful personality.

Since they were steady customers at Juanita's, the host welcomed them and signaled for Cristina to take them to their table.

"Hey, sweetie," her pop said. "How about we start with the usual—cold beer, warm chips and hot salsa."

"I take it you guys are regulars," Amber said.

"This is Pop's home away from home. They're probably building his burrito as we speak."

When the beer arrived, they placed their order. Then her pop raised his bottle. "To getting out of the house."

"Cheers," they answered.

Barbara, who had all but shoved Amber aside to take the seat next to Shep, told him, "You're welcome to get out of the house any night you want. If these girls won't bring you, just pick up the phone and I'll come get you."

"Trust me, Barbara. You can have Pop any night you want him."

"I second that," Amber added.

For all his insistence that they were only friends, Joy saw a sweetness in her father's eyes when he looked at Barbara. It wasn't the look of devotion he'd shown her mother all those years, but there was interest and genuine friendship, enough to suggest there might be more for them down the road.

"See how they treat me? They should be ashamed." He turned to Amber. "Did you tell Joy about your test?"

Test…it took Joy a few seconds to realize he was referring to the GED practice test Amber had taken the night before at the library. "I forgot to ask. I was asleep when you got home."

"Last night was the math part. Un-freaking-believable! The whole test took almost two hours. He'll probably come back and tell me I should be in the sixth grade."

"When will you find out?" With a pointed look, Joy snatched the basket of chips from her father's hands and passed them on to Amber and Barbara.

"He'll have it scored by tomorrow. I have to take the grammar and writing test next. Then on Saturday I do science, social studies and reading."

"Is that going to be your schedule, three days a week?"

"Pretty much. Tuesday and Thursday from five to nine, and then on Saturdays from nine to three. But I'll only have to study the parts I don't pass."

Joy nodded, working it out in her head that she could be home with her pop for those hours. "That should be fine."

"What worries me is that I won't be getting home until about nine thirty. And you can't stay up that late, Joy."

"I can come over if you need me," Barbara said.

"It's no big deal," her father said. "I'm usually watching TV by that time, and they both have cell phones if I need anything…but you're welcome to come over and sit whenever you want. It's probably a good idea to have someone from the outside world check on my well-being every day."

Dinner arrived and her pop ordered another round of beers.

"Make mine iced tea," Joy said. "I'm driving."

"Make his iced tea too," Amber told the waiter.

"What the hell? I'm not driving."

"No, but you're taking anti-inflammatory medicine that makes your stomach hurt. I read on the package that alcohol makes it even worse. You don't need an ulcer on top of what you've already got."

"She's right, Pop." Joy was immensely impressed, not only that Amber had read the warning labels, but that she'd stood up to her father in front of everyone. It was hard to believe this was the same girl who, only a couple of weeks ago, wouldn't even clean up after herself.

With a sullen look, her father acquiesced. "No more Goobers for you."

* * *

In a move that had gotten to be old hat, Amber tugged on Shep's shorts to help him swing into bed. Then she went into his bathroom to collect the towels, giving him privacy to strip down to his boxers and T-shirt for the night. She had no problem coming around when he needed help getting dressed or dried off after his shower, but that didn't mean they were married.

"You dropped salsa on your sling. I'm going to toss it into the wash with these towels tonight."

"Good! I can sleep late."

"Like that would ever happen. Joy barely beats you out of bed and she's up at four o'clock." She started the laundry and came back to see if there was anything else he needed before she went to bed.

"Let's just hope that burrito goes to sleep," he said.

"Thanks for that mental image. Say, you and Barbara were looking pretty chummy there. Anything you want to share?"

"What do I look like, one of those Kardashians? I keep my business to myself."

"Interesting…got some business, do you?"

"I like Barbara," he confessed. "We've been friends for thirty-some years. Her husband Hank was a good man. I know she's lonely. I guess I am too, but I'm carrying a lot of baggage here."

"Seems to me like she knows that already."

"Yeah, well…" His words were dismissive, but the look on his face gave away his interest. "I'll say this for her. She passes all the tests."

"What tests?"

"You know, all that stuff you put on your list that matters. She likes Joy. She and Hank never had any kids, but she took to Madison"—he snapped his fingers—"just like that. And like tonight…she fits in like family."

"I think it's sweet that Madison calls you Grandpa Shep."

"God, that kid…I remember the first time Joy brought her out to visit. She was only five and I halfway expected her to freak out about seeing the wheelchair. Once she figured out I still had a lap, she was good."

"Like Skippy."

He chuckled. "Yeah, it didn't hurt that I kept a few Goobers in my pocket…or in Skippy's case, bacon bits."

"You've been bribing my dog all this time? I thought he just didn't like me anymore." She got an extra blanket from the closet and spread it across the bottom of the bed where he could easily pull it up if needed. "In case your feet get cold."

"Ha! Good one. I'm going to steal that. So what about you and Joy? Something going on there I should know about?"

"What the hell? Why would you even ask?" The idea that he'd picked up on her interest caused her to smile, no matter how hard she tried not to.

"Don't give me that bullshit. I've been watching you two."

Amber didn't care that he'd noticed her looking at Joy. She was far more intrigued by what he'd seen that made him think Joy had been looking at her. "I think you're seeing things. Maybe we ought to back off those meds."

"I'm seeing things, all right. I'm seeing that Joy spends all her weekends at home instead of going out with women."

"Maybe that's because her old man's gimpy and she thinks she ought to be home with him. And besides, she had a date this afternoon, somebody named Dani."

"Pfft. Dani's no date. She came along with us once to Great America—that's one of those amusement parks—and all she did was watch everybody else ride. Hardly spoke to Madison. Joy isn't going to go for somebody like that."

The way Shep and Joy went on about that child, Amber figured she must walk on water. "That kid means a lot to you guys."

"Family is family."

Amber wouldn't know anything about that. But if her feelings for Joy were to go anywhere, she understood she'd have to fall in love with this Madison kid as well.

CHAPTER FOURTEEN

Joy struck the perfect balance between her clutch and accelerator to hold the hill at Filbert and Hyde. When traffic cleared, she turned left behind a streetcar and started slowly downward toward the bay.

"I can't believe you just did that," Amber said. "If I'd been driving a stick shift on that hill, we would've rolled all the way back to Oakland."

"You get used to it. What did I tell you about San Francisco? Isn't it the most beautiful city you've ever seen?"

Amber couldn't argue with that. The movies and travel guides didn't do it justice, especially when they'd gone up to Twin Peaks and watched the fog creep over the Golden Gate Bridge. "I've never seen anything like it. It's got so much character. It's more like a person than a city."

Joy nodded thoughtfully. "Good way to describe it."

They'd eaten dinner in Chinatown and were making one last loop through the city at sunset before joining what Joy had described as throngs of commuters heading east across the Bay Bridge. Spending the afternoon together this way had been an unexpected treat, made possible when Shep and Barbara decided to take in a matinee movie and then dinner.

All day, Amber had been focused on any sign that Joy was interested in her. Whatever Shep had seen between them was still a mystery as far as she was concerned. Joy was her usual friendly and attentive self, but no more than usual, and hardly more than she was to everyone else.

One encouraging sign had come about by accident. Amber spilled her purse as she was getting ready to get out of the car at Twin Peaks, and before she could collect everything, Joy had walked around to open her door. It could have been simple impatience, but then she'd done that when they returned too, and that made it seem chivalrous.

"We'll come back some weekend when we have time to walk around. There's a lot more to see."

"Ever since I was a kid, I associated San Francisco with earthquakes. Don't you ever worry about them?"

"You mean like the one we had back in eighty-nine? One of my mom's friends was killed."

"Now you're just trying to scare me."

"If I'd been trying to scare you I would have added that she was on the Nimitz Freeway, which is the road we took to get over here. That's where most of the fatalities were." They started across the Bay Bridge. "And a whole section of this bridge fell out."

"Oh, shit." Amber shuddered. "Now you're freaking me out. I don't know how y'all can stand it."

"Every place has its problems. Didn't you guys get flooded a few years ago in Nashville? I remember seeing pictures of Opryland under water."

"God, that was awful. The Cumberland River just kept getting higher and higher. It didn't reach our apartment because we lived up on the second floor, but Molly's car almost floated away."

"See, I'd rather have earthquakes than floods any day. It happens and it's over in less than a minute. I'd be the one freaking out if I had to watch water coming up around my house and didn't know how high it was going to get. And the other thing about earthquakes is you don't have to dread them. There's only so much you can do to prepare. It's not like those hurricanes you have to watch for three or four days till they're on top of you. Give me earthquakes anytime."

Amber still couldn't see how she didn't live in mortal fear for her life. But then, the stories Joy and Shep had told about landing planes on a carrier deck in rough seas said a lot about both of them. "You navy types don't scare easily, do you?"

"There's a lot to be afraid of in the navy, but you just do your job and trust everyone else to do theirs." Joy grew quiet, peeling off toward Alameda when they emerged from underneath the upper deck of the bridge. "I'm scared of losing people I care about."

"Like your mom?"

"My mom, my pop…and I always worry about the people I'm responsible for on the planes, or when I was on the aircraft carrier. The one who keeps me awake nights is Madison."

"Isn't Syd taking good care of her?"

"I suppose, but I'd rather be doing it myself. I think I could do a better job."

"You really want to be a mom that bad?"

"Not just a mom. I want to be Madison's mom. If I had it to do over, I wouldn't have given up so easily. I thought it was best for her at the time, but now I think she'd be better off with me and Pop."

Amber had given up her baby so he'd have a conventional life—two parents with good jobs, a nice house and enough money that he'd never have to do without. Joy was lots of things, but conventional wasn't one of them. Before she realized it, she'd let out a groan.

"What's that supposed to mean?"

"Just…I was…" She was caught without a decent lie. "Do you really think it's a good idea to bring a kid to a home where you're sleeping out in the backyard?

"Jeez, it's not permanent. I usually stay in the house, but I moved out there when Madison came to visit so I wouldn't wake her up at four o'clock in the morning. And in case you haven't noticed, I'm out there now because somebody else has my room." There was a teasing edge to her voice.

"You didn't have to do that for me. I told you I'd sleep out there."

"Oh, no. You're the one getting paid to look after Cranky Pants in the middle of the night."

"He's not so bad if you've got enough Goobers."

They pulled off the Nimitz Freeway and into the neighborhood, where Joy slowed the Jeep considerably. "I don't intend to live with Pop forever, but I might want to stay close in case he needs me. I had my eye on a house on Fountain Street last year but I hemmed and hawed too much and someone else bought it."

"I wouldn't worry about your dad if I were you. I hear wedding bells in his future."

"Yeah, maybe. I like Barbara."

"Then you'd be off the hook."

"It doesn't feel like a hook, but I know what you mean. I never worried about Pop while I was in Norfolk until my mom got sick." She pulled around to the carport in back. "But if he got married again, he'd be okay. And who knows? I might put in for a transfer back east to be close to Madison again."

That would certainly be an ironic twist, Amber realized. Even if she got training and a good job out here, she'd have nothing at all invested in California if Joy left.

* * *

It was after eleven on the East Coast, way too late to check in with Madison. Joy intended to call her the next morning but talking about her with Amber made her want to connect now, if only for a few seconds. Rather than call she did the next best thing, which was to watch a video she'd taken of Madison shouting into the Grand Canyon in hopes of hearing an echo.

What would Madison think of Amber? Joy had been reluctant at first to let her know she'd picked up a stranger on the side of the road, and the more time that passed without saying anything made it that much harder to broach the subject. Once she did, Madison would probably get silly and say Amber was her new girlfriend.

The idea made her face heat up, not because it was far-fetched, but because she could imagine herself getting tongue-tied trying to answer. Of course Amber wasn't her girlfriend but that would lead only to more questions, like why wasn't she?

Because…Amber didn't like girls that way. Joy wasn't totally sure that was true. The only time Amber ever mentioned her ex-boyfriend was to call him an asshole, and she wasn't shy at all about her sexual taste for women. Whether she preferred one or the other wasn't even the real issue. Amber seemed to prefer what she happened to need on any given day, and that made Joy unwilling to take a chance. Syd had been that way too— whether she admitted it or not—and left the moment a better opportunity came along.

Then there was her father's observation that she was always looking for a damsel in distress. Joy admittedly loved the feeling she got from coming to the rescue. It was one of the reasons Dani hadn't appealed to her, because Dani didn't need anyone, at least not in the desperate sense. She was strong and independent, and even the one time they were intimate, Joy had been left with the feeling that she hadn't brought anything special to the party. Whatever Amber's experience had been fooling around with her girlfriends, it was nothing compared to how Joy could make a woman feel when there was love between them.

A crack of thunder startled her and she closed her laptop.

"Come on, Skippy. It's okay." It was Amber's voice just outside her camper door.

Though the yard was lit only by the porch light, Joy could see her crouching figure underneath the deck. "You need some help?"

"He's afraid of thunder. He ran under there."

Huge drops of rain begin pelting them as Joy tried coaxing him out with a cracker. Amber grabbed his collar the moment he came within reach. A bolt of lightning lit up the yard and they raced to the camper door with Joy shouting, "Let's get in here."

Once inside, she dried off and handed Amber a fresh towel.

"Thanks. Where the hell did that come from? I've been here nearly six weeks and haven't seen a drop of rain, and then all of a sudden the bottom falls out of the sky."

"Welcome to fall in the Bay Area. Once it starts, it can last for weeks. Just be glad you don't work outside like I do."

"Speaking of where I work, I hope Shep didn't get caught in this."

"He's a big boy. I don't think he'll melt."

"Maybe he's holed up with Barbara making some lightning of his own."

Joy put her hands over her ears and shook her head. "If he is, fine…but please don't make me think about it."

Amber set her towel aside and leaned back against the cushion of the dinette seat, her nipples straining against the wet cloth of her tank top. "Bet you didn't know he's been thinking about your love life. He asked me the other night if there was something going on between you and me."

A deep breath…then another. "What did you tell him?"

"That I thought it was all in his head because I hadn't seen anything…and trust me, I've been looking." She leaned across the table until she was only inches from Joy's face. "So if you're trying to tell me something, you're being way too subtle."

Joy tried to swallow and found nothing but air. "I wasn't…I didn't…it probably wouldn't be smart."

Amber's bravado dissipated instantly and she leaned back again, folding her arms over her chest. "That's too bad. I kind of liked the idea, but I can see why you'd have problems with it.

You want someone with a better track record who can take care of herself."

"It's not that, Amber." Just hearing her disparage herself made Joy want to reach out and prove her wrong. "I like you... and of course I've noticed you. How could I not? You're a pretty girl, you're fun to be with...but I didn't want you saying yes just because I have power over your job. It wouldn't be right for me to push myself on you."

Before she knew what was happening, Amber was beside her, pressing into her chest and forcing her backward on the couch. "What if I said it was okay for you to push?"

Joy surrendered to her kiss, tuning out all the warning sirens in her head. Amber was an adult, capable of making her own decisions, and after six weeks on the job had to be secure enough to know she didn't have to do this. That made it okay to enjoy, and Joy squirmed in the tight space to pull Amber onto her lap, never breaking their kiss.

It was only when Amber's hand slid upward to cup her breast that the ringing bells made themselves heard.

"No...no." She grasped the hand and held it at bay. "I can't do this with you, Amber."

"Seemed to me like you were doing it just fine."

With a gentle buck, she nudged Amber out of her lap and onto the bench beside her. In just those few moments, it was as if the temperature in the tiny camper had gone up twenty degrees.

"It isn't as simple as that, not for me." There was a lot of baggage she could unpack to explain what was stopping her, but those six years she'd lost with Syd weren't Amber's fault. The lessons she'd learned, however, were ones she'd never forget. "I'm a lesbian. I never made a choice to be this way. I just discovered it in myself and accepted it. I need to be with someone who understands that, and who feels the same way."

"So I'm not gay enough." Amber was clearly offended.

Joy sighed. "Being gay isn't just about sex. It's a whole lifestyle. We see the world differently."

Amber abruptly rose and wrapped the towel around Skippy. "Got it. Maybe I can take a course and get certified."

She didn't even bother to close the door as she sprinted into the house beneath a downpour.

* * *

Joy was probably right after all, Amber realized. All she'd accomplished with her daring kiss was to put her job at risk. There was an uneven distribution of power between them—Joy had it all. And as usual, she couldn't just accept Joy's reservations with maturity, or even a dose of humor, which would have defused the awkwardness. No, she did what she always did, which was to get off a parting shot that made rational discussion impossible. No wonder she'd been fired from practically every job she'd ever had.

After making sure Shep wasn't home yet, she pulled off her wet shirt and pants and slung them over the shower rail to dry. If Joy didn't like her mess in the bathroom, that was just too damn bad. Wrapped in only a towel, she'd started for her room when the back door suddenly opened.

"I just got a call from Pop. He's at the hospital with Barbara. She had a reaction to something she ate at dinner." Joy was still in her jeans but now with a dry shirt and a raincoat. "I need you to come with me so you can bring Pop home. I'll wait until we see what's happening with Barbara and then I'll drive her car home...with her in it, I hope."

Concern for Barbara trumped everything else on the short ride to the hospital, and neither of them brought up the incident in the camper or how it had devolved into a spat. Joy adopted her usual take-charge persona, making sure Amber knew to park beside the ramp when they got home if it was still raining instead of in the carport. Then she scanned the hospital layout and indicated the best place to transfer her father into the car so he wouldn't get wet.

In the emergency room waiting area, Shep sat at the end of a long row of chairs, his hair and jacket still damp from the rain. He was clearly distraught.

"Is she okay, Pop?"

"Jesus, I'm glad you're here. Yeah, they gave her a shot. They want to keep her a little longer but she's already better."

"That's good, Shep," Amber said, draping her arm around his shoulder as she took the chair next to him. Regardless of her situation with Joy, Shep was her primary responsibility, and this was where she needed to put her energy and focus. "How about you? Are you okay?"

"Fucking useless is what I am," he grumbled. "There she was—turning purple, for Christ's sake—and she had to help me into the car before she could drive herself to the emergency room."

Joy squatted in front of him and took his hand. "You're not useless, Pop. You know this is just temporary until your shoulder gets better. Then you'll be back to doing everything for all of us again, just like you always have."

"She's right, Shep. Any other time, you would have had it all under control. You're already a lot stronger than you were a few weeks ago and it's only going to be a couple more months before you'll be back to your old self."

If he was placated at all, he didn't show it. Instead, he looked at Joy and tipped his head in the direction of the nurses' station. "Go check on her again, will you?"

As he dismissed their words of reassurance, Amber's heart broke for the old guy. For the first time since she'd known him, he seemed to be feeling sorry for himself.

"Would you like to go home? I can take you. Joy said she'd wait and bring Barbara's car."

"I think I'd rather stick around if it's okay with you. I want to make sure she's all right."

"That's fine too. What about if when we get home, I stay over at Barbara's tonight just to keep an eye on her? Joy could sleep in my room."

He looked up and nodded, finally showing a bit of eagerness. "That's good. And maybe I should stay over there too. She has a recliner in the living room I can sleep in, but I'll need some help getting this chair up the back stairs."

Joy returned looking visibly relieved. "The doctor said the antihistamine did exactly what it was supposed to, and she's doing just fine. They want to watch her for another thirty minutes or so and then she can come home with us."

Amber walked Joy to a private area of the lobby and filled her in on their plans for the night, expecting a pushback. Joy would probably want her father in his own bed, and would be just as adamant about being the one to take charge of Barbara... since she always took charge of everything else.

"He really wants to do this, Joy. It'll be easy. I can sleep on the couch over there in case either of them needs help."

"That was good thinking. He'd be up all night if he wasn't right there watching over her. It'll put his mind at ease, and it'll put mine at ease if you're there with both of them."

There was something different in Joy's expression, and it was more than gratitude. It was respect.

"Look, Joy...about what happened earlier. I'm sorry I spouted off. Whatever reasons you have...they're okay, and you don't have to explain them to me. You guys have been really nice and I should have left well enough alone."

Joy put her hand on Amber's shoulder—like a big sister. "Don't worry about it."

"I won't. From here on out, I'm just going to focus on doing my job."

CHAPTER FIFTEEN

"I don't get it, Madison. You've always gotten good grades in math. What's different this year?"

"I hate it," the child whined from the computer screen. Joy had never seen her so disgruntled about school. "It's too hard and my teacher gives too much homework."

Though Joy felt bad about giving Madison grief over school, especially on a Saturday morning, it was obvious Syd wasn't helping her over this rough patch. From where she was sitting, she wasn't even sure Syd was doing anything at all.

"School's supposed to be hard, honey. If it weren't, you'd already know everything and you wouldn't have to go."

"But it's not fair. Even when I try real hard, I still get the answers wrong. Luke says I'm stupid because I'm half black."

Joy bit her tongue to keep from saying something obscene about Luke, who had been in Madison's class since second grade. "Someday Luke will grow up and be ashamed of himself for saying that. In the meantime, all you have to remember is that I've known you a lot longer than he has, and I think you're very smart."

She was visibly cheered by the praise, grinning into the camera of her tablet. "I got a B-plus in spelling. I missed 'protein' because I thought it was supposed to be 'i' before 'e' except after 'c'. What's the point of memorizing all the rules if you're just going to break them?"

"Good question. If I knew the answer I'd be a genius." Joy didn't want to spend any more time nagging Madison about school. "What are you doing today? Is the sun shining?"

"Yeah, but I can't go outside. Mom and Mitch went to get some new tires for his Camaro. He loves that car like it's a person."

"You're home by yourself?"

"It's *okay*," she said, emphasizing the word. "I'm not a baby. Besides, it's just for a couple of hours and I'm not allowed to do anything but play with my tablet and watch TV."

Joy didn't like it much, but it wasn't entirely unreasonable to leave a nine-year-old alone for a little while in a familiar place. "Fine, but what are you supposed to do if there's an emergency?"

"Call you."

"I'm too far away to help. What if the toilet runs over and you can't get it to stop?"

"Ewww!"

This was exactly what worried her—Syd hadn't even prepared her for the simplest of problems. "Is Tara's mother home?"

"I guess."

"And you have her number?"

"Yes!" Madison made a face and groaned.

"Okay, okay, okay." Except it wasn't, and Joy would follow up with Syd to make sure there were plenty of procedures in place if something went wrong. The trick would be doing it without coming off as critical, since Syd would deal with that by telling Madison not to call her anymore when she wasn't home.

The important piece was Madison's safety, not their prickly relationship.

Madison asked, "Where's Grandpa Shep?"

"He's over at Barbara's." She related the story from the night before, including the fact that her father had stayed to keep an eye on his friend. That let her segue into introducing Amber. "Did I tell you about Grandpa Shep's helper? Her name's Amber Halliday, and she's from Kentucky."

"When did she come?"

"Uh…right when he got out of rehab." She didn't want to trigger too many questions, hoping to avoid the whole story. "He needs help getting around in his chair because he can't use his bad shoulder. What would happen if he tried to wheel himself with only one arm?"

Madison placed a finger on her chin as she thought about it. "He'd spin around in circles!"

"And he'd drill a hole all the way to China. So Amber helps him get in and out of his chair, and she pushes him wherever he needs to go."

"That's why you're always in the camper when you call me."

"Correct-o! Amber sleeps in your room so she can get up if your grandpa needs anything. And she helps him with all his exercises, which means she stands over him and cracks the whip until he does them like he's supposed to."

"Is she mean?"

"No, she's nice. He taught her how to play backgammon, just like you."

"Aww, that makes me want to be there. I tried to show Mitch how to play, but he didn't like it. He only plays stupid video games where soldiers shoot people or blow them up."

Joy's dislike of Mitch was now cemented, as was her loss of respect for Syd. Whatever those two were doing together, it wasn't conducive to raising a child, especially one who was struggling in school.

"You know, I haven't talked to your mom for a while. How about if you ask her to give me a call?"

"You won't get me in trouble, will you?"

"How would I do that?"

"I'm not supposed to tell you stuff about Mitch…and I can't say anything about you either when he's here. I don't think he knows Mom used to have a girlfriend."

That was Syd in all her self-loathing glory. Of course she hadn't told Mitch about the nature of their relationship. "I won't get you in trouble. I just want to ask if you can come out to visit for Thanksgiving, and maybe Christmas too. Would you like that?" Since Syd was head over heels about Mitch, she'd probably welcome the chance for more time alone with him, and Joy wasn't above taking advantage of it.

"Please…please! That would be so cool."

"Just tell her to call me when she gets home." It was all she could do to keep a pleasant smile on her face as her anger toward Syd roiled. "I guess I need to go check on Grandpa Shep and Barbara. I want you to get Tara's number right now and keep it by the phone in case you need it."

"Okayyyy," she said, rolling her eyes. "If I come, do I get to sleep in the camper too?"

"That depends. Do you really want to get up at four o'clock in the morning when you're on vacation?"

"On second thought…Amber can sleep with you and I'll take her bed."

"You think so, do you?"

"You need a girlfriend, Joy."

She hoped Madison's screen didn't show off how deeply she was blushing. "I'll be sure to warn her that you like to play matchmaker. I love you."

In their usual signoff, she kissed her hand and touched the screen, and Madison did the same.

As she closed her laptop, she heard voices outside the camper door. Barbara, looking rested in a casual knit pantsuit, was pushing the wheelchair up the ramp.

"Hey, how are you today? Did that reaction clear up?"

"Good as new," Barbara answered. "The restaurant neglected to let their customers know the secret ingredient to

Friday's potato chowder was Thursday's leftover lobster bisque. At least I had only a taste before I started getting a reaction."

"I'm so glad you're okay." Joy held the back door open. "Where's Amber?"

"She had class today," her father answered. "Not that she doesn't have class other days. She's a classy gal."

Joy glanced back at the carport. "But the car's still here."

"She took the bus…not the brightest move considering it's supposed to rain again this afternoon, but she didn't want to take my car in case I needed to go somewhere. Some people are too stubborn for their own good."

Stubborn, indeed. This sudden flash of independence likely had nothing to do with leaving the car in case they needed it. It was probably left over from their episode in the camper last night, and it bore Amber's usual stamp of immaturity. If she couldn't have the relationship she wanted, she wanted to prove to Joy how far she could go in the opposite direction.

* * *

Instructor Lee Bowman was cute in a teenage heartthrob sort of way, short brown hair with a matching mustache and trim goatee, and the longest lashes Amber had ever seen on a guy. It was easy to imagine the girls in his high school social studies class going gaga over him. He certainly seemed to like the young women in the adult education class, bending low to help with problems in their workbooks, while standing upright to help the men.

He'd been over twice to check on Amber's work, but hadn't spoken to her because she was in the midst of a timed practice test. Now she'd finished and was waiting for him to tell her how she'd done on the parts she had taken earlier in the week. Today's tests were hard but she felt good about her work. The only subject she was really worried about was math, the test she had taken on Tuesday. She'd spent the last seven years forgetting almost everything she'd ever learned about numbers other than what it took to make change.

It irked her to watch Lee hanging over Wendy, a girl of about twenty who'd failed the GED test twice already. Even more, she was bothered by Wendy's flirtatious response, as if sucking up to Lee would help her do better on a standardized test. If she was dumb enough to think that, it was no wonder she couldn't pass.

Considering what she'd told Joy about her previous relationships with Archie, Molly and Corey, Joy had probably been right to worry about what was behind Amber's advance the night before. Not long ago she might have been just like Wendy, trying anything to get an advantage in the form of extra help. Guys especially were so easy to manipulate. Wendy had only to smile and cross one pretty leg over the other, and Lee would practically sit down and do the workbook for her.

Joy wasn't so gullible, and she didn't answer to sexual urges the way guys did. She just gave of herself out of the goodness of her heart. No one had ever offered Amber security the way she had without expecting a piece of her in return. It was one of the main reasons her feelings had grown the way they had. What she wanted from Joy was free from any sort of trade-off.

"So, Amber," Lee said, smiling in a way she decided was sleazy. "How did you do?"

"Not too bad, I think. I'm more worried about the test I took the other night."

"Yeah, lots of people have trouble with math, and it looks like we've got some catching up to do. But the good news is you did great on your grammar and writing sections, so I don't think we'll have to work on that anymore. You should be able to pass that part of the test on the first try."

At least there was one thing she didn't have to worry about. But the other... "How bad was my math score?"

"You did all right on the basic parts...addition, subtraction, multiplication and division. Not so good on algebra and geometry. We can start on that next week, but in the meantime, you should take the workbook and skip all the way to Chapter Six. That's only five chapters you have to master."

Five chapters actually seemed manageable. "Let's just hope I did okay on the tests I took today."

"I'll have those graded when you come back on Tuesday. If you can't wait that long, we could meet for coffee on Monday."

His seedy invitation wasn't much of a surprise, but her surging anger was. A person in his position shouldn't be hitting on a student, not when he had the power to withhold his help, even though it was his job. But for once, she controlled her temper.

"I can wait until Tuesday," she said as pleasantly as she could.

"Oops, I probably should have asked if you had a boyfriend."

"No, I really don't go for guys."

"Oh." He looked wounded for a second, and then mildly amused, as if her statement was the only way to reconcile her rejection. "See you Tuesday then."

Lee Bowman was officially an ass.

* * *

Despite the hoodie Amber wore over her head as she stepped out of the Alameda Free Library, Joy recognized her from the tight, ragged jeans and flimsy sandals. Someone needed a trip to the shoe store before the wet winter set in.

She had been mildly surprised when Amber accepted her offer of a ride once it started raining, but she knew better than to assume things between them were rosy again. Their text exchange had been short and to the point, not the playful back and forth they usually shared.

Once in the car, they traded a few clumsy pleasantries, with Joy asking about the test and Amber asking about her father. It was strained and subdued, not unlike the call she'd gotten from Syd, who didn't want to talk about the holidays today, probably because Mitch was there. She'd promised to call back later in the week, and Joy was bracing for a confrontation over losing even more time with Madison.

Her issues with Syd would wait, though. She needed to clear the air once and for all with Amber. "I'd like to talk some more about what happened yesterday."

Amber shrugged and glanced at the car door, as if emphasizing her captive presence. "I'm not going anywhere."

Joy's instinct was to push back, to demand that she actually try to have a mature conversation for a change, without her childish comebacks and blasé attitude. All that stopped her was the assumption it would cause Amber to dig in even deeper. "Look, I feel like I need to explain what I was feeling, because it didn't have anything to do with you. I wanted that kiss just as much as you did, maybe even more. The other stuff I was saying though, all that about needing to be with a lesbian...it's real. I don't want to get dumped on again. I invested a lot of my life with a woman who left me for a man because she never really considered our relationship to be permanent. It was only until what she really wanted came along. I happen to believe Syd's a lesbian, but she doesn't want to be, and that's all that matters in the end."

"Oh, I get it. Syd didn't know what she wanted, so neither do I."

"I think you know what you want now, Amber. You have feelings for me, but for how long? I don't want to get involved with a woman just to bide my time or fool around. If there isn't a chance it can turn into something serious, then it's just a waste of everybody's time."

"Everybody's? What gives you the right to decide what's a waste of my time?"

Amber, it seemed, had a reflexive need to treat every word as a criticism, challenge or threat. "Can you just try for a minute not getting so defensive about every single word I say? I'm not trying to attack you or put you down. Like I said, this is about how I feel about me, not you. If you really aren't interested in that, I'll shut up and we can just pretend none of it happened."

For almost a minute, it seemed Amber had decided on that route. Then she drew in a loud breath and harrumphed. "You want to know what it looks like from where I'm sitting? You say it's about you and you aren't trying to attack me, but you've already made up your mind about who I am and what I want. You're not giving me any credit at all for having feelings of my own. And you also said you didn't want this to be about power, but it is…because you aren't giving me any. You want to be in charge of everything."

"But I'm not trying to be in charge of you. I'm just looking out for myself, like anyone else would do. You've done it too." As soon as the words left her lips, Joy knew she'd chosen the wrong point to emphasize. Before Amber could fire back, she pulled over to the curb, shoved the stick shift into neutral and yanked the emergency brake. "I didn't come here to argue like this. I just wanted you to know that I like you, but I don't want to get hurt again."

That was the plainest, most straightforward way Joy could think of to put herself out there. She wanted to take a chance, but she needed to hear Amber say she had feelings for her, not just sexual desires. If there was a chance for a serious and long lasting relationship, she was more than willing to try.

Amber shivered and wrapped her arms around her waist, prompting Joy to turn on the heater.

"Look, Joy. I know just as much about getting dumped on as you do. I was left in a parking lot with a suitcase, for fuck's sake. And before that, Archie walked off and left me four months pregnant, knowing damn good and well I couldn't raise a kid without him. So, yeah…I try to look out for myself, and I'm not going to let you make me feel ashamed of how I did it."

"You shouldn't. I didn't mean anything like that." There probably wasn't much point in dragging this conversation out any longer, since it had only made things worse. She put the Jeep in gear, but before pulling out, added one last bit she hoped would salve any hard feelings. "Just for the record, I never once felt like you were trying to take advantage of me. You've earned every dime from the work you've done with Pop, and we couldn't have gotten along without you. I like you very, very much. I also respect you, and if I weren't so scared of getting my heart handed back to me with a pike through it, this wouldn't even be an issue."

Amber looked away, and for a moment Joy thought she was still annoyed by where the discussion had gone. Then she sniffed and wiped her face with the back of her hand. Tears... but why?

As tempting as it was to reach out and comfort her, Joy resisted, unwilling to risk setting off another defensive response. Maybe it was best, she thought, to let it all die down so they could get back to normal and leave this distrust at the doorstep. Then she'd try to talk it over again because in her heart she wanted to find a way to do this.

CHAPTER SIXTEEN

"You're cheating," Amber yelled. "I don't know how, but nobody rolls doubles four times in a row."

"It's my righteous living," Shep countered, walking the last of his stones off the backgammon board.

"Righteous, my ass. I bet your friends down at the American Legion are enjoying this little break from having their pockets picked." She counted out pennies for the stones she had left on the board and pushed them across the dining table.

"I hear the Jeep. My daughter's come to save me from your scurrilous accusations."

Amber looked past him out the back window to see Joy walking into the camper. After almost a week, the atmosphere was back to normal between them, insomuch as normal was pretending they'd never kissed or voiced any sort of attraction for one another.

In its place, the new normal also included Joy showing a side of herself she'd kept hidden—not just friendly, but sweet and amazingly supportive.

On Sunday she'd insisted on Amber taking the day off just to pamper herself—and to shop for the winter shoes and clothes she'd left behind when packing for the bus tour. Then on Monday and Wednesday, she'd not only handled dinner and cleanup, but also shooed Amber out to the camper so she could do her schoolwork without the interruptions of TV and chatter. Add to that a spontaneous ice cream run for everyone and two long walks with Skippy, and it seemed Joy was bending over backward to please her.

Whatever the reason behind Joy's new outlook, Amber was more than happy to see it, and found herself lying awake at night thinking of ways to return the sentiment. One night after Joy had gone to bed, she made brownies and sneaked them into her lunch bag. Then on Wednesday—Joy's usual laundry day— she stripped the sheets in the camper and washed them, along with everything in the hamper, making sure to carefully fold all of the shirts fresh out of the dryer so they wouldn't wrinkle.

The upshot of all this mutual saccharinity wasn't merely the return to a good working relationship over the issue of Shep's care. Nor was it simply a renewal of their friendship. Both of those had come about, but for Amber there was also a smoldering undercurrent of temptation that threatened to erupt at any moment. She wanted to walk out there right now and demand another kiss.

If this was Joy's idea of looking out for herself, it was maddening. How could she act like this knowing how much Amber wanted her? It was as if she was flaunting it, saying, "Look, but don't touch." All because Amber wasn't gay enough.

Maddening!

"Hi, guys!" Joy had changed from her uniform into jeans and a long-sleeved denim shirt. "Did I miss anything important on *The High-Strung and the Useless*?"

"Jesus, I almost forgot!" her father said. "*The Final Countdown* comes on at four."

Joy looked at Amber and rolled her eyes. "It's an old sci-fi movie about an aircraft carrier. It was filmed on the *Nimitz*, which is one of the carriers Pop worked on for a while when it was in port. He has the DVD but he still watches it every time it's on TV."

With Joy's help, he switched over to the recliner, where Skippy jumped into his lap immediately. "Watch it with me."

"Sorry, Pop. I've already seen it about twenty-three times. I think I'll find some other way to amuse myself."

"Madison still grounded?"

"Yep, till Sunday, she said. No calls, no emails." She looked at Amber and tipped her head in the direction of the back door. "If you want some peace and quiet, come on out to the camper. You can bring your school stuff."

Amber looked at Shep, who was settled and content for the next two hours. After a couple of minutes, she followed Joy outside with her workbook, but stopped on the deck for a cigarette. Intermittent music and talking emanated from the camper, which meant Joy was either watching TV or surfing the web. It was possible she didn't actually want company but Amber couldn't resist popping in. If there was even a tiny window of opportunity, she wanted to pick up the conversation where they'd left off last weekend, and vowed to herself to park the attitude and actually listen for a change. Joy had a right to her doubts, and if Amber wanted more from their relationship, it was up to her to put those doubts to rest, not to challenge their validity.

As soon as she entered the camper, Joy closed her laptop and put it into the bin beneath the dinette. "You can have the table." Still sweet and supportive, as she'd been all week.

"I don't have to take it. I thought maybe we'd give that talking business another try."

"That talking business?" Joy smiled gently.

"Yeah, I've been thinking a lot about why I got so upset last week. The main reason, I guess, is because that's my normal reaction when I don't get my way."

Joy, who had made no move to sit, leaned against the bathroom door and folded her arms, apparently satisfied to let Amber do "the talking business" on her own.

"The other reason was because you didn't believe me. I thought if I told you something—like when I said that time I liked girls better than guys—you ought to just take my word for it. The thing is, I can't go back and undo all the bad decisions I made with guys like Archie and Corey. But I can change my mind about how I felt."

"Are you saying this is not just a temporary feeling? That you're a lesbian after all?" Her tone wasn't as skeptical as it had been last week, but there were still traces of doubt.

"I honestly don't know about all the labels, Joy. I didn't grow up around a lot of gay people." The second she said that, she recalled the whispered rumors about some of her classmates in high school. "Actually I probably did, but all the kids in my part of Kentucky get funneled into whatever kind of life other people think they're supposed to have. If they want to be different, they have to want it bad enough to leave. It's the only way. I left home before I ever had to deal with what they'd think of me being with another woman. In fact, I don't have to answer to anyone like that ever again. I'm twenty-four years old, and if I want a girlfriend, I don't need permission…and I don't have to sneak around about it. There won't be anybody pulling me in another direction and I'm not going to secretly pine away for some other kind of life. I may not be ready to get married this week, but I wasn't just fooling around with you for the fun of it. I have feelings."

It seemed like hours before Joy finally responded with an exasperated sigh. "Well, if you can't commit to a wedding this week, then just forget it."

With the soft chuckle that followed, all the tension between them evaporated.

"I want a traditional Jewish wedding," Amber said.

"You aren't Jewish!"

"What's that got to do with anything? I like how they carry people around in chairs on their shoulders."

Joy stepped closer and slid her arms around Amber's waist. "Does this mean we can kiss again?"

If she had it to do over again, she'd have skipped the cigarette. "God, I hope so."

Her memory of their first kiss faded instantly as she experienced the delicious feeling of Joy's mouth closing over hers. The difference this time was Joy taking charge and giving off all that power Amber had fantasized about feeling. All she could think of was Joy sweeping her off her feet and onto the bed three feet away.

Her attention darted between the soft, warm tongue that prodded her mouth, and the sliding hands that explored her backside. Joy's focus seemed to shift as well, alternately urgent and in retreat, as if she kept changing her mind about whether or not to continue.

"I wish we had more time," Joy moaned. Though it seemed she was trying to hold back, her hands slipped under Amber's overshirt and tank top and rose slowly until her thumb brushed the side of her breast. "I don't think I can wait."

"Then don't." Amber disentangled from their embrace and wasted no time shedding all of her clothes, leaving them in a pile on the floor.

Joy's eyes left her only to peel back the covers on the bed.

Amber climbed into the lair and lay on her side to watch Joy undress. The muscles in her shoulders and chest were unlike any she'd ever seen on a woman. Her slim hips and powerful thighs made her look like a world-class athlete, and when she stepped out of her panties and stood to her full height, Amber burned in anticipation of being underneath such a hard body.

"You are something," she uttered. It wasn't only beauty that she saw. It was power.

For someone who'd never been able to articulate what she wanted from a lover, the answer began forming in her head as soon as Joy pressed against her atop the cool cotton sheets. This moment turned her on like nothing she'd ever felt—lean, hard muscles in a perfect package of smooth skin with a tender, feminine touch.

Never breaking their kiss, they writhed against one another as if caressing with their whole bodies. Amber opened her legs to let Joy nestle between them. As they slowly rocked together, she grew more conscious of her excitement. In only moments, her center might explode without Joy even touching her.

As if reading her thoughts, Joy shifted slightly lower, breaking the heated friction between their mounds. Her lips then painted deliberate kisses to the top of Amber's breasts.

The loss of contact against her center was tempered by the tingling of her nipple as Joy raked it with her teeth. Just when Amber thought she could stand it no more, Joy switched to the other, leaving a moist, cool trail across her chest.

"You're making me crazy," Amber murmured, cradling Joy's head in her hands, unable to decide whether to draw her back for more kissing or urge her downward for what she knew would finish her off.

The decision was taken out of her hands when Joy lowered herself again, this time stopping at the hollow just inside her hipbone. With her eyes closed, she brushed her lips across the sensitive skin to the apex of Amber's legs, where she paused to draw a deep breath, as if savoring the scent. After an excruciatingly long few seconds, she finally lowered her lips to tease Amber's throbbing center.

Amber drew her arms high above her head in total surrender, reveling in the feel of Joy's warm tongue as it slid through her folds. She opened her eyes to diffuse the sensations in hopes they'd last longer. Instead they intensified as she momentarily locked eyes with Joy, who wore a look of pure lust. It was only seconds before the vibrations spiked and a loud moan escaped her lips.

Joy slowed but never broke contact, working gently until another climax erupted, and then more. It was only when Amber shook her head and went limp that she crawled up and wrapped her in a strong embrace. "I couldn't have waited any longer for that."

Tucking Joy's head beneath her chin, Amber lay still, letting her body fall back to earth one pulsating spasm at a time.

The ceiling of the sleeping compartment was barely two feet above her head. This was Joy's private domain, and there was something profound about finally being allowed to share it after all this time.

Her fingers trailed leisurely across Joy's broad shoulders. "If that was a sample of what we've been missing, I'd say we've wasted a lot of time."

"We have plenty of time in front of us," Joy whispered.

Amber appreciated her choice of words. She hadn't said there was time left, implying their relationship might end when Shep's care was finished. It made all the more clear what Joy had meant when she said she wanted something serious. They'd crossed an important bridge.

Or at least they were halfway there.

She nudged Joy onto her back and let her hands wander her torso. Even relaxed, the muscles were firm and defined. The pride Joy took in her body was worth more than just vanity points to Amber. It was a symbol of the enviable self-discipline that permeated her whole life.

"Joy Shepard...you have the most amazing body."

"And it's all yours."

"Good, because I plan on taking it." She began by swiping a finger between Joy's legs and holding it between their faces. Then she licked one side, offered it to Joy and pulled it away at the last second to finish cleaning it with her lips. "Mine."

With a look she hoped was sultry, she lowered her mouth to Joy's rose-colored nipple, sucking it until it was rock hard. Then she flicked it several times with her finger.

"Would it surprise you to know I'm a terrible tease?"

"Careful...I have a very long memory," Joy said.

"That's good. I wouldn't want you to forget any of this."

With deliberate attention to even the tiniest detail, Amber explored Joy's body, paying special notice when a kiss or touch resulted in a whimper or squirm. Though she hadn't yet reached the more intimate spots, she'd drawn an excited response to the trail of kisses from the inside of Joy's knee to the top of her thigh.

Joy was ready but Amber wasn't. She skipped over the places that cried out for attention to come face to face again, where they kissed with even deeper passion than before. This was that rare part of intimacy she relished, where it was about the person and not just her body.

"I'll do anything you want, any way you like. Just let me stay right here for now so I can kiss you when you come."

Joy answered by pulling her into another kiss as she arched her body upward under Amber's searching hand.

She was slick and swollen, and Amber easily slid two fingers inside, only to draw them out and circle her hardened knot. Each time she traced the route inside and out, Joy grew more aroused, rocking her hips in a climbing rhythm until suddenly she squeezed her thighs together and groaned.

Amber sought out her lips for a kiss, at the same time burying her fingers inside to feel the contractions. Not only did it strengthen their connection, it also gave her a heady feeling of confidence and self-worth. *She* was good enough to make love with someone as decent as Joy Shepard.

"I will never question your lesbian credentials again," Joy said, tightening her embrace as she nuzzled beneath Amber's chin. "If you weren't one before, I'll vouch for you at the next official membership meeting."

"I'm not nearly finished with you." She wanted to bury her face in that warm, wet center and feel all those same sensations with her tongue.

Amber's distinctive cell phone ring erupted from the pile of clothes on the floor.

"Someone has a terrible sense of timing," she said as she tumbled from the bed.

"Could have been a whole lot worse."

"Operator...what's your emergency?" She could hear the TV in the background, a jingle for car insurance.

"I don't think I can hold on much longer without a burger and fries from Pearl's," he stated drolly.

Amber held the phone to her chest and repeated his demand.

"I'll go," Joy said, adding with a whisper, "assuming I can still walk."

"Anything else, Your Majesty?"

"I wouldn't mind a beer, if you think my poor system can tolerate it."

"Okay, I'll be there in a minute."

Joy was mostly dressed by the time she ended the call, but Amber couldn't resist the urge to press her naked body into Joy's arms one last time before their magic afternoon ended.

"Does this mean we're girlfriends?" she asked.

"What it means is everything has changed." Joy cupped Amber's face in both hands and planted a tender kiss on her forehead. "We can have this only as long as we both take care of it. It's up to us."

Where Amber had been expecting a trite reply, she'd gotten so much more. No one had ever spoken to her with such depth of thought and feeling, and it gave her a renewed sense of hope that this time she had gotten something right.

CHAPTER SEVENTEEN

"For the love of all that's holy, that hurts like a motherfucker!" Shep groaned as he raised his arm to shoulder level. His incision had healed, and his doctor was satisfied that the pin in his shoulder was now sturdy enough to begin range of motion exercises.

Joy felt sorry for his pain, but her overriding emotion was relief at not being responsible for pushing him through his routine every day. Instead, she watched from the comfort of the dining room table where lunch was a bowl of cereal with strawberries Amber had washed and sliced.

"That's what happens when you hold it one position for two months," Amber said. "Grin and bear it. The therapist said ten times, three times a day."

"The bastard pops in once a week like the Pain Fairy and then skips out after he's told everybody what to do." He let his arm fall limply to his side. "I'm through with this bullshit. I'll do some more when it stops hurting like a son of a bitch."

"Fine, we'll both quit. No more exercises for you. No more dumping your piss jug for me."

He snarled and resumed his feeble arm lifts, yelling even louder to make sure they both knew how much it hurt.

Joy had to admire Amber's tenacity and resolve. Whether her pop admitted it or not, he was getting stronger because of her staunch refusal to let him slide. It was hard to believe she was the same person who, only two months ago, had no sense of discipline or responsibility. Equally amazing was how Joy's feelings for her had gone from doubt to admiration and more.

"Three more and you get a handful of Goobers," she taunted, standing just out of his reach as she rattled the box.

"How about we shove those Goobers right up your—"

"Say, Pop...what did Madison have to say this morning?" Joy had missed the call when she'd gone to the gym. With Amber now intimately studying her body from head to toe, she felt especially motivated to keep it in top shape.

"Barely a word. It's almost like she's afraid to talk. What the hell is that all about?"

"I don't know for sure, but apparently Syd told her not to talk to anyone about the new boyfriend—anyone probably meaning me—or about anything at home, including the fact that her so-called mother doesn't help her with her homework now that she has better things to do." This was the only place Joy could vent her anger. "And Madison isn't supposed to say anything about me in front of Mitch. I think Syd's afraid he'll dump her if he finds out she's actually a lesbian, and she's making sure Madison knows how shameful that is."

"I have an idea how to fix that—three helicopters and a Navy Seal extraction team."

"I wish."

Amber doled out ten Goobers and put the box back in the refrigerator. "You should just call the guy and tell him. Be done with it, and take the pressure off Madison."

"I would never see her again." Joy explained how the law worked in Virginia. Her only connection to Madison was out of the kindness of Syd's cold heart.

"That's just fucked up. How does Madison feel about it?"

"She's a kid. She loves both of us and doesn't like having all these stupid rules."

It was more complicated than that, but Joy didn't want to talk about what she thought would be the ideal solution, which involved her moving back to Newport News so she could see Madison several times a week. Ultimately, she might do that, but there were now two others to consider in her life besides Madison.

"I'm going out to the camper to give her a call."

When she was sure her father was looking the other way, she shot Amber a quick wink. It was ironic to be talking about Syd's secrets when she and Amber were keeping their own, but they'd agreed to let the news of their relationship emerge gradually and without fanfare.

With a fresh cup of sugar-infused coffee, she booted up her laptop and tapped the icon to call Madison, the only person in her video contact list. Her smile faded instantly when Syd's face appeared on the screen.

"What's up? Where's Madison?"

"We need to talk. I was going to call you later today, but I told Madison to come get me if you called first."

"Is she still grounded?" Joy did her best to keep the ice out of her voice.

"No, you can talk to her in a minute, but I need to tell you a little about what's going on." Syd turned away and told someone—apparently Madison—to close the door behind her. "Madison's getting out of control. She's started acting up at school, and here at home too. She won't do her homework, and even when she does, it's like she doesn't try at all. I've caught her in I don't know how many lies, and then last week I walked in and found her rummaging through my nightstand. She knows better than that, but she's not listening to me anymore. It just started about a month ago and she won't tell me why."

Joy was sure she knew the reason but didn't dare speak his name. It was only natural that Madison would be jealous of a new boyfriend when her mother stopped spending time with her. "Do you want me to talk to her?"

"It's way past that, Joy." Syd shook her head and sighed. "Mitch just got orders to the Sixth Fleet."

Headquartered in Naples, Italy. That would certainly fix the problem.

"He'll probably be there three years, maybe even more, so I was thinking this was a good opportunity for Madison to get a fresh start."

It was as if a stone dropped in the pit of Joy's stomach as the implication hit her, and she felt tears rush to her eyes. The thought of not seeing Madison for three years was enough to make her sick.

"I really think she needs a change of scenery, Joy. How would you feel about her coming out to California for a while?"

Joy was so stunned she could barely breathe. Surely she had misheard. "You want her to come here? For how long?"

"I don't know…it depends. You know how the navy is. If we want to live in base housing, we have to get married. But even if we live off-base, I wouldn't want to take Madison to a place like Italy unless she's a navy dependent, and Mitch just isn't there yet, especially with her acting out like this."

It was classic Syd, focused solely on what she wanted for herself. Without conscience, she was offering to give up her own daughter in order to go to Italy with Mitch. What made it surreal was that Joy didn't care about her motives at all as long as she ended up with Madison.

"How soon?"

"He has to be there by the third of December. It would be easier if we could get the navy to move all of us at one time."

That was less than six weeks away. "I can be there by next weekend. Can you have her ready to go by then?"

"I don't know. I'd have to get Friday off to withdraw her from school."

"I bet I can do that over the phone after I get her enrolled out here," Joy offered eagerly. "But you need to see a lawyer and get the paperwork finished by Saturday. If you're going to be all the way over in Italy, I should be her legal guardian."

"You still have the hospital papers from Carrie, don't you? Those should be good."

"I don't think so, Syd. That was Carrie giving both of us parental rights, but now that Madison's your adopted daughter, I think we'll need some sort of temporary transfer of guardianship."

"I didn't..." Syd looked back over her shoulder in the direction of the door, and then lowered her voice. "I never followed through with the legal adoption on account of Johnny, because he didn't want to take on somebody else's kid. Good thing, I guess, since he was scum."

And somehow, it had slipped her mind for over three years to share that bit of critical information? Joy wanted to scream obscenities at the narcissistic, lying sack of self-centered shit but still she managed to swallow her fury. Whatever she felt about Syd wouldn't matter at all once she got Madison, especially if Syd had made no formal effort at adoption.

"Once we get to Italy, if we go ahead and get married and Mitch agrees to adopt, then we'll probably want Madison to come live with us. And, of course, there's always a chance—as much as I hate to say it—that things won't work out with Mitch. If I end up coming back to the states early, I'll want her back with me in Newport News."

"Of course." Of course that's what Syd wanted, but Joy wasn't actually agreeing to anything, especially since she'd just realized she had just as much claim to Madison as Syd, and always had. "Let's do this. I'll get plane reservations for next weekend and you get her stuff packed."

Syd nodded and glanced behind her again. "I don't want to tell her yet. She's been so disruptive that I'm not sure how she'll react."

"What, you want me to show up out of the blue and tell her she's coming with me?"

"I know, it sounds ridiculous, but I think it would be easier on her if she didn't have too much time to think about it. She's crazy about you and Shep, and I think she'll be excited."

In other words, Syd didn't want to deal with the fallout from Madison realizing that she was being dumped.

"We'll make like it's a big surprise," Joy said.

Syd was so focused on herself that she probably didn't notice the phoniness in her words, or if she did, she didn't care. After agreeing to connect later in the week when Joy had her flight plans firmed up, she turned the phone over to Madison.

"Am I in trouble?" the girl asked.

"Why would you ask?"

"Because you and Syd never talk, and she's been mad at me about *everything*."

"Mad isn't the right word, sweetie. We're both worried about how you're doing in school."

Joy could hardly curb her giddiness at knowing what changes were right around the corner. No more suffering without Madison because Syd was in a snit, and no more having to suck up just for the privilege of seeing her. The gloves were coming off.

After pasting a kiss on the screen, she disconnected and dialed a number on her cell phone, which went to voice mail.

"Dani, it's Joy. Remember that national network of professionals you told me about? I need the number of an adoption attorney in Virginia."

* * *

Amber rested her head against Joy's thigh and used her finger to outline the triangle of pubic hair. Though Joy was obviously spent, Amber wasn't yet ready to leave the sensual place.

Something had to give soon. It was past ten o'clock—well past the hour Joy needed to be asleep in order to be up at four—but there was no other private time they could escape to the camper, especially under the guise of Amber doing her schoolwork. Not long after dinner tonight, Shep had turned in early to watch a movie and had fallen asleep. That created this rare opportunity, but Joy would pay the price for it tomorrow.

"I should go and let you get some sleep."

"Come up here." Joy opened her arms. "This will be easier once Madison gets here. Then you'll have an excuse to be out here in bed with me."

The news about Madison's imminent arrival had come as a shock. The fact that Joy hadn't even talked it over with her before agreeing to it told her all she needed to know about priorities, but realistically speaking, what could she have said? That she wanted Joy all to herself? The poor kid got enough of that from her mom and the boyfriend. What worried Amber more was that she wouldn't fit in once Joy, Shep and Madison were together again. It was just her luck to fall for someone who was suddenly being pulled in a different direction.

Amber wanted to be part of that direction too. In fact, she wanted be part of the family, and clearly that meant welcoming Madison with open arms and hoping for the same.

"One of these days, we have to tell your pop that we're sleeping together. I bet he asks you what you could possibly see in someone so cruel."

"He should know by now what I see in you," Joy said softly, her hands stroking Amber's back in a tender way that threatened to put both of them to sleep. "I'll talk to him Tuesday night when you head off to school. If I know Pop, the only thing he'll say is what took you so long."

"And what's Madison going to say?"

Joy chuckled and gave her a squeeze. "She's been telling me to get a girlfriend. I think her favorite part will be having three people pay attention to her. That'll be a big change after being invisible."

Amber wished she shared Joy's optimism. She'd never been all that good with the babies and toddlers at Harmony's daycare, but she'd surprised herself lately. If she could handle an old crank like Shep, she could probably handle anyone.

"My shirt's around here somewhere," Amber said, groping in the dim light that came through the window by their bed. Her hand came to rest on an iron box. "What's this? Is this where you keep the dirty magazines?"

Joy produced her shirt from beneath the pillow. "That's my gun safe."

"Cool." She ran her hand along the compartment. "Is the key here too?"

"It's a combination lock…seven-one-two, which happens to be Madison's birthday."

"Good to know you keep it so close. I'll be careful not to disturb you during a bad dream. You might blow my head off."

"Not funny. As useless as I was the one time I tried to use it, I might as well get rid of it."

"I don't know how you can say that. You practically saved my life."

"I could've done that just as well with a baseball bat to the back of that bastard's knees. At least I wouldn't have run the risk of getting shot."

"You're being too hard on yourself."

"What's so weird is that I trained for nine years in the navy to be ready for a situation like that, and it didn't make a bit of difference. You see somebody you care about in trouble and everything you know goes out the window." Joy hugged her tightly. "I couldn't stand it if something happened to you."

"It didn't." Amber reluctantly disentangled and climbed down from the bed to get dressed.

Joy slipped on the shorts and T-shirt that passed for pajamas just as Amber's cell phone rang.

"What's up, Shep?"

"Can't…breathe."

"We'll be right there!" Amber was halfway out the door when Joy's feet hit the floor behind her.

They dashed up the deck and through the house to his bedroom in the front of the house, where he was flipping the channels with the remote while petting a slumbering Skippy.

"Movie must not have been very good. I think I fell asleep."

"Are you okay?" Joy asked, her eyes darting around the room.

"Sure," he answered. "Say, how did you get here so fast? I thought you'd be asleep."

That's when Amber noticed the smirk on his face. The whole episode had been a ruse to get both of them to come running. She smacked him with his own pillow. "You're an asshole."

"Me? I called out for Amber and nobody answered so I picked up the phone. What's with the secrets? And don't bullshit me. I know you weren't out there studying at this hour."

"We were going to tell you, Pop. We were just talking about it, in fact. We just wanted a little more time to ourselves, that's all." Joy plopped on the end of his bed, causing Skippy to raise his head, but only for a couple of seconds. "Oh, sorry…did I sit on your foot?"

"Smartass." He stuffed the pillow behind his head. "I don't care what you do, but I'm not an idiot."

"Fine," Amber said. "But the next time you pull a stunt like this one, I want you to remember what happened to the little boy who cried wolf."

"Aw, you won't let somebody come in here and eat my sheep, will you?"

"No, but I'll mix Skippy turds in with your stupid little Goobers, you ornery old man." No longer concerned about hiding her affections, Amber patted Joy on the back. "You should get on to bed. I'll deal with this delinquent."

"I'm not afraid of you," Shep snarled playfully after she'd gone. "The only way you'll get my Goobers is to pry them out of my cold, dead hands."

"I could cut your hands off too!"

His eyes grew wide. "That's very cruel."

"So is faking a heart attack, and nearly giving both of us one. What the hell were you thinking?" She scooted a chair close and sat down, blatantly propping her bare feet on his bed. "You okay with Joy and me?"

"Sure, why not? You're okay for a hillbilly. Just don't go screwing it up. And if you don't know what that means, you'd better find out quick. Joy doesn't need that kind of shit. She's a good girl."

"I know that. She's the best person I've ever been with in my whole life." With their secret out in the open, she felt brave enough to share the fears that had been building all day. "What about Madison? You reckon she's going to be okay with it?"

"She's a smart one. Don't think you'll be sneaking anything by her because she'll be on to you."

"I won't be sneaking around. I just want her to like me. If she doesn't, then I'm screwed, because I can see what she means to Joy, and to you too."

"Just be yourself, Amber. Kids see right through phony shit, which is probably why she's acting out around Syd's boyfriend. She'll probably be jealous because she's used to being the center of attention around here. You'll have to give a little because you're the grownup."

She was willing to give a little, as long as she wasn't the one turning invisible.

He tipped his head toward Skippy. "And don't forget it's always good to have a little bacon in your pocket."

CHAPTER EIGHTEEN

With a creamy, sweet latte in hand, Joy entered the lobby of the mostly empty office building. A quick check of the directory by the elevator confirmed she was in the right place. There on the third floor was the person she was to meet: *Lynne Pierce, Esquire*.

Eschewing the elevator for two flights of steps, she found the door slightly ajar and let herself in. "It's Joy Shepard. Anyone home?"

"Confounded piece of worthless junk!" The invective was followed by what sounded like a kick to an inanimate object.

Joy followed the booming female voice to a room off the reception area where a round-figured woman of about sixty was doing battle with a copy machine. "Lynne Pierce?"

The woman turned, and in that moment, her scowl disappeared, replaced by a smile. Short gray hair and wire-rimmed glasses framed her face, and she was dressed casually in a tropical shirt with Capri pants and sandals. "You have any trouble finding the place?"

"No, the directions were good. Thanks for seeing me this morning. I couldn't get here from California until late last night."

"No problem." She shuffled down the short hallway to an office. Judging by the books, papers and sticky notes in virtually every corner of the room, she was juggling a number of different cases.

"So, Ms. Pierce...did you have time to look over my questions?"

"Call me Lynne, please. And yes, I did. Dani Hatcher is the squeakiest wheel I've ever met. If I ever need someone to cut through the noise and get something done, I'm going straight to her." She hoisted a stack of books and documents and let them drop noisily onto the edge of her desk. "I retrieved a copy of Carrie Larson's will from the courthouse, and it looks pretty clear that she intended for both of you to be Madison's guardians."

"We were in a relationship back then."

"True, but with you going back to California, I think Ms. Koehler could make a pretty good case that you're the one who abandoned your responsibilities."

"That's not what happened," Joy blustered. "I only left Newport News because I needed to help take care of my mom. I would've come back after she died but Syd had already asked to start adoption proceedings because she was getting married. Supposedly this guy adored Madison. I hated the idea of giving her up but I wanted what was best for her, and I thought that was a family. No matter what, Syd can't say I haven't been responsible because I've sent money every single month for her support, and I see her at least three or four times a year."

"Interesting. Did you know Syd was also collecting survivor benefits from the navy for Madison? That might explain why she hasn't gone through with the adoption. Those would have stopped."

Typical Syd—everything to her advantage.

"Did you ever sign any papers giving up guardianship?"

Joy shook her head emphatically. "Nothing. She told me after her divorce that her ex-husband's part of the adoption was never finalized, but she didn't say anything about her own. I always assumed it went through, but evidently that was just a con so I'd think she had all the power to make decisions about Madison."

"Possibly. Carrie's will was all I turned up that was registered in the State of Virginia. If she ever filled out any adoption papers, they never got filed, which means they're worthless. Besides, nothing would have gone through without you surrendering guardianship."

She was impressed that Lynne had done so much homework on her case in such a short period of time. "Are you saying she couldn't have adopted Madison without my permission?"

"Correct. A legal guardian either has to surrender rights or have them terminated by a court."

In other words, her own plans for adopting Madison were pipe dreams because Syd would never sign over guardianship. "So there's really nothing I can do to get Madison."

"I wouldn't say that at all." Lynne stretched her arms above her head, leaning back so far in her chair that Joy feared she would fall over. "Adoption could be tricky, but you have just as much right to physical custody of Madison as she does. What works against us is the fact that Ms. Koehler could make a very strong argument for the least disruptive outcome, which means Madison staying with her here in Virginia."

"That's just it, though. Syd isn't planning to stay here. She wants to go to Italy with her new boyfriend, and Madison's become an inconvenient obstacle...for now, anyway."

Lynne plopped a fresh yellow legal pad on her desk and began scribbling. "Tell me all you know about that."

Joy related the story of Mitch getting transferred to Naples and Syd's hopes of getting married someday, complete with his reservations about Madison. "I don't want Madison's future hanging on whatever this Mitch guy wants. All I know about him is that he plays violent video games and doesn't seem to want anything to do with her, and both of those make him a loser as far as I'm concerned. And I damn sure don't want Madison ripped away from me a year or two from now whenever Syd waltzes back into town after getting dumped. Madison needs a permanent home where somebody will always be there for her. I think that's with me, not Syd."

"What if Syd changes her mind and decides to stay here with Madison?"

"Yeah, I've thought about that." It was tempting just to go along quietly with Syd's current plan, since it would mean Madison could leave with her tonight. At the very least, they'd get maybe a year together, and she could always refuse to relinquish custody. "The problem is that it'll happen again with the next boyfriend and the one after that. She may not try to leave Madison with somebody else, but she'll push her off to the side just like she's doing now, and probably punish her if she tells anybody her mommy used to have a girlfriend."

Lynne shoved the books aside and leaned back again, folding her arms. Then a slow grin crossed her face. "Maybe we can use some of that paranoia to our advantage."

* * *

Joy wound through the residential neighborhood, checking to make sure Lynne's tan Chevy Malibu was behind her. Though all the streets looked alike, she knew the neighborhood like the back of her hand from her years sharing this house with Syd. She parked her rental car at the curb, leaving enough room for Lynne's sedan behind her.

The attorney had made a quick stop at her home to change into a smart business suit. She was here to make a forceful impression.

"You really think this is going to work?" Joy asked.

"What have you got to lose? You're going to file for adoption anyway, right? From what you've told me about this woman, she makes critical decisions on the spur of the moment, and she puts her own needs first. The only way she can do that today is to sign this guardianship release form. Anything else means we go to court for a long, long time. Leaving the country with her boyfriend won't be an option, and her life as a lesbian will be an open book."

"Couldn't she argue later that she signed under duress?"

"Perhaps. But after today Madison will be with you in California and the burden will be on her to file suit out there. I'm betting she won't bother to do that."

Joy wished she shared the attorney's confidence, but Syd was so impulsive there was no way to predict what she would do. It wouldn't surprise Joy at all to learn she'd had a fight with Mitch in the last two days and changed her mind about the whole thing. What Joy had going for her was the determination to see this all the way through. If Syd were actually willing to fight this out, it meant Madison was more important to her than Joy thought. At least that would be good for Madison, and it would put an end once and for all to Syd's shameful denial. Whatever the outcome, Joy was prepared to exercise more authority over decisions about Madison's upbringing.

Syd met them on the porch. Her dark hair had grown and she looked as if she'd started working out again. She was a slave to whatever man she was trying to impress, so it was easy to deduce that Mitch liked physically fit women with long hair. Nothing about her stirred even the slightest spark of interest for Joy. Mitch could have her.

With a suspicious glance toward Lynne, Syd said, "Madison's over at Tara's. She doesn't know anything about this yet. I wanted it to be a surprise."

Surprise, nothing, Joy thought. Syd's intent was to orchestrate the transfer in a way that minimized the amount of time she actually had to confront the consequences.

"Syd, I'd like you to meet Lynne Pierce. She's my attorney and she's brought some papers for you to sign."

"I don't really think any of that's necessary. Like I told you on the phone, the papers Carrie signed gave both of us guardianship."

"Precisely," Lynne said. "These papers would relinquish yours. My client, Ms. Shepard, wants to formally adopt Madison, and having you sign a release would make it a speedier process."

Syd's mouth dropped open in shock as she looked from one to the other. "Forget it. I never said I was giving her up permanently. It's only until I get settled with Mitch."

Joy felt her jaw twitching with anger and she took an even breath to steady herself. "No dice, Syd. Madison isn't some puppy you can send out to the kennel while you work things out with your boyfriend. If you want her, you're going to have to fight for her right now. I have as much legal right to her as you do, and I can't wait to tell the judge that you tried to palm her off so you could go to Italy with Mitch."

Lynne reached into her briefcase and extracted a stack of papers. "Ms. Shepard wants Madison to have a permanent home and stable family. In accordance with her rights as legal guardian, she'll be filing for adoption immediately. If you wish to contest that, you'll need to be present for court hearings."

"You goddamn bitch!" Syd was shaking with fury. "This isn't even about Madison at all. It's about you getting back at me for leaving because you can't accept the fact that I'm not like you."

"This has nothing to do with your prior...lesbian... relationship," Lynne said, her halting cadence suggesting deliberate antagonism. "It's about what's best for a nine-year-old girl."

"And what's best is putting her needs in front of yours for a change," Joy added.

"How dare you!" Syd seethed. "I love Madison and you damn well know it. I'm the one who took care of her when she was barely out of diapers and you were out to sea half the time. If you cared as much as I did, you would have left the navy for her instead of waiting for your mother to get sick."

The accusation stung, but Joy had grown up in a navy family and knew it was possible to be both a parent and a sailor. Besides, she didn't have those obligations anymore. "Madison always knew where I was and why. What are you going to tell her about why she can't come to Italy? Some lie about how you're going over there first to get settled? She's not stupid. Sign the papers and let's make her feel good about this."

Syd was clearly struggling with the immediacy of Joy's demands, just as Lynne had predicted she would. Missing out on the glamour of moving to Italy was a steep price indeed. With her lower lip quivering, she looked over the release form. "If I sign this, will I still get to see her? I want holidays and vacations like you have now."

"It's not a joint custody agreement," Lynne clarified. "It's a release."

"I want her to be my daughter, Syd...my family. I won't do anything to discourage her visiting you if that's what she wants, but she deserves to belong somewhere. You had your chance to adopt her and you didn't follow through. You should ask yourself why."

Lynne tugged on Joy's sleeve. "I told you it was a long shot. We need to get back to my office and finish the paperwork to contest guardianship before you have to catch your plane. I want to file first thing in the morning."

Those were the magic words and Syd angrily scratched her signature across the bottom of the form. "You're despicable, Joy Shepard. I hope you rot in hell."

There was no way to feel good about what she'd just done. Nonetheless, it was all Joy could do not to smile.

* * *

As the events of the past few days filled her thoughts, Joy couldn't muster an ounce of regret for the heavy-handed way she'd handled Syd. For four years, she'd tiptoed around her ex's bad moods and petty grievances, thinking she had no power to assert her guardian rights. It didn't bother her one bit to see the shoe on the other foot now, and for real this time. It was a long, complicated process to finalize the adoption, but at least the path was clear.

The moment Syd signed the papers, Joy's suspicions about her ambivalence toward Madison were confirmed. Syd loved her, but not enough to sacrifice her own dreams for a glamorous life as the wife of a navy officer. If she and Mitch got married, which was probably more likely now, Madison might drop off her radar altogether, especially if they had children of their own.

"What time is it?" Madison mumbled as she raised her head from Joy's lap.

"Eight twenty-seven Pacific Time." Joy had been tracking their descent for the last twenty minutes and estimated they were only minutes from final approach into Oakland International Airport.

Madison had duly cried when they left the home she'd known for the last six years, but her tears stopped before they ever made it out of the neighborhood. Since then she'd been giddy with excitement about getting back to Oakland and her Grandpa Shep. Without any prompting at all, she'd vowed to make the honor roll and keep her room clean, causing Joy to wonder if Syd had threatened before to send her away.

None of that mattered now. Madison was never going to feel unwanted again.

"Sit up a minute. I want to talk to you about something." The cabin lights were dim but she could see that Madison was listening. "You okay about what happened today?"

She nodded. "I guess."

The story she and Syd had agreed to share was that her real mother had intended for both of them to be her guardians. Now that Mitch was going overseas, Joy had insisted it was her turn to care for Madison, and Syd had reluctantly agreed. That way Madison felt loved by both, and she was clearly ecstatic to move to California.

"Remember when I told you about Amber, the woman who's taking care of Grandpa Shep? You said I should get her to be my girlfriend, so guess what?"

"But you don't need a girlfriend now. I want you to be with me."

"I will be, and so will she. She's excited about meeting you. I've told her all about your kooky songs and games. She's as silly as you sometimes."

By the crease on her forehead, Madison was far from enthusiastic about the news. If anything, she was distressed, and Joy thought she knew why.

"Sweetie, I know Syd spent a lot of time with Mitch and sometimes you felt left out. That's normal for adults and I know it's hard to understand. But it isn't going to happen with Amber and me. You're number one, kiddo, and we all want to spend time with you."

"I want to sleep in the camper with you."

"No, I have to get up too early. If I wake you up, you'll fall asleep during your math class."

"I fall asleep then anyway," she said with a grin.

Joy tousled her hair and guided her head back into her lap as the landing gear dropped. She had some mild concerns about their unconventional household, but not about her ability to be a good parent.

Amber had proven her knack for adapting to just about anything, so Joy was confident she would work out her relationship with Madison. They might even bond over having to do homework together in the afternoons, and they'd certainly join forces to tease her father. Once Madison moved into the bedroom, Joy would have Amber to herself all night, every night. Not a bad arrangement, though it was time to consider building on an extra bedroom—a big one with a private bath and walk-in closets.

Though it all seemed to be falling into place, she didn't want to get ahead of herself. Bringing a nine-year-old into the home wasn't the ideal way to start a romantic relationship that she hoped would last, but Joy had faith they could work it out.

"We're going to land soon, but I have a couple more things to tell you. You listening?"

Madison squeezed her hand without looking up.

"I'd like to adopt you. That means Grandpa Shep would be your real grandpa, and I'd be your real mom. You'd never have to wonder about who your family was, or who loved you no matter what. Would you be okay with that?"

"I thought I already was adopted."

"Yeah, so did I. But it turns out that's harder in Virginia than it is in California." Another lie she and Syd had concocted to soften the blow of separation. "That's why it's better for you to be with me."

"Does that mean I'd call you Mom instead of Joy?"

"I'd like it if you did, but it might be hard to get used to. I'd sure like to tell everyone you were my daughter instead of my goddaughter."

"That would be really cool."

The wheels touched down on the runway, but Joy's heart soared to hear that Madison liked the idea. "And there's something else you might be interested in...Amber has a dog, and he just loves your grandpa."

Madison sat up suddenly, clearly excited more by this tidbit than with just about anything that had happened today. "What kind of dog?"

CHAPTER NINETEEN

It was another damp morning, the kind that chilled Amber to the bone. How Joy worked outside in weather like this all day was a mystery to her. She could barely stand the half-mile walk to the elementary school and back, and it wasn't even November yet.

"Wait up, Madison," Amber called as she tugged gently on Skippy's leash.

The girl looked very cute in the dark pink skinny jeans Joy had bought her as a welcome-to-California present. Though she'd arrived with plenty of clothes, many of them were too short or too tight—not a fashion statement, but a sign that Madison was hitting a growth spurt. Even the purple sneakers Shep had bought for her birthday only three months ago now cramped her toes.

"I know the way by myself," she sang without looking back.

Amber cursed under her breath. Madison had known her all of four days and already had figured out just how to get under her skin.

It was Thursday, their third day walking to school together, a task Amber had volunteered for as an opportunity to bond with Madison. Too bad the bonding wasn't going well. Joy had warned that Madison might be distrustful at first because of her experience with Mitch. There was little doubt she was jealous, even though Amber had been extra careful about not showing affection for Joy whenever Madison was around...which happened to be practically all the time, since they both went to bed at eight thirty. At least she had Joy to herself while they slept, along with a few moments of groggy cuddling when Joy woke up at four a.m. The weekend couldn't come fast enough.

"I know you can get there all by yourself, but Skippy and I like walking with you."

"How do you know what Skippy likes?"

Why was this child always so antagonistic? She refused to drink anything if Amber had already poured it in a glass, even if she ultimately poured a second glass for herself. Without fail, she went back to her room to change clothes if Amber dared to compliment what she was wearing. Then there was her challenging reply to virtually every question or statement. How the hell was anyone supposed to make conversation?

"Because he always wags his tail and holds his ears flat when you're close by. He doesn't do that unless he likes somebody."

"I bet he puts his ears down when he's scared."

"Maybe, but he doesn't wag his tail."

Skippy chose that moment to live up to his name, skipping happily at the end of his leash to a clump of grass that clearly looked to him like the perfect dog toilet. He twirled around a few times before finding just the right spot as Amber fished in her pocket for a plastic bag to clean up after him.

Madison continued down the sidewalk.

"Hold up a second!" Amber's shout was to no avail. If anything, her plea caused the child to walk even faster. "Hurry up, Skip."

By the time she'd scooped up the mess, her youthful charge had rounded the corner out of sight. Amber hustled to catch up, only to realize that Madison was now running and almost a full block ahead of her. Skippy's short legs couldn't possibly keep up so she tucked him under her arm and began jogging desperately. There was a busy street at the end of the next block—too busy for an obstinate nine-year-old to cross by herself.

Panting from exertion, Amber stopped when she reached the crosswalk and frantically scanned the area. How had Madison disappeared so quickly?

Skippy's sudden barking and squirming alerted her to a presence over her shoulder.

The giggling child stepped from behind a parked car, filling Amber with both relief and fury. "That was not funny."

"You can't run very fast because you smoke," the girl taunted.

Amber wanted to smoke Madison's behind with a switch but she managed to keep her temper in check, since an angry reaction would only give Madison more encouragement to push her buttons. "That was dangerous. What if a big dog had started chasing you? I wouldn't have been able to help." There were lots more serious consequences than that but she couldn't bear to think of them, and didn't want to fill the child's head with such frightening thoughts.

"I'm not afraid of dogs. If I stopped to pet him, he wouldn't bite me."

"But something even worse could have happened. Joy and your Grandpa Shep asked me to walk you to school, and they aren't going to be happy to hear you ran away from me."

"Aw, don't be a tattletale. I was just playing. I won't do it again," she pleaded. It was the only time she'd shown any inclination to behave herself.

Except tattletale threats made lousy leverage, Amber grudgingly acknowledged. They might make her more compliant in the short run, but the resulting animosity would cancel out any good effects. This brat was the center of the Shepard universe, and Amber needed to get along with her, even if it meant being the butt of her pranks.

"Okay, kiddo. You've got a deal. I won't tell on you and you won't run off while I'm busy doing Doggie Duty."

"Poopy Duty."

"Doggie Doody Duty."

Whatever it took, Amber would find a way to connect with Madison. Only last week, she had begun to feel like part of the family with Joy and Shep. Now she was the odd one out.

* * *

"I'm proud of you for finishing your math homework," Joy said. "I know it's hard, but you're really smart and you're going to catch on soon."

She pulled the blanket up to Madison's chin and smoothed her unruly hair against the pillow. Left unsaid was her disappointment that Madison had told her the homework was finished only to confess when Joy asked to look it over that she'd done only half. They'd had a brief talk about honesty and the importance of working hard in school, followed by a focused effort on Madison's part to slog through the math problems until she finally grasped the concept of rounding remainders to the nearest whole number.

It would take patience to get her past this fibbing stage, and Joy couldn't help faulting Syd for letting it get this bad. Once Madison settled into her new routine and felt secure that all the grownups in her life cared about her, she'd stop acting out for attention.

"Maybe you can work with Amber tomorrow. She usually has math homework too."

"I like it when you help me. Besides, Amber isn't as smart as you are."

Joy had already picked up on a tinge of jealousy regarding Amber and blamed it on leftover anxiety about Syd and Mitch shutting her out. To allay Madison's fears, she'd made a special effort to spend lots of time with her each night until they both went to bed.

Amber was the one who disappeared most evenings. On the nights she wasn't in class, she joined them only for dinner and spent the rest of her time studying in the camper. Joy hoped that would change when she finished her GED, though she'd probably sign up for something else after that.

"You know, Amber's smart about lots of things. You should ask her sometime about Gus Holley. She actually knows him."

"I don't care about Gus Holley anymore. His music sucks."

Joy shook her head. "That is not a nice word. Can you choose a different way to say that, please?"

"I don't like it."

"That's better. I was going to see about getting tickets for the three of us to go to Gus Holley's concert next month, but it sounds like I only need two."

"I want to go! I love Gus Holley. I was just kidding. I know all his songs."

Joy laughed and tickled her through the covers. "Sweet dreams. Love you."

They signed off with a kiss to the fingertips and a touch and she returned to the living room.

"I'm going to bed, Pop. You need anything?"

He tipped his head in a gesture to have her come closer. In a voice too low for Madison to overhear, he asked, "What's with all this lying stuff? She told Amber this morning you said she could walk to school by herself. That didn't sound right to me so I pulled rank and said she couldn't."

"I never told her that." She slumped on the couch and ran her hands through her hair. "I think she's just testing her limits, seeing what she can get away with. She backs down right away when you call her on it. By the way, Syd also told me she'd caught her rummaging through her drawers too."

"No kidding. I found one of my old navy hatpins on her book bag this morning. I didn't mind her having it but not after she'd swiped it out of my dresser, so I took it back."

"I'll talk to her about that tomorrow. Who knows what all she had to do to get Syd's attention? It may take a while to break her of those bad habits."

For now, she needed to give Amber a heads-up that Madison was prone to bending the truth, and she should use her best judgment if there was any doubt. Getting Madison up in the morning and ready for school was above and beyond the job of taking care of her father, but circumstances were different now that they were trying to be a family.

Joy asked, "How is she dealing with Amber? Are they getting along?"

"They aren't smacking each other," her father deadpanned.

"Not exactly a ringing endorsement."

"Madison can be contrary over trivial stuff but Amber keeps her cool. It may take them a while to become friends, but that won't be Amber's fault."

"Sounds like I need to talk to her too."

"I wouldn't worry about it too much. I never thought I'd like Amber all that much when she first got here, but the little scamp grows on you. They'll work it out."

That much Joy understood. Amber was a totally different person from the miserable destitute she'd picked up in Louisville, all because she and her pop had shown faith in her and given her a chance. Madison needed that faith now but she too would come around eventually. Amber would win her over the way she'd won everyone else.

* * *

A faint light shone through the camper window as Amber slowly closed the back door so it wouldn't make a noise. Not only was she worried about waking Joy, there was also the matter of Madison, whose bedroom was just a few feet away. She was later than usual getting home but she had big news. Unfortunately, it was news that would have to wait until morning.

In the living room Shep snored softly in his recliner. A college football game droned in the background.

As quietly as she could, she took Skippy out to the front yard for a quick break, and then steered a sleepy Shep to bed. This used to be her private time, the only window of the day that was hers alone. She'd always relished carrying a snack into the bedroom with a supermarket magazine on country music stars, poring over pictures of Gus Holley onstage or out with his gorgeous wife Michelle. The nostalgia for her days in Nashville was a mere remnant now. Her new life was in Oakland and her private time was in Joy's arms.

On her way to bed she couldn't resist taking a moment to gaze at the sleeping child, whose innocent expression was as soft as a rose petal—the polar opposite of the thorn she'd be when she showed up in the morning for breakfast. Amber straightened her blanket and tucked her stuffed rabbit underneath.

Out in the camper, she slithered into her nightshirt and crawled into bed beside Joy, who immediately rolled over and kissed her on the forehead.

"I thought you'd never get here."

"You aren't even awake."

"Mmm...I'm awake enough."

Enough for what, Amber wondered. Always ready for a sexual adventure, she reached under Joy's shirt to tickle her stomach.

"Not that awake. But I miss you on the nights you go to class."

"I'm sure Madison appreciates having you all to herself every now and then. I know I would." Even in the dark, she could tell her statement had gotten Joy's attention. "Don't take that the wrong way. I'm not saying I'm jealous or anything... just that I look forward to being out here alone with you when we're both awake."

"Me too, sweetheart. We didn't get a lot of time to ourselves before Madison came along. I'm sorry about that."

"It couldn't be helped." It was quite the benevolent response, and technically true. That didn't mean she liked having Madison around. In fact, it bugged her that Joy hadn't even talked to her before dashing off to bring her back to California. Not that she would have put up any real resistance—other than to remind Joy that her experience in caring for children left a lot to be desired—but it would have been nice had her feelings been considered.

Joy's arms tightened around her and another kiss landed on her head. "I'm so glad you understand that. I don't know what I'd do if you didn't."

Amber knew but didn't want to think about it. No way would Joy turn her back on Madison, certainly not for a romance barely off the ground.

"I never dreamed I'd wake up someday and be somebody's mother," Joy said. "I had eight weeks of boot camp in the navy and that was like growing up overnight. Now I feel like a raw recruit again, but eight weeks of training with Madison won't be near enough. It's going to take me months to get the hang of this."

"More like years," Amber said. "Think of all you have to look forward to…driver's license, tattoos, birth control…"

"Oh, please. I wonder how many parents actually pray for their daughters to be lesbians."

"Don't know, but I catch myself every now and then thanking God for the fact that you are."

"Same here. Which reminds me…I have a plan for tomorrow night. It's Friday, so I'll let Madison stay up an extra half hour, but when nine o'clock comes, we're putting the old man to bed and coming out here to get reacquainted, even if it takes all night."

Just her luck, Amber realized grimly. "I'm not so sure about the all night part."

"You're tired of me already?"

"I was going to tell you tomorrow. I passed the math pretest I took last Tuesday, so Lee thinks I'm ready to take the real GED on Saturday. It's an all-day test, but I won't have to go back to class again until I get the results. That should be about two weeks."

"Wow, you weren't even in class a month. I told Madison you were smart. You ought to be the one helping with her homework. I've forgotten nearly all the math I ever learned."

In the first place, Amber had offered to help, only to be rebuffed by Madison, who she suspected might be sandbagging in order to get more of Joy's attention. And in the second place, she was sitting for the GED on Saturday. That was *her* big news, and it bugged her how Joy had changed the subject and made it about Madison.

This crap was getting old.

* * *

Joy groped in the dark for the buzzing alarm clock that occupied the same shelf as her gun safe. After a yawn and a stretch, she settled her arms around Amber, who had rolled into her chest to snuggle.

The last few weeks had brought rapid changes for both of them. They'd barely had time to establish their relationship before Madison moved in, but Amber had taken it all in stride. Joy felt lucky to have found a loving partner who could help with the challenges of parenting.

"Hey, sweetie. Wake up a minute."

Amber wriggled out of her grasp and sat up. "What's wrong?"

"Nothing, relax." She guided Amber back to the pillow and kissed her. "It's been a crazy couple of weeks. I've been so busy that I forgot to tell you something important. I love you."

Several seconds of silence passed before Amber reacted, and not with an expected smile or hug. Instead, her eyes filled with tears and she shook her head with what looked like disbelief. "That's not something I've heard a lot in my life."

Of course it wasn't, not with a cruel family or guys who had used her up and turned her out. There was no telling how much Amber could give someone who returned her loyalty and trust.

"You're going to hear it a lot more now," Joy said. "I'm so proud of you, and I'm grateful for all you've done for my pop, and now you're doing it for Madison too. You're a good person and I'm lucky I found you."

"I love you too. You're the only one who's ever believed in me."

Of all the things she could have said, nothing else would have made Joy feel as proud. Putting her faith in someone who'd shown so little aptitude and initiative had been a huge risk, but she knew from the navy that giving a slacker responsibility was usually all it took to bring out their best. "That's because you made a believer out of me. I can't wait to see what you do next."

"If you had an extra fifteen minutes, you wouldn't have to wait."

Joy reached beneath the covers and began stroking the warm skin on the inside of Amber's thigh. "Breakfast is so overrated."

CHAPTER TWENTY

Sweat poured off Shep's brow as he turned his chair on the concrete driveway between the carport and the deck. "How many is that?"

"Nine down, six more to go." Amber watched his endeavor with admiration. Only three days after getting clearance to start wheeling himself, he was up to fifteen laps, with a goal of adding five more every day. "What is it about thirty-three laps that makes it your magic number?"

"The parade route's a half-mile long," he answered, huffing. "I've been carrying one end of the banner for American Legion Post Number Nine for the last twenty-one years. No way am I going to let Brady Hawes take my spot. His chair's electric, for Christ's sake."

That stubborn pride ran in the Shepard family, Amber noted. Joy had freaked out when she'd found her dress pants too tight, enough to tack on an hour to the end of every day so she could stop at the gym. Apparently, this Veterans Day Parade was a big deal in Alameda.

As Shep approached her for the turn, she held out a handful of Goobers and dropped them into his open mouth. "Too bad I can't run along beside you in the parade. You'd do anything for Goobers. I noticed Madison likes these too. I had to hide them in the vegetable bin. No chance of her finding them in there."

"She's a pistol, that one," he wheezed. "Never saw a kid adapt so fast to being in a new place."

Of course she'd adapted, Amber thought. Who wouldn't with that kind of red carpet treatment?

Shep paused to catch his breath. "It must have been tough on her with that worthless mother of hers...probably talks to her more now on the computer than she did when they lived together. And that sorry excuse for a boyfriend...how did the navy end up with a cad like that? He's just the sort of asshat who'll put himself first on a ship when he gets in a jam."

Amber leaned against the ramp to the deck, cupping her hand to light a cigarette. Seconds later, she savored the heady rush of nicotine hitting her bloodstream.

Shep turned at the carport and started toward her. "Hey, I just realized that's the first time I've seen you light up today."

She'd been trying to quit, but hadn't told anyone in case she failed. "That's because I've cut back. I'm down to only five a day, but these cravings are driving me up a wall. I might have to postpone this till I get finished with all my school stuff. It makes it hard to concentrate."

"That's nuts! You've already got the hardest part of quitting behind you. Why the hell would you want to go through it again?"

"Because that's bullshit. The hardest part is when you get to zero." She took another deep drag and blew it away from him as he approached. "I'm still trying to figure Madison out. I can't tell if she likes me or not."

"She probably doesn't, but it's not personal."

"She told you that?" Amber asked anxiously.

"Nope." He wiped his face with a towel before spinning and starting back toward the carport. "You upset the order of things. That kid loves me to pieces, but I practically fall off the face of the earth when Joy walks through the door. That's what you're up against."

"I know, and that's why I get the hell out of the way. I don't even show my face until it's time for dinner. Then I clean up the kitchen and go hide in the camper until she goes to bed. What more can I do?"

"Could be that's part of the problem. You need to let Madison know you belong here too. Stick around and watch some TV with us after dinner, or maybe we could all play a card game. Don't let her shove you out of the picture. The best way to show her you aren't a threat is to hang out with us."

"Pfft! I don't see what that's going to accomplish. Every time I come around, she latches onto Joy like a magnet."

"Yeah, but you've got to give Joy a chance to tell Madison what she wants. It's her job to balance all the parts."

"Joy doesn't need that kind of stress at the end of the day."

"Horse hockey. Joy handles stress just fine. Besides, how else is the kid…going to learn that you being here is okay?" he said, huffing as he spun his wheels forward. "Joy has to show her… and she has to set down some rules about how to behave. She can't…teach her anything about you if you're out here in the camper with your head up your ass."

Shep sure had a way with words. Fortunately, it was a way Amber understood. "Fine, I'll hang out tonight and see what happens." She smoked the last of her cigarette—all the way to the filter—and dropped it into an empty soda can on the deck.

"That's fifteen laps," he said, gathering his strength for one final burst up the ramp. "Madison won't make it easy…but stick with it and she'll come around. You get through this and… giving up them coffin nails will be a piece of cake."

Amber answered a cell phone call from Joy and told her, "Your pop's been doing laps around the backyard. You working that hard at the gym?"

"I haven't even broken a sweat yet. That's why I'm calling. I got hung up after work talking to one of the other crew chiefs, and now I'm running a little late. Can you go meet Madison?"

Amber rolled her eyes at no one in particular and checked her watch—plenty of time to get to the school before the final bell, but Madison wouldn't be happy about it. "Sure. Shep and Barbara want to order a pizza from Bowzer's, so we don't have to worry about cooking dinner. Take your time."

"Thanks. Oh, and I've been letting Madison walk the first couple of blocks by herself. I wait for her at the corner of Lincoln and Versailles, right there by the fire hydrant."

"I know where that is." It was one of Skippy's regular stops in the morning. "See you back here a little later."

With Shep growing more independent every day, Amber didn't have to worry about leaving him to shower on his own. Her bigger concern was over what would happen in a couple of weeks when he got released from therapy altogether. She should have her GED results by then, and if she passed, she'd have a few more options on the job front. None of them paid as well as this one, but even a few hundred dollars a week would be enough to get her by while she looked into getting the right kind of job training.

Working with Shep on his exercises had been both fun and interesting. Seeing his progress every day made her a believer in physical therapy, so much that she'd looked into what it would take to become certified as a physical therapy assistant—two years of college. But the average salary in Oakland was over $50,000, and more important, there were lots of job openings. A part-time job on top of school would make those two years fly, as long as Joy agreed it was worth the investment. She didn't want to take advantage of her home situation—like she always had in the past.

Getting out of the Shepards' house all day for work and school had lots of advantages. Mainly, it took her out of the running for Madison's babysitter-in-chief, a job she'd never wanted in the first place. For generous room and board, however, she owed it to Joy and Shep to lend a helping hand where she could.

Skippy tugged her to the fire hydrant and commenced his routine of sniffing, sprinkling and sniffing some more. In the distance, children began to appear from the school. For a moment, she thought she'd glimpsed Madison, who was wearing her bright pink pants again with a white shirt and blue backpack. She waved, but as the children drew closer, there was no sign of the gangly girl in pigtails.

For more than fifteen minutes, Amber waited, growing ever more impatient until the last cluster of schoolchildren walked past. Then she tugged Skippy's leash toward the school, her eyes scouring every direction for a group of girls playing in a driveway or on a porch. Only a handful of stragglers remained in the schoolyard, none of them Madison.

Panic set in and she anxiously called Shep.

"Two minutes earlier and you'd have caught me in my skivvies."

"Have you seen Madison?"

"She's not with you?"

"She never walked by the meeting spot. I got here before any of the kids did, corner of Lincoln and Versailles, just like Joy said. I thought I saw her in the distance but when the kids came by, whoever it was disappeared."

"You don't think she got in a car with somebody?" He sounded as fretful as she. "Hang on a sec. I think I hear Joy pulling in."

Amber waited a few more frantic moments before Joy came to the phone.

"What do you mean you never saw her? Didn't you go where I told you to?"

"Of course I did! She never showed up." She explained once again about the girl she saw in the distance. "But then she mingled in with the other kids and when they walked by, she wasn't with them."

"She didn't just disappear into thin air. I'll drive through the neighborhood. You go back to the corner and wait."

Amber cringed at the agitation in Joy's voice, but this wasn't about either of them. A nine-year-old was missing and they had only a couple of hours of daylight to find her.

* * *

Before Joy even made it to the end of Garfield, she spotted a small figure trudging along the sidewalk toward the house. A closer look confirmed it was Madison, and she heaved an enormous sigh of relief. She drew her Jeep even and tooted the horn while simultaneously calling her father to report everything was okay.

"Where have you been?" she demanded, still more worried than cross.

"I had to walk home all by myself. Why didn't you come meet me?"

"I was at the gym and I asked Amber to wait for you at the corner. Didn't you see her?"

"She wasn't there. I stood there for a few minutes, but then I got scared of being by myself so I walked home."

The house was less than half a block away. "I'm sorry, honey. Amber must have gone to the wrong place. Go on home and start your homework. I have to go pick her up."

"I'll go with you," Madison said eagerly, and started to climb into the passenger seat.

"No, I want you home. Grandpa Shep was worried, and I need to figure out how this happened."

"I was right there waiting and she never came. She must have gone to the wrong place, like you said."

Joy was almost disappointed to find Amber at the fire hydrant. Had she been at the wrong corner, it would have explained how the two of them had missed each other.

"Madison's at home."

Amber got in and patted her chest as if to slow her heart rate.

"She said you weren't here and she got scared and walked home by herself."

"That's crazy. I would have passed her on the sidewalk. I'm telling you, I was right here but she never came by."

"That doesn't make any sense." Madison had been playing fast and loose with the truth lately, but Joy had a hard time believing she could have found her way home on another street. "Did you walk up to Versailles a different way? Northwood, maybe?"

"No, I came straight up Lincoln like we always do. The only time I ever went down Northwood was in the car with you."

Maybe Madison had just gotten confused about where she was going. On the other hand, perhaps Amber had dawdled for a smoke, or turned her back to chat with someone.

"I've been thinking about letting Madison walk to school and back by herself," Joy said. "Some of the other kids on our street do it, but after what happened today, I'm pretty sure she's not ready for that."

"I agree. She scares me half to death sometimes when she runs up ahead of Skippy and me. I'm worried she'll try to cross the street where there isn't a crossing guard. Traffic's pretty busy in the morning with all the people driving up to the school."

"You let her run up ahead?"

"I don't let her," Amber snapped. "She does whatever she wants, and if I say anything to her, it only makes it worse. About the only way I can get her to listen to me is by threatening to tell you she's misbehaving. Makes me feel like a third-grade tattletale."

"So why haven't you told me any of this? Did you stop to think I might have been able to straighten her out? She's a smart kid and I can get her to listen to reason. You can't keep these things from me, Amber."

By her jutting chin and crossed arms, Amber was fuming inside. She probably had a whole string of curses and rants she was dying to let fly, but in the last few weeks she'd learned to control her explosive temper. No doubt she felt powerless because of her situation, and while Joy hated lording that sort of authority over her, the issue of Madison's safety wasn't negotiable.

She pulled into the carport and turned off the engine. "Amber, look…I'm not mad. I just got really scared when we didn't know where she was. If something happened to that kid… God, it would kill me."

Amber stewed a few more seconds before flinging open her door. "Just so you know, I was scared too. Enjoy your dinner. I've got stuff to do in the camper."

A temper tantrum. How nice.

* * *

Distracted by the growling in her stomach, Amber tried to make sense of the California Driver's Handbook. Her Tennessee license was good for two more years, but most potential employers would probably want proof she was a resident of the state.

Still smarting from her confrontation with Joy, she tried to figure out how she'd screwed things up. Joy was right that Madison probably couldn't have found her way home on another street. Maybe her watch had been wrong, or she'd been so wrapped up in her thoughts that she missed seeing Madison pass her on the other side of the street.

Whatever had happened, one thing was abundantly clear: She wasn't responsible enough to be left in charge of someone's kid, and if Joy hadn't known that before she certainly knew it now.

The back door banged at eight o'clock, a half hour before Joy's usual bedtime. She entered the camper with a slice of pizza on a paper plate. "I sent Madison to bed a little early tonight. Thought you might be getting hungry."

The aroma of pepperoni and onions reached Amber's brain immediately, causing her mouth to water. It was all she could do not to snatch it off the plate and swallow it whole. "Thanks, I could use a pick-me-up. I can't believe how many traffic rules you guys have. Am I going to have to know it's a hundred-dollar fine to smoke with a kid in the car? Can't I just promise not to do it?"

"To the first question, yes. To the second, I don't think that will help you on the test."

Joy slid in beside her at the dinette and draped an arm around her shoulder as she ate. "I talked to Madison about listening better and doing what she's told."

Amber had hoped they'd all just drop the whole subject and go on about their business. "Great, now she knows I ratted her out. She'll probably hate me even more."

"She doesn't hate you. Jealous, yes. But I think that's normal for a kid who's been through what she had to put up with from Syd. She knows I'm crazy about you, and that jealous streak ought to pass when she realizes it won't have any effect on how I feel about her. Besides, I didn't say anything about what you told me. When I saw her on the sidewalk this afternoon, I told her to go straight to the house and start her homework, and instead she came home and got Pop to play a game with her. It was the wrong day to disobey and I let her know it."

Amber wasn't proud of her feelings at the moment, but she was glad to hear that Madison didn't totally walk on water. Maybe getting yanked down to earth by someone she idolized would do the trick. It certainly had for Amber.

"I'm sorry about what happened today, Joy…"

"It all turned out okay and that's what matters." She pushed Amber's hair back and nuzzled her neck. "Actually, that's not all that matters. You matter, and I should be the one apologizing for today. I was scared and I overreacted."

Amber had rarely been on this end of an apology. In the three years she'd spent with Corey, the word "sorry" had never left his lips. Same with her parents, and not a single crazy boss she'd ever worked for had apologized for their bullshit. She frankly wasn't used to having someone else accept blame, and Joy's sweet words nearly made her cry.

She allowed herself to relax in Joy's embrace, sorry she had wasted the night alone in the camper when she could have taken Shep's advice and joined the family. "I understand, honey. It was terrifying. You totally get a pass for that. I'm sorry I was a jerk about dinner."

"It's okay. There was more pizza for us."

Amber managed only a weak chuckle. Smoothing over the day's events fixed only a few of the symptoms, not the underlying cause. "I'm worried about things between me and Madison. How am I going to live here with you if I can't get her to accept me?"

"You're borrowing trouble, sweetheart. She's always been the center of attention in this house, so it's going to take a little time for her to get used to having someone else around. But she will, especially when she sees how much I love you. I think we just need to start doing more activities together."

"That's what your pop said."

"He's right. You've got a break from classes right now. Come hang out with us."

Amber nodded gamely.

"And by the way, I was saving this for a surprise, but…" She produced three tickets. "Gus Holley, next Saturday. Tenth row."

"Oh, my gosh!" She hugged Joy's neck. The tenth row probably wasn't close enough for Corey to see a Fuck You sign, but she didn't care about Corey anymore. What she had with Joy erased all the crap she'd ever had to deal with.

"Look, I know you didn't bargain for any of these headaches with Madison, and I'm sure it's crossed your mind to run for your life while you still can. I wouldn't blame you if you did, but I hope you'll give it some time. And don't be afraid to talk with me about how you're feeling. You're not the only one who's new at this."

"Okay." At least it put to rest her fear that Joy would realize this wasn't going to work and throw in the towel. With her declaration that she wanted Amber to stick it out—and tickets to Gus Holley—the day couldn't have ended much better. Unless…"I don't suppose there's more pizza."

CHAPTER TWENTY-ONE

With a smug grin, Madison snapped her next to last card, a red six, on top of the pile.

Amber checked the fan of cards in her hand, leaned forward, and in a voice barely above a whisper, calmly stated, "You forgot to say Uno."

"Aaaaaaay!" Madison screamed before grudgingly drawing two more cards from the pile. "This game's never going to end."

It was a miracle they were playing a game by themselves at all, but Shep and Joy had been right to encourage Amber to spend more time inside the house with the rest of them. While Madison hadn't exactly done an about-face, her demeanor had softened to the point that she no longer went out of her way to be cheeky. It wasn't the same as being warm and friendly, but anything was an improvement over the open hostility she'd shown in her first couple of weeks.

Skippy barked suddenly at the sound of Shep's bedroom door opening, but then his tail flipped with excitement as the chair rolled into the living room.

With an unexpected feeling of reverence, Amber rose to her feet at the sight of his dark gray uniform, pants pinned neatly underneath his thighs, and a jacket adorned with ribbons and a gold braid at the shoulder. In his hand was a folded garrison cap with his Legion number on it.

She nodded toward Madison, who was sitting with her back to the living room. "Check out your grandpa Shep. He looks pretty doggone handsome."

Madison leapt from her chair and into his lap. "I want to be in the parade too."

"Sorry, pumpkin. This one's just for veterans. You'll have to wait until you grow up and join the navy."

"I don't want to be in the navy. I want to be in the marines. Their pants are blue with a long red stripe."

"A jarhead, huh? Fine, but you better be nice to the sailors, or they'll leave you hanging out there without any air support."

"I could be in the air force."

"I bet you can be anything you want," Amber offered. The girl had no idea how lucky she was to be growing up in a house where she had noble role models like Shep and Joy.

Shep rolled his chair to the front window. "Any sign of Barbara?"

"She called while you were in the shower," Amber explained. "She should be here any minute."

The Veterans Day Parade was one of the biggest events in Alameda. Over a hundred thousand veterans, most of them navy, lived in the community, having spent much of their careers working at the now-closed Alameda Naval Air Station. Today's events included a half-mile parade down Hornet Avenue followed by a program aboard the USS *Hornet*, a retired aircraft carrier that was now a National Historic Site. If the weather cooperated, they'd finish with a family picnic in Franklin Park. Amber had packed the cooler full of drinks, but Barbara was bringing lunch for all of them—fried chicken, potato salad and baked beans. It was almost enough to make Amber homesick for Nashville.

Shep twirled his chair toward the front door, with Madison still in his lap. "Let's go out on the front porch and wait for Barbara."

The sight of Shep in his American Legion uniform had triggered an unusual surge of patriotism for Amber. She always felt a mix of pride and sentiment when country musicians, including Gus Holley, sang tributes to the military. Soldiers and their families were more of a theme than a presence in the Nashville music circle, whereas Shep and Joy were the real deal.

The sacrifice Shep had made for his country was extraordinary, and even more profound because he'd allowed—encouraged, in fact—his daughter to follow in his dangerous footsteps. The Shepards lived their lives as though patriotic debt was the most important thing in the world. Amber didn't exactly get that, but she nonetheless envied their conviction. She'd never believed in anything so grand.

"Everyone ready to go?"

The voice from the kitchen startled her and she whirled around, gasping at the sight of Joy in uniform. Her dark blue pants were perfectly creased down to the tops of her polished shoes, and her matching jacket draped from her broad shoulders. On her chest were three rows of colorful ribbons beneath impressive silver wings.

"Wow."

"See something you like?"

"You look amazing. If you came to bed dressed like that, there's no way I'd let you take it off."

"Good to know." Joy looked past her at the others on the porch before pulling her into an embrace. "I have to admit I was nervous about what you'd think."

"Are you kidding? Why?"

She shrugged. "I don't know. Some people are weird about the military, like we're all just a bunch of warmongers, so I couldn't figure out where you came down. All you've ever said about it was how silly I was to iron my T-shirts."

"There is that." Amber traced her fingertips along the winged pin, which ironically read Air Warfare. "I've talked a lot with your pop about the navy. We went through that aircraft carrier book over there and he told me all about what it was like working on a ship. Notice I didn't use the B-word."

"There's hope for you yet."

Though both had tossed off a couple of frivolous lines, there was a far more serious undercurrent to what Amber was feeling. "I also asked him how he kept from worrying about you when you enlisted, especially when you took such a dangerous job. He said you were the kind of person he'd want out there on the carrier deck if he were there...and I knew exactly what he meant. I felt that way the night you showed up out of nowhere to save my sorry ass."

Joy squeezed her and planted a kiss just above her ear. "You're my damsel, Amber. I won't ever let anything happen to you, not as long as you let me share your life."

Wow, again. That sounded almost like some kind of proposal. "I'll be your damsel, but I want to learn to take care of you too. And I want you to be proud of me."

"I already am."

Madison burst through the front door and hugged Joy possessively. "Barbara needs help with our picnic."

"I'll do it," Amber said, disentangling from Joy's arms. "Wouldn't want you to get anything on that spiffy uniform."

Joy nudged Madison to follow. "Go with her, honey. They could use your help. We'll bring the car around front."

"I want to stay with you and Grandpa Shep," the girl whined.

Stooping to Madison's eye-level, Joy cupped her chin and sternly repeated, "Go. Help."

A few days ago, Madison would have pouted and sulked, but the talking-to she'd gotten from Joy over not listening seemed to have made a lasting impression. Compared to last week, she was almost cheerful.

Even more surprising was how she clung to Amber when they got to Barbara's. Joy and Shep would always win Madison's attention if they were anywhere near, but Amber liked knowing she might come in third under certain circumstances. They hauled a cooler and two grocery bags to the curb and waited for the car to emerge from the backyard. When it did, Amber was astonished to see Shep behind the wheel. "Oh, my gosh!"

Joy got out to help load the supplies into the trunk and directed Amber to take the front passenger seat. "I want you to watch how he does this."

A bar with handgrips on both sides had been affixed to the steering column with wing nuts. It guided a pair of rods—one to the brake, the other to the accelerator—allowing Shep to steer with one hand and control the car's speed with the other.

"I'm a little out of practice, so you guys better buckle up tight."

Despite his warning, he drove so smoothly that Amber even closed her eyes to see if she could feel any difference between Shep and an able-bodied person. The very idea that he was anything but able-bodied was absurd. There was very little he couldn't do for himself, and the fact that he now could drive officially meant he no longer needed her help.

She turned to look at Joy in the backseat. "Looks like it's time for me to find a new job."

Shep snorted. "Hey, you never know. Maybe someone else will fall ass over teakettle today."

A veteran in an American Legion uniform like Shep's was guiding cars into a vast parking lot near the start of the parade route, where they separated. Amber walked with Barbara and Madison to a sunny spot along the wide avenue leading to the port, where they spread out a small blanket and sat down to wait. It was twenty minutes before the sound of a marching band signaled the start of the festivities.

A color guard marched by first, bringing observers to their feet. Veterans in the crowd saluted, and Amber copied Barbara by placing her hand over her heart. Behind the flag bearers, an active duty detail of young sailors marched in a smart, clipped formation, most dressed in dark blue uniforms with wide collars and square-knotted ties. The handful of women in the group wore uniforms like Joy's.

The band, which turned out to be from a local high school, whipped up the crowd with a rousing "Anchors Aweigh" just ahead of the Grand Marshal, a retired *female* admiral, Amber noted proudly. The cheers that erupted as her convertible Humvee rode past swelled Amber with gender pride, and she couldn't resist pointing the woman out to Madison. "That could be you one of these days."

The crowd enthusiastically hailed the first float, a decorated flatbed truck that held a couple of dozen World War II veterans who waved tiny American flags and tossed candy to the children. Amber made sure Madison got some, but gripped her jacket like a tether to keep her from wandering too far into the street.

One after another, veterans groups filed past, most in uniform like Joy and Shep, but some wearing civilian clothes. Banners, flags and bill caps identified the various campaigns— Korea...Vietnam...Desert Storm.

"Here comes Grandpa Shep!" Madison yelled excitedly.

All of the veterans in his group, American Legion Post 9, wore the same garrison cap, if not the entire uniform. He smiled their way as he rolled his chair proudly by. "Hope you brought the Goobers!" he shouted.

There were only a few more groups to come. The USO... the Red Cross. Where was Joy?

Then the largest contingent of the day came into view to thunderous cheers, a group of comparatively young men and women marching behind the unified banner of Operations Iraqi Freedom and Enduring Freedom. The sight of several wheelchairs clustered near the front sent a shudder through Amber as she thought again of Joy's dangerous duties. The group's uniforms ran the gamut from Marine Corps dress blues to khakis to the blue camouflage work suits like those Joy said they wore on the ship. Amber spotted her right away about halfway back, thanks to her white peaked cap.

As Joy walked past, she dropped her otherwise somber demeanor to wink at Amber and wave to Madison.

The final group was a Junior ROTC program from the same high school that provided the band. Their lines were as straight as those of the active duty sailors, and their steps as crisp.

All around Amber, people were folding their chairs and dispersing, some back toward the parking lot and others in the direction of the massive aircraft carrier docked at the end of the street. She wondered if any of them were feeling the same emotions as she. There was certainly pride and gratitude, but for her, the most remarkable impression left by the array of soldiers—past, present and future—was admiration and respect.

For the first time, she realized it was the foundation of her love for Joy, and though she'd been put off earlier by her rigid, compulsive nature, it was clear Joy's self-discipline was what had made her able to perform the dangerous job she'd had in the navy. Shep was right—she was exactly the person you'd want around if you had to depend on someone.

* * *

Joy and her pop waited near the gangway to the USS *Hornet* as the program spectators filed in from the parade route. "I just realized something," she said. "When Amber gets here, I can walk aboard with her holding my arm just like all these other people. I never thought I'd see the day."

"Anybody gives you any shit, send them to me. I'll kick their ass."

"With what?" she asked with a chuckle. "You know, I've done this parade four years in a row, and I realize what makes it special isn't marching with all the others. It's having somebody in the crowd watch for me to go by."

"I know what you mean. I always got excited when I knew you and your mom were somewhere up ahead waiting for me. I got that little thrill again today."

"From Madison or Barbara?"

The arrival of their party saved him from having to answer, but the smile on his face was enough to confirm it could have been either.

"What took you guys so long?" Joy asked. "We'll probably have to stand in the back."

Amber chucked her father's shoulder. "You okay with that?"

"Good one! How about hauling me up the gangway? I'm worn out, and I have to save something for the sack races at the picnic."

Joy could hardly contain her pride as they pushed the wheelchair aboard ship. It was obvious Amber was awed by the sheer enormity of the massive gray deck.

"I can't believe this monstrosity actually floats."

"This one's just an *Essex* class. The *Nimitz* carriers like the *Teddy Roosevelt* are even bigger."

Amber looked in every direction, shaking her head. "Remind me never to take you on a tour of any of the places I used to work. Trust me, no one wants to see the back end of a Taco Loco."

Madison squirmed between them and took Joy's hand. "I've changed my mind again. I want to be in the navy like you and Grandpa Shep."

"That's my girl," Joy said. "Where did your grandpa go?"

"He's with Barbara." She pointed to chairs in front of a speaker's platform, where Barbara sat at the end of a row beside the wheelchair. "Let's go sit down."

Though Joy relished the opportunity to show off the ship's grandeur to Amber, she didn't want to make Madison feel left out. "Amber and I are going to stand in the back and let some of the others have the chairs. You can stand with us, or you can go sit with Grandpa Shep, but whatever you do, you have to stay there until the program's over, and you have to be still and quiet."

The prospect of sitting won out, probably because Madison knew she'd get away with more fidgeting if she sat with her grandpa.

Joy hooked Amber's arm through hers again and nodded silently toward two women on the back row who had turned to smile. It was clear they too were a couple, and were also celebrating perhaps their first chance to wear the uniform of their country without having to hide their love for one another.

Amber had no idea what profound freedom Joy felt from being able to do that.

After the invocation, Amber's fingers suddenly tightened around her forearm, and she leaned in to whisper, "Thank you."

"You're welcome. What did I do?"

"This…nine years of it. I don't think I've ever really thanked a veteran before." Her voice quivered and she wiped the corners of her eyes with her fingertips.

Joy was too moved to answer, afraid she too would be overcome with emotion. Until that moment, she hadn't realized how important it was that Amber truly respected who she was, and what she'd done with her life.

CHAPTER TWENTY-TWO

From her stealth position behind a tree, Amber watched as Madison approached the fire hydrant on the corner, craning her neck to look for Joy. She could all but see the wheels spinning inside the girl's head when she spotted her, as if considering a quick backtrack before she was seen.

"Hey, kiddo."

"Where's Joy?" Not exactly a friendly greeting, but at least she hadn't run in the opposite direction.

"Union meeting. She'll be home in about an hour." She relieved Madison of her backpack as they started toward the house.

"Why didn't you bring Skippy?"

"He was asleep with your grandpa."

A dark-haired boy zipped along the sidewalk on his bicycle, causing both of them to jump into someone's yard to escape being run down. "Hey, y'all," he yelled, his voice an exaggerated drawl, obviously meant to mock Madison's southern accent.

"Butthole!" she yelled.

"Whoa, watch the name-calling." Amber would have said something far worse. "Who was that?"

"Jason Perini. He thinks he's hot snot, but he's just a cold booger."

She didn't dare point out that boys that age usually teased the girls they liked. "Let's play a game, Madison. You ever play Truth or Dare? You pick whichever you want, and then you either have to do what I dare you to do, or you have to answer my question with the truth."

"You do it."

"Okay, I'll go first. I pick Dare. You dare me to do something and I will."

Madison stopped on the sidewalk and scratched her chin thoughtfully. Suddenly her eyes lit up and she pointed to Amber's pocket. "I know! I dare you to eat a cigarette."

"Ew! That's disgusting."

"I dare you!"

This would probably make her sick, but it was worth it if she could get Madison to play the game.

"Fine." It wasn't as if she'd never lit the wrong end of a cigarette and gotten specks of tobacco on her tongue. She readied her mouth with lots of saliva to make swallowing easier and pinched off an inch of tobacco. "Just a bite, though. Keeling over dead would take all the fun out of the game, and you'd have to drag my body home like a sack of potatoes."

Madison giggled. "This is going to be so gross."

"Okay, here goes." The bitter taste of tobacco leaves filled her mouth as she soaked the blob with spit and swallowed it whole. "I think I'm going to be sick."

"Yuck! That's worse than vegetables."

Amber smacked her lips to rid her mouth of the foul taste. "That was sickening, but now it's your turn. Truth or Dare?"

"Truth!" Obviously wary of subjecting herself to a vengeful dare, Madison walked right into Amber's trap.

"Okay, so I get to ask a question and you have to tell me the truth. No fibbing."

"As long as I don't have to eat a snail or something."

"So...where did you really go the last time I came to meet you at the corner? I was waiting for you right where I was supposed to be and saw you coming down the street, but then you turned around and went the other way." Amber wasn't absolutely sure about all that, but figured she could force Madison into coming clean if she was forceful enough about her version of events.

"I was there too but you didn't see me."

"No, you weren't. And I just ate a nasty old cigarette"—she coughed for effect and made a sour face—"so you have to tell me the truth."

Madison walked ahead a few steps and then stopped and turned around. "I walked with Melanie. She lives on that other street and she said I could get home that way. But then I got lost and went the wrong way around the circle."

"How did you find your way home?"

"A crossing guard...she told me how to get to Garfield."

That explained why it had taken her an extra fifteen minutes to get home, but not why she'd gone that way in the first place. "How come you didn't want to walk with me and Skippy?"

The girl shrugged, likely realizing that an honest answer in this case would show her as not being very nice.

"Are you going to tell Joy? She'll be mad at me."

"No, but I bet she'd be disappointed because you told her a fib about me not being there to meet you." To say nothing of the fact that she'd gotten Amber in trouble, which had probably been her sole intent.

"That's even worse. I'd rather she be mad at me than disappointed. But you promised not to tell her."

Amber had hoped to clear her name, but couldn't do that without telling Joy. She could, however, leverage it to make Madison behave in the future. "I won't, but you have to make a promise too—that you won't ever do anything like that again. Friends don't get each other in trouble, and we're pretty good friends now. Right?"

Madison's head bobbed up and down in an eager nod. Whether it was a pact of genuine friendship or merely an effort to avoid being ratted out to Joy, Amber didn't care. All she really wanted was an end to the shenanigans.

Jason Perini appeared again at the corner on his bike and Amber tugged Madison off the sidewalk, though she'd been tempted to stand her ground, knowing he would have dodged them at the last second rather than risk crashing.

"You're a smelly brat!" Madison yelled. "I can't stand him. I want to make him stop."

"Does he bother you at school too?"

"He bothers everybody. He's a bully."

"Bullies only act tough to make everyone afraid. Sometimes you just have to stand up to kids like Jason and let them know it's not working. If he realizes you aren't scared, maybe he'll leave you alone."

"What if he doesn't?"

"If it gets to be a big problem, you should tell Joy. She could talk to your teacher about it, and maybe your teacher would talk to Jason's parents."

"But that's tattling."

"Tattling isn't always a bad thing." Amber didn't dare share the fact that she'd kicked the crap out of a bully in sixth grade as her classmates cheered, but she hoped for Madison's sake that one of Jason's other victims was brave enough to take him on. "Just try to stand up to him and see if that works. If it doesn't, we'll talk it over again and try to think up something else."

As they neared the house, Madison asked, "I'm supposed to call Syd today. Can I use Joy's laptop in the camper?"

Joy was generous with her computer, so Amber readily agreed. "You can bring it into the dining room if you want."

"Grandpa's TV makes too much noise."

She couldn't argue with that. "Okay. Joy should be home in an hour or so, and your grandpa wants to make spaghetti for supper."

"Yum!" Madison tore through the front door and greeted her grandpa and Skippy before disappearing into the camper with her backpack.

"She's in a good mood," Shep said. "Wonder what kind of mood you're going to be in when you open this?"

Excitement and dread filled her as she saw the envelope from the testing service. Either she was now a high school graduate or a flunky doomed to suffer through another round of classes before she could retake the test. If it was the latter, she could cross off most of the jobs she'd seen advertised.

Nervously, she tore open the envelope. Language arts, mathematics, science...only one score mattered. *Overall Status: Pass.*

"Woo!" Amber tossed the papers into the air as Skippy ran for cover. "I'm officially a high school graduate."

"Atta girl! Let me see."

They looked over the results again. As expected, most of her scores were quite high, but she'd barely squeaked by on math. Close didn't matter.

"I need to text Joy." Her hands still shaking, she pounded out the news on her phone. Within seconds, it rang.

"That's fantastic! We should go out to dinner to celebrate, just you and me. I'm on my way home now."

"Wow, a date with my girlfriend." Amber would have been just as happy to celebrate her feat with Shep's spaghetti, but a real date with Joy made it extra special. "Hey, Shep. I'm going to hop into the shower for a few minutes. Will you keep an eye on Madison? She's out in the camper talking to Syd."

"Hope she's telling her to jump in the lake."

Amber headed out to the camper for her toiletries and clothes, eager to share her news but expecting Madison to pout about not being allowed to come along on their date. "I passed my test, and Joy's taking me out to dinner to celebrate. That means you and your Grandpa Shep get all the spaghetti to yourselves."

Clearly startled by her sudden presence, Madison hurriedly covered something in her backpack. There was no laptop on the dinette table to suggest she had been video chatting with Syd.

Amber's eyes were drawn immediately to the bed, which was wrinkled from someone having crawled on it. She certainly hadn't left it that way, and when she moved to straighten it, she saw that Joy's gun safe had been moved from its usual place on the shelf by her pillow. "Madison, how come you were crawling on the bed?"

"I wasn't."

A lie. Obviously she'd been fooling around with the gun safe, and Amber wasn't going to let that go. Kids had no business handling guns, even if they were locked up. "Were you playing with Joy's lockbox?"

Madison didn't answer, which was just as good as a confession as far as Amber was concerned.

"You shouldn't go messing in other people's things." When Amber slid the case back to where it belonged, she was startled to realize it was unmistakably lighter than usual. She picked it up and shook it—nothing rattling inside. "Oh, my God…did you open this box?"

Again, no answer.

"Please tell me you didn't…" She tugged the backpack from Madison's grip and looked inside. Sure enough there was Joy's pistol. The ghastly image of one child being shot by another while others screamed raced through her head. "Oh, my God… oh, my God, Madison!"

"I was only going to borrow it. I wanted to show it to Jason so he would be scared and leave me alone. That's what you told me to do. You said I should stand up to him."

Overwhelmed with horror, Amber shrieked, "You don't ever threaten anyone with a gun! You're a child, for gosh sakes. Joy is going to freak out."

"You can't tell her! She'll get mad at me and I'll get grounded."

"You deserve to be grounded. I can't believe you did this! You went into her private things and opened a box that had a lock on it. How did you even...?" With shaking hands, she reached into the backpack, wrapped her palm around the grip and removed the gun.

Bang!

"Fuck!" Amber dropped the gun on the floor and clutched her thumb, sure it was broken from the recoil.

In the same instant, Madison screamed and covered her ears, instinctively drawing her feet up onto the bench.

"Are you okay?"

Madison nodded rapidly, her eyes wide.

Suddenly the door flung open and Joy appeared. "What the hell just happened?"

"I was just—"

"Amber was showing me your gun and it went off!"

"Madison!" Amber barked.

Joy sharply ordered the girl to her room and turned her glare on Amber. "What the hell were you thinking? You could have killed somebody. You had no right to—"

"No right to what? Take your gun out of her backpack?"

"How did she get it in the first place? You're the only one who knew the combination."

"Yeah, right," Amber said, laying on the sarcasm. "No way would such a *brilliant* child be able to figure out that your secret code is her birthday. She was going to take it to school and scare a bully. You're lucky I noticed she'd been crawling on the bed."

Joy was breathing so fast, Amber thought she might hyperventilate. "What was she even doing out here by herself? You were supposed to be watching her."

"You expect me to follow her everywhere she goes? She's nine years old, for fuck's sake, not two. Who's watching her in her room right now?" She didn't blame Joy for being upset but she wasn't going to take the fall for Madison, not this time. "I hate to break this to you, but Madison lies, and she sneaks around and goes through people's stuff. You can't trust her."

"I can't trust anybody," Joy yelled. "Why didn't you just send her inside and wait for me to get home? You don't know how to handle a gun any better than she does."

Amber counted to ten—getting only as far as three—and as evenly as she possibly could, replied, "All I could think about was taking it away from her."

"Unbelievable." She squatted and fingered the hole in the floor. "Of all the irresponsible things you've ever done, this one takes the cake."

Amber whirled around and grabbed her rain jacket and purse. She'd had enough of this. "Nice to know you're keeping a list."

"I'm not keeping a list. Don't be such a—"

"You know what? Just stop telling me what to be. My job was to take care of your father, not your kid. If I'd wanted one of those, I wouldn't have given mine away." She pushed past Joy and stormed out the door, unsure of where she was headed. All she wanted was to get away.

CHAPTER TWENTY-THREE

"I want the truth, Madison," Joy said sternly. She was still shaken from hearing the gunshot as she walked toward the camper.

"Amber was showing it to me and it went off."

"Which one of you took it out of the box?"

"She did. She was telling me about how I needed to stand up to Jason Perini. He calls me a jungle bunny because I'm half African-American." Madison jutted out her lip in a blatant play for sympathy. "Amber said I should take it to school and scare him with it."

Not a word of that could possibly be true. Even at her most immature, Amber would never have been so reckless as to play with a gun in front of a nine-year-old.

Joy sighed and moved toward the bedroom door. "This is so disappointing...especially since we had a long talk about lying just a few days ago. I think you need to stay in here and think about it some more. I'll come back later and maybe you'll be ready to tell me the truth."

She closed the door behind her and walked into the living room where her father muted the TV so they could talk.

"Did you get anything else out of her?" he asked. He'd heard the commotion earlier and rolled out to the deck just in time to see Amber stomp off.

"Just one lie after another. Makes me want to call Syd and apologize for all the nasty things I said about her. Madison's a handful, all right. No wonder Syd wanted a break."

"What I don't get is how the gun went off in the first place. Those damn things don't just shoot themselves."

"I don't know, Pop. That's what I got so mad about with Amber. If she didn't know what she was doing, she had no business picking it up to begin with." She huffed facetiously to realize they had literally dodged a bullet. "Too bad she didn't stick around to explain her side. She just left us to clean up the mess."

"Can't say as I blame her for running off," her pop said. "If you're sure Madison's the one who's lying, then you were pretty hard on her. She's been knocking herself out to help ever since Madison got here."

Maybe so, but she'd made it loud and clear that she wasn't interested in doing that anymore. That was a deal breaker as far as Joy was concerned.

* * *

"Ow!" Amber muttered to herself, gently massaging her swollen thumb after flicking the remains of her cigarette into the damp street. Regardless of what she'd let herself believe about building a life with Joy, their relationship apparently wasn't deep enough to upset the fairytale version of Madison as a perfect child. The kid had gotten exactly what she wanted—she'd driven a wedge between them and forced Joy to choose sides. From the first day she'd shown up in California, Amber never stood a chance.

It was probably for the best. Joy had shown her true colors today, a controlling streak that shifted blame wherever she wanted it to fall. At her core, she was still a chief petty officer or a ground crew chief used to giving orders, not all that different from someone like Corey who dictated the terms because he held all the power.

Whether Joy admitted it or not, she'd done exactly that too.

As a light sprinkle became a steady drizzle, Amber flagged down the first city bus she saw. It didn't matter where it was going since she wasn't headed anywhere in particular. This one happened to be an express to San Francisco, which would take at least an hour at sunset. All the commuters from San Francisco and Oakland seemed to swap sides at the end of the day. At least she was dry and warm for the time being and her bus pass was good for eight more rides, enough to kill a whole evening until she figured out what to do with herself.

That question wasn't just rhetorical. Her current situation wasn't all that different from being dumped at a truck stop in Kentucky with a suitcase, except this time she had more or less dumped herself, the way she usually did when she was fed up with a rude and unreasonable boss. Now she needed not only a job but also somewhere to stay, and it had to be a place that would let her keep Skippy. Or maybe she ought to just leave Skippy with Shep. If she could give up a baby so it would have a better life, surely she could do the same for a dog, especially one that preferred someone else's lap anyway.

The practical difficulties of finding a job and a place to live were all that kept her from wallowing in despair. Only hours ago she was soaring on cloud nine, her future taking shape and her heart finally fulfilled with someone as wonderful as Joy. This relationship was supposed to be the one that lasted. If it could fall apart in only minutes over what was clearly an accident, then it had never been real in the first place.

She got off at the Embarcadero, picked up a couple of newspapers and boarded a bus back across the Bay Bridge, this one heading to Berkeley. There weren't many job ads for people with virtually no skills or education, but there were lots of apartments for rent, and several people looking for roommates. A couple of those offers were reasonable and included utilities, but she needed that elusive job first.

There was one live-in caretaker job but when she called the number, it had already been filled. At this point it was doubtful she could depend on Joy for a reference anyway. Though she'd done a good job with Shep, a potential employer would ask if she was responsible, and Joy had made her opinion on that pretty clear.

In hindsight, it was stupid to reach into a dark backpack and pull out a gun without even knowing whether or not it was loaded and cocked. If only she'd left it in the backpack and sent Madison inside like Joy said, none of this would have happened. Sadly, good judgment wasn't her strong suit.

When she stepped off the bus in Berkeley, one of the first things she noticed was a Help Wanted sign in the window of a Chinese restaurant. Three doors down was a copy shop also asking for help. That's how she'd found work before, either word-of-mouth or by walking up to the counter and asking for an application. She could do that now…but not here. Berkeley was overrun with students and apartments were expensive. The only places she could afford to live and work were in Oakland or Alameda.

Boarding her last bus back to Alameda, she congratulated herself on having a plan. Starting tomorrow she would ride through some of the decent neighborhoods in the area and search for Help Wanted signs. With over three thousand dollars in the bank from her work with Shep, she could rent an apartment or room nearby and be totally on her feet within a few days.

She'd have to pick up a new phone right away, a prepaid one. The battery in this one was all but dead, and besides, it was on Joy's account. She'd return it when she went back to gather her clothes.

The idea of seeing Joy's angry face again brought a rush of tears, and she fought to keep her sweet memories of their weeks together from ripping her heart out. How would she ever be able to trust her feelings again?

The bus dropped her in front of the library just as Lee Bowman was walking out.

"Amber! I was wondering if I'd ever see you again. You should be getting your test scores any day."

"They came today, in fact. I'm officially a high school graduate."

"Congratulations." Like her, he was wearing a raincoat, but not carrying an umbrella. "How about I buy you a beer to celebrate?"

Mindful of his flirtatious ways, Amber hesitated before deciding a beer in a nice, warm bar was better than walking around in the rain. Besides, she hadn't yet figured out where she was going to sleep tonight. If she got up the nerve to go home to Garfield, it would have to be after ten when everyone had gone to bed.

At the Hobnob, a local pub, she slid into a booth opposite Lee who ordered beers for both of them.

"This is a celebration for me too," he said. "Whenever one of my students passes the test, it makes me feel like I've done something worthwhile."

"You deserve to celebrate. I think anyone who helps people reach their goals is doing something worthwhile. I've been working with a man who hurt his shoulder." She told him about Shep's condition and injury, and all the therapy he'd done to regain his independence. "He did all the work, but I felt good because I helped him."

"We'll drink to that too." Lee raised his bottle and clinked hers. "So what are you doing out on such a rainy night?"

She shrugged and started to peel the label off her bottle. Though willing to admit she had misjudged Lee—actually he was turning out to be a pretty nice guy—that didn't mean she wanted to share her personal problems with him. "I'm sort of scouting around for my next job."

After three beers, she'd managed to tell most of her story, including the fact that she'd stormed off in a huff and wasn't even sure she had a place to stay the night.

"Look, I don't want you to worry about that. I've got plenty of room at my place." He patted her arm, not like a lecherous flirt...more like a friend. "I wouldn't offer that to just anyone but I liked you right away because you were hardworking and focused on improving yourself. And a lot more mature than most of the others who show up for GED classes, I might add. I respect that in people."

Amber knew the drill—a place to stay in return for...

* * *

Each time Madison told her story, the details grew more outlandish. It was fascinating to hear her lie so brazenly, and Joy could see how frustrating that must have been for Amber. No wonder she had stormed off in a huff.

It was almost nine, well past Joy's bedtime. Most likely Amber was at the library, the one place she knew well and felt comfortable. It was open until ten and Joy wouldn't be at all surprised if she stayed out that late so she wouldn't have to deal with anybody when she came home. After stewing all this time, she probably wouldn't come crawling into bed later anyway. If she were Amber, she'd crash on the couch inside the house. It would take time and patience to rebuild the trust between them.

On the other hand, maybe Amber was the sort of person who settled down and put quarrels behind her quickly. They'd never had a fight this big before, so Joy had no idea what to expect.

The more she thought about what her father had said, the more she realized she owed Amber an apology. It was only an accident, at the most a simple lapse in judgment. Joy had been so upset at the time she could barely remember what she'd said...something about not being responsible. Calling Amber irresponsible was probably the most insulting thing she could have said. Furthermore, it wasn't fair, not given the leaps and bounds Amber had grown since she'd gotten to California.

Her calls to Amber's cell phone went straight to voice mail, likely because it was turned off. If she'd wanted to talk, she wouldn't have left in the first place. Joy had no choice but to let the anger run its course.

She found herself lying awake and listening for Amber's return. After two hours, she got up and sneaked into the house, thinking she'd find her on the couch. By midnight, she accepted that Amber had found another place to stay.

This rift was a bigger deal to Amber than she'd thought.

* * *

Buzzed…not drunk. Still, it was good she wasn't driving.

Amber ground out her cigarette on the sidewalk and tossed the butt in the trash bin that Joy had pulled to the curb for tomorrow's pickup. The defiance and anger she'd felt when she left the house this afternoon had passed, replaced by sadness and a deep sense of loss. Though she'd barely had enough of Joy to call it love, what they'd had was by far the most special of all her relationships. Joy was the one she wanted to take care of and keep. Now it was like a dream come true had been dangled within her grasp and suddenly snatched away. No matter what she accomplished in her life, Joy would always see her as the useless screwup someone else had cast off.

At least she'd had enough pride in herself to resist falling back on her old habits. She could have been sound asleep in Lee's bed right now, with absolutely no sense of urgency about finding a job or another place to live. She was finished with subjugating herself. The next time she moved in with someone, it would be on her terms.

A lamp had been left on in the living room, a likely sign she was welcome to return. While that was fine and good, it was negated by the fact that, from the porch, she could see a pillow and blanket laid out for her on the couch. In other words, she needn't bother coming out to the camper. That ship had sailed without her.

Not that she was surprised. But it still hurt. After four months of doing exactly what she was supposed to do with Shep—and even going the extra mile with Madison—Joy owed her more respect than this. But Amber wasn't going to beg for it, and she wasn't going to settle for the scraps left over at the end of the day after everyone else got what they needed. The next time she saw any of them, she planned to have a job and a place of her own.

As quietly as she could, she opened the side gate and peered around the corner of the house where a floodlight on the deck lit up the whole backyard. Walking on the grass to soften her footsteps, she sneaked to the carport and climbed into the backseat of Shep's sedan. There she curled into a ball and spread her rain jacket to cover as much of her body as it could. Not exactly cozy, but warm enough. Joy wouldn't see her at all from the driver's side of the Jeep when she left at four thirty, and she could slip into the camper and change before anyone else was up.

She could manage this for a couple of days, three at the most. By then she hoped to be settled somewhere else. Maybe if she kept herself busy, it wouldn't hurt so much.

CHAPTER TWENTY-FOUR

Joy burst through the back door and looked around the house, seeing only her father, who sat in his recliner with Skippy. "What time did Amber come by?"

"I never saw her."

"She was here, all right. I found the clothes she was wearing yesterday in the laundry bag in the camper, so she must have stopped by to change." She was relieved to find Amber's other belongings still in the drawers, but disappointed to realize she didn't yet feel ready to stick around and talk to anyone. "Looks like I really blew it, Pop."

"Shit happens, you know," he said.

"Yeah, and this time I was the one who shot off my mouth. How's that for irony?"

"I remember one time when I snapped at your mother, she popped me on the hand with a wooden spoon and reminded me that not everyone was in the navy. That was her way of telling me I wasn't her boss."

That was exactly what Amber had been afraid of all along, that Joy had all the power in their relationship. "I didn't mean to come off as bossy. I was upset about Madison and didn't even stop to think how I was making her feel. Now she won't take my calls or answer any of my texts."

"She'll be back. I'm holding her dog hostage."

Joy checked the clock in the kitchen, noting it was almost time to meet Madison. "Did you have any trouble getting Madison off to school?"

"Nah, Barbara walked with us. We went halfway up Lincoln, and then Madison went the rest of the way with some of the other kids. They've got crossing guards practically the whole way."

"Yeah, I know. I guess I can let her start walking by herself." She pulled on a blue navy hoodie and started out the front door. "Maybe I'll talk about it with her on the way home. If Amber shows up, please ask her to stay."

Joy didn't stop at her usual corner, continuing instead all the way to the school, where Madison greeted her with an apprehensive look. They hadn't talked since last night when it was still obvious she wasn't telling the truth.

"How was school?" she asked. She'd concluded there was only one way to deal with this troublesome penchant for lying.

"Fine. I said my sevens today…multiplication tables."

"Good for you." Joy took Madison's hand as they sauntered down the sidewalk. "Sweetheart, I've been thinking a lot about what happened yesterday. It upsets me that you still haven't told me the truth, but I'm not going to ask anymore. I just want you to know that I don't believe you. I yelled at Amber yesterday for something that wasn't her fault and that makes me feel ashamed of myself."

Madison looked away, but Joy was determined this would be more than a scolding. She wanted an end to these lies once and for all.

After slowing until the other kids were out of earshot, she stopped and bent low, placing her hands on her knees to look Madison in the eye. "I love you very much and I know you love me too, but it hurts my feelings when you lie to me. I forgive you this time but that's it. No more lies. Do you understand?"

The girl nodded, blinking back heart-wrenching tears. "I'm sorry."

"I appreciate you saying that. Now we need to apologize to Amber too, both of us."

"Okay," she said meekly.

Joy had no idea if that would be enough to persuade Amber to come back. Her outburst about not wanting children might only have been frustration talking, but it was undeniable that she'd withdrawn since Madison arrived. That was Joy's fault for not doing more to make both of them feel loved and wanted, and that's what she had to fix. If Amber truly wasn't interested in helping to raise Madison, there was little hope for their relationship.

* * *

"...And this is a temporary address. I'm staying with friends right now," Amber said, pointing to a line on the form she'd just filled out.

The store manager, a tall African-American man wearing a gray polo shirt and neat black slacks, eyed her application for counter help at the Postal Plus shop. "But the phone number's good?"

"Yes, sir." Getting a pre-paid cell phone had been her second stop this morning, right after a trip to the bank to withdraw two hundred dollars to get her through the next few days. Between the phone and a new bus pass, she was already down to only eighty bucks.

"I need to show this to the owner when he comes in to close up. He'll probably decide on somebody today or tomorrow."

"Okay, great. Thank you very much. It was wonderful to meet you." She smiled as she walked backward out the door, her best customer service face firmly fixed.

This Postal Plus job was by far the best of all she'd come across so far. It would be nice for a change to work in a place where the staff wore ordinary uniforms that didn't smell like onions or baby shit. She especially liked that the store was neatly arranged and the floor was clean, a far cry from the convenience store she'd worked at where employees crammed stock onto shelves wherever it fit, and the tile floor was so dirty it could have sprouted crops. This job—seven to four, five days a week—would be perfect.

There was one more row of stores in this, her fifth strip mall today. Besides being physically exhausted, her feet were swollen and screaming with every step, but she'd applied for work in eight different places. One of those—full-time cashier at a busy discount store—was a solid offer if she showed up for training on Monday, but the job was good only for the holiday season. Still, it was good to have a sure thing in case nothing else panned out.

Less certain was her living situation. Yesterday she'd been hell-bent on finding a place of her own, anything to get out from under the Shepards' roof. As her anger dissipated and her job prospects rose, the full force of losing Joy had hit her like a tidal wave of despair. Unlike her past relationships, this romance hadn't come out of necessity. It had grown from gratitude to admiration to love, and for the first time in her whole life, she was free to have sex with someone without feeling that it was an obligation. Joy was the only person who'd ever treated her with respect, and along with her father, had shown her what it meant to be strong, capable and, most of all, honorable.

If I'd wanted a kid, I wouldn't have given mine away.

Classy. That made it sound like she didn't want Madison around at all. It wasn't like that...exactly. Sure, she wanted private time with Joy, but what mattered more was proving that she could be trusted with responsibility. That was hardly possible if Madison didn't listen to a word she said.

Once again, she'd done something rash in the heat of the moment. How many bridges had she burned at work or with friends just so she'd get in the last hateful word? Joy had never struck her as someone with a high tolerance for bullshit like that. It was doubtful she had the capacity to forgive stupidity.

But maybe it wasn't too late.

Amber liked her chances a lot better if she could go home with a job. Work that took her away from the house most of the day would solve a lot of problems, especially if she tacked on night classes too. Now that Shep was his old self again, he could take over the task of handling Madison, and Joy wouldn't have to worry about her screwing things up again.

A job…a job…a job. Nothing mattered more.

Three more stores and she'd have to call it a day. It would be dark before she got to the next shopping center and the Help Wanted signs were hard to see.

Then came the question of where she would sleep tonight. It wouldn't kill her to camp out in the car again but the couch was a cushier option. And maybe Joy had cooled off enough to talk. Amber had.

* * *

Madison's bedroom door opened a quarter-inch and her feeble voice called, "Can I come out and show you something? It's important."

Joy was putting away the last of the dinner dishes. She hadn't yet decided on Madison's full punishment for handling a gun, but for now she was confined to her room. "You may not. I'll come in there when I finish."

The door closed and Joy looked at her pop, who nodded grimly. "Hang tough."

It was harder than she'd ever imagined—a delicate balancing act to teach her right from wrong in a loving, supportive way. Until now, the time they'd spent together had always been during cheerful vacations from the drudgery of homework and chores. More important, Madison had never had to share her with anyone else.

Her cell phone rang with a call from an unfamiliar number, and she nearly let it go to voice mail, but since it was a local area code, she answered.

"Hey, it's Amber."

Joy immediately stepped out on the deck for privacy. "Where are you?"

"Waiting for a bus. I was wondering if it was okay for me to come home."

"Of course! Stay there and I'll come get you."

"No, that's all right. It's a straight shot from here to the corner. I'll be there before long."

"You didn't have to leave, you know. This is your home. It's where you belong." She had so much to say and didn't know where to begin. "I'm so sorry, Amber. I know you were telling me the truth and it was all just an accident. I never should have yelled at you. I was just so upset that I wasn't thinking right."

"I said some stupid things too…that bit about not wanting Madison. I'm really sorry I said that."

Joy cast her eyes upward and said a silent prayer of thanks. "I'm so glad. I don't know what I would have done if you'd really felt that way."

"I know what you'd have done, but let's not go there," Amber said with a soft chuckle. "I got a job."

So that's what she'd been up to.

"That's fantastic, sweetheart. I know you're going to be good at it, whatever it is." She meant that. Amber had proven herself, erasing all the doubts Joy had harbored when she first took her on as a hapless hitchhiker. "Come home. I promise we'll sit down and talk everything out. I'm not going to let Madison come between us. She'll just have to accept what you mean to me."

"I understand where she's coming from, but I'm starting to think it'll all work out."

Elated, Joy went back inside. "Amber's coming home. She says she got a job."

Shep smiled and scratched Skippy's ears. "You hear that, boy? Your mama's back." He looked at Joy. "A good job is exactly what she needed. She's been cooped up here too long with my sorry ass anyway. It'll do her good to get out of the house."

It also signaled the end of their deal that had brought Amber here in the first place. She no longer had to feel that she was working off her debt like an indentured servant. She was here now because she wanted to be, and because Joy wanted her here too.

No doubt there would be more hurdles with Madison—

Joy suddenly remembered that Madison had wanted to show her something. She knocked and opened the door a crack. "May I come in?"

By the mess in the room, Madison had been busy with scissors and colored markers. "I made this for Amber," she said. It was yellow construction paper, folded in quarters with three swinging windows on the front.

Joy opened the windows one at a time to form a simple message: *I am sorry*. "This is nice, Madison. I'm sure she'll appreciate it, but it may take a little time for her to trust you again. You'll have to show her that you really mean it."

"I'll walk Skippy and clean up his mess…and I'll let her pick all the TV shows."

It pleased her that Madison had been thinking about how to make up for the trouble she'd caused, but Joy wanted the feelings to change along with the behavior. "You remember what I told you this afternoon about how much I loved you?"

Madison nodded.

"Nothing will ever change that, I promise." She sat on the bed and pulled Madison onto her knee. "I also love Amber, and sometimes I want to be alone with her, like to go out on a date or something. It doesn't mean we don't love you, or that we don't like being with you. Grownups need private time together every now and then, but I promise it won't be like it was with Mitch and Syd. You don't have to be jealous. We're a family now, and that means all four of us care about each other." She chucked Madison gently on the chin. "So you better get used to it, kiddo."

"Is Amber going to be my mom like you?"

Joy wanted to say yes, but knew she'd have to win Amber over on that one. "We'll have to see about that. But yeah, I think if they let Amber and me get married someday, then we both ought to be your moms."

The idea was novel enough to Madison to be exciting, though that wasn't quite the word Joy would use to describe what she felt. The last two days had made her realize just how ready she was for a step like that.

Voices in the living room signaled Amber's arrival, and Joy guided Madison out the door first so she could present her card.

By her tired face and drooping shoulders, Amber looked as though she'd been gone much longer than two days. Her hair was limp, her eye makeup smudged, and her wet clothes needed a tumble in the dryer. The look on her face however was pure satisfaction, if not triumph. Finding a new job was obviously just what she needed for a sense of self-determination and freedom. It was good for Joy too, since it meant Amber was here because she wanted to be, and not because she had no other place to go.

She'd never been one for public displays of affection, especially in front of her father, but she couldn't resist the urge to give a welcoming hug. To her relief, it was returned with just as much enthusiasm, and it took a conscious effort to set her emotions aside long enough to separate and acknowledge the others in the room. "Madison has something for you."

"I made you a card," she said, her small voice clearly contrite. She stepped forward and presented it. "I'm sorry I blamed you for stuff. I was afraid I'd get in trouble."

Amber read the card and smiled gently. "This is very nice. I appreciate your apology." Sincere but guarded, exactly what one would expect until Madison earned her trust again. "I was a whole lot more worried about you playing with Joy's gun than I was about the lying. I hope that never happens again."

"It won't."

Joy nodded in agreement and addressed Madison. "I know it won't because I got rid of it this afternoon...turned it in to the police station. There's still the matter of punishment but we'll talk about that this weekend. Now get your bath and go on to bed."

"But tomorrow's Saturday."

"Bath and bed," she repeated firmly. "I'll be in later to say goodnight."

Madison, looking both ashamed and worried, wrapped her arms around Joy's waist. "I love you."

"I love you too, baby."

She followed with a hug to her grandpa, and then surprised everyone by hugging Amber too. "I'm sorry," she said again.

"I know. It's okay." Amber kissed the top of her head. "Sleep well."

Whatever soul-searching Amber had done over the past couple of days had produced a remarkable change. Gone was the immature hothead who lashed out when she felt threatened or challenged. In her place was a calm, thoughtful young woman who seemed at peace with herself and the world around her.

Or maybe she was just tired.

"Let's go talk," Joy said, holding out her hand. The moment they reached the camper, she made up for her earlier restraint, pulling Amber into a long, deep kiss. "Please don't ever run off like that again. I've been worried half to death."

"I was fine."

"You should have called me."

"My phone died and I didn't have a way to charge it."

Joy could have pushed it—if Amber had wanted to call, she would have found a way—but she was glad just to have her back home and she didn't want to fight anymore. "You're here now. That's what matters."

"I love you." With both hands cupping Joy's face, Amber kissed her again. "Nobody's ever believed in me before, and it means the world to me that you do. I just want you to be proud of me."

"I already am, and you should be proud of yourself too." She helped Amber out of her damp coat and led her up to the bed. "Come lie with me. I want to hear everything. Where have you been all this time? Where did you stay last night?"

Amber chuckled as she kicked off her shoes. "Mostly I rode all over the Bay Area on the express bus just to stay out of the rain. Then I came home and saw the couch made up in the living room. I figured you didn't want me in the camper so I spent the night in the backseat of your father's car."

Joy was astonished to hear that her friendly gesture of leaving the blanket and pillow out on the couch had been misinterpreted. "You were so mad when you left, I figured you wouldn't want to sleep with me. I swear to God, if you'd crawled in this bed last night, I would have held you just like this."

"Yeah, well...I'm not exactly famous for making rational choices, but all that's going to change now. This is the new me."

"Don't change too much because I'm pretty crazy about the old you."

She looked down into Amber's eyes and pushed her hair from her face. Any other night, lying together on the bed like this would have led to lovemaking, but tonight was about healing from their sharp words and hurt feelings, and reaffirming the kind of life they wanted together.

"Amber, I really, really love you."

CHAPTER TWENTY-FIVE

Amber finished the arduous task of drying her thick hair and gathered her toiletries to take back to the camper. She and Joy had almost gotten carried away earlier, but Joy's promise to kiss Madison goodnight gave her the opening for a much-needed shower before they turned in for the night.

"Thanks for looking after Skippy," she said to Shep, who was watching a college football game from his recliner.

"Who are we kidding? He's my dog now."

"I can see that."

"So what's this new job of yours? You find some other cranky old coot in a wheelchair?"

She laughed and reached over to scratch Skippy. "No, I specifically asked if there were any cranky old coots involved before I turned in my application. I'll tell you all about it tomorrow."

When she reached the camper, Joy was already in bed, but the bedside lamp was still on. Amber dropped her robe and slid nude between the sheets, drawn instantly to Joy's smooth, warm skin. "I missed you."

"I was always here...and I always will be."

Always was another word Amber had missed in her life, and her heart swelled to think she'd grow old with someone as wonderful as Joy.

"So when are you going tell me about this new job?"

All evening, Amber had been dying to share her big news, but was waiting for just the right moment. She rolled Joy onto her back, and with equal parts trepidation and pride, gave her the biggest news of her life. "I joined the navy."

Joy's face flickered first with amusement, then confusion. "You're not serious."

"Oh, but I am. I went to a bunch of shopping centers today and put in applications all over the place. The very last one turned out to be a recruiting office and it felt like an invisible hand just pushed me right through the door. I go for testing and career counseling on Monday, and then I have to get a physical."

"But you haven't signed a contract yet, right?" Joy asked anxiously, squirming to sit up. "Amber, you can't just decide something like this on the spur of the moment. There's a lot that goes into a commitment like that. We need to talk this over."

"I know, that's what the recruiter told me, and that's what we're doing now." She urged Joy back down to the bed. "It was weird. I was shaking all over when he handed me that letter of intent, but the moment I signed it, it was like...yeah, this is exactly what I want to do with my life."

"With your life? What about our life? The navy's at least a four-year commitment. Is that what you need? To get away from us for that long?"

"What I need...what I need is to feel as good about myself as you do, and to go to work every day knowing what I do is important. Until now I've always looked to somebody else to take care of me, but no more. On Veterans Day...gosh, seeing you all dressed up in your uniform and walking across that carrier deck like you owned it...I was just so crazy proud of you.

I want somebody to feel that way about me. I want *you* to feel that way about me."

Joy's eyes filled with tears, but then a broad grin crossed her face. "I can't believe you're doing this…but yeah, I'm going to be crazy proud of you too."

"The timing's good on this, Joy. Madison's had a tough time and she needs a lot of attention right now. More important, she needs it from you. It's better for everyone if I don't interfere with that."

"But what about you and me? I already told her we were family now, and she has to accept that. She will."

"And so will I, but I need for her to respect me in my own right, not just because I'm your girlfriend."

"God, Amber." Joy squeezed her so hard that her spine popped in two places. "I don't know whether to lock you in the closet or re-enlist. How am I supposed to sleep at night when all I can think about is you being surrounded by pretty women in uniform?"

Amber goosed her in the ribs. "Why would I look at anyone else when I know what's waiting for me at home? I could worry about you too but I won't, not if we promise each other this is what we want."

"This is so wild," Joy said. "You left here yesterday afternoon madder than a wet cat, and now you sound like you just climbed down from a Buddhist retreat. How did this happen so fast?"

"The answer was there all along. I just didn't know it until it was staring me in the face." Amber crawled on top and let their warm bodies meld beneath the covers. "You're my hero, Joy. I look at you and get swallowed up by these waves of love and admiration. I can't help but want to be like you."

"Sweetheart, I love and admire you too."

"But I don't feel that way about myself, and that's what this is about. I need to respect myself before I'll ever believe other people do. I'm ready to grow up and take responsibility, and this is how I want to do it. But I need your support for it. I won't go if you don't think I'm up to it, and I won't go if it's going to put our love at risk." That was hard for Amber to even think about, let alone say. She wanted Joy's blessing, but she also needed the assurance this would be her home and family no matter what. "You have the whole weekend to think about it before I sign the contract, and seriously, I won't go if it means losing you."

Joy pulled her into a kiss that left no doubt about her feelings. "I don't need to think on this all weekend. You joining the navy is crazy. It's also awesome...and brave, and I'm behind you a hundred and ten percent."

"You mean it?"

She laughed softly. "I can't believe it. This is so wild. I grew up dreaming about being like Pop and working on an aircraft carrier. Now I get to be like my mom too, a navy wife."

"I like the sound of that."

"Good, because I'm not letting you out of here without a promise. This country's going to get its act together one of these days, and I expect you to stand up with me and make it official. I'm old-fashioned that way."

Only hours ago, Amber had thought she had nothing— no job, no home and no one to call her family. Now she had a future with the woman she loved and a potential career that would bring her pride and satisfaction. That made it the best day of her life. "I'll say yes to anything if it gets you back in that uniform."

* * *

"Eight weeks of basic training at Great Lakes," Amber said as they all worked together to get breakfast on the table. "That sounds cold."

"Only if you get a chance to go outside," Joy said, shuddering at the memory of her first two months of navy life. "Nearly all your training is indoors because most of the time you're in the navy, you're below decks on a ship."

"Indoors is good because I'm scheduled to go in January."

Shep, who was flipping pancakes from a large griddle onto a platter, laughed haughtily. "I did basic in San Diego, but I remember a guy from Great Lakes saying the RDC hauled his ass out of the rack in the middle of the night to shovel snow."

"What's an RDC?" Madison asked.

"A Recruit Division Commander. He's the boss at basic training," Joy explained. Then she glared at her pop. "Could you watch your language, please?"

"Why? Madison knows better than to say 'ass' at school. Don't you, kid? There's a reason they call it having a mouth like a sailor. You're the one that's messed up."

"That's because I had Mom's influence, and Madison is going to have mine."

"I don't like bad words," Madison said primly. "How old do I have to be to join the navy?"

"Eighteen," Amber said. "The recruiter said I'd probably be one of the oldest ones in my unit. Is that good or bad?"

Joy and her father answered simultaneously, each giving a different response.

Shep set the platter on his lap and wheeled to the dining table, where Amber and Madison had set out plates and utensils. "It's good because your RDC gets fed up with all those wet-behind-the-ears teenagers. He'll be glad to have somebody who's been around the block already."

"And it's bad because they'll probably expect more of you and yell even louder if you don't give it to them," Joy said, following behind with a tray of bacon. "But they'll find a reason to yell at you anyway, because that's the whole idea of boot camp."

"I wouldn't like that," Madison said. "I'd probably start crying."

Shep tousled her hair. "That would only make it worse. It's like a shark smelling blood in the water."

"The hardest part for *some* people"—Joy nudged Amber with her elbow—"is holding their temper when the RDC is ripping them a new one over some microscopic detail, like writing a crooked stencil in their underwear."

"Okay, I got the message. It's going to be a humbling experience and I need to keep my mouth shut. I only have to survive eight weeks of abuse, then it's off to A-school for training in my field."

Joy had to admit, now that the shocking news of Amber's enlistment had settled in, it was exciting to think about what her future held. "What did you tell the recruiter you were interested in?"

Amber looked at Shep and grinned. "I told him I wanted to be a physical therapy assistant."

"Hah! Pity the poor sailor that gets hurt on your watch," he said. "You better hope they don't call me for references."

"I told him I had a little experience, and that I hadn't killed you...yet."

"She's only joking," Joy whispered to Madison. "The Hospital Corps trains at Fort Sam Houston in San Antonio."

"That's what he said. And after that I'd probably go to one of the medical centers to get experience, like in San Diego or Bethesda. I could stay there permanently or end up at one of the bases, or even on a ship."

"There you go," Shep said, shaking a spatula at her. "Your first mistake is believing one word your recruiter said. The second you walked out of there, he probably laughed and tossed you over in the ship's company pile. Those are the grunts, but they're the backbone of the navy. Without those guys, the ships don't sail."

"Please tell me he's kidding," Amber said. "He said I was supposed to take some kind of job placement test next week."

"He's kidding...sort of. The navy's first priority is whatever *they* need. The best way to get the training you want is to show an aptitude for it. You can study ahead of time for the test next week to make sure you qualify for what you want, but it's still not a guarantee you'll get it."

Amber pushed back from the table. "I can't be wasting my valuable time chitchatting with you people. I need to go study, or I'll end up loading torpedoes on a battleship. That's not the sort of skill that gets you a job in the real world."

"I don't know about that," Joy said. "If you can load torpedoes, you can probably load baggage too."

"Nah, she'd be too careful."

"Can't argue with you there, Pop." Joy started collecting the plates. "Madison and I will clean up the kitchen so you can start studying."

"Okay, but I have a favor to ask first. You have to come out to the camper."

A private favor? It wasn't like Amber to flaunt their relationship in front of the others, but things were changing so fast she didn't know what to expect.

Once inside the camper, Amber went straight for the laptop. "I guess I need to download some articles to study."

"Need some help?"

"No, I wanted to ask if you'd reconsider letting Madison come to the concert tonight."

Joy shook her head. "No way. She's grounded."

"I know, but this is really special. Maybe you can give her two more weeks without TV or going to bed at seven thirty. It's just that she really likes Gus Holley and that's one of the few things we have in common. It would go a long way toward helping us be friends."

"The very first time I have to get tough with her, and now you're asking me to give in."

"You can be Badass Mama after I'm gone. Please?"

Please was the magic word coming from Amber, especially since she didn't ask for much. The *after I'm gone* part, though... that would take some getting used to.

* * *

"Hold up Joy's cell phone," Amber screamed. Gus had done one encore already but she knew there would be another, since he still hadn't done his classic hit, "In the Doghouse."

Madison waved the lighted phone high in the air, chanting *Gus! Gus! Gus!* with fifteen thousand other people. Her first concert was one she'd never forget, and Amber was thrilled for helping to give her a special memory.

"Here he comes again!" Joy yelled. It was painfully clear all through the night that she wasn't much of a Gus Holley fan, but she gamely clapped and cheered along when everyone else did. She also sprang for three T-shirts and Gus's new CD.

Amber's biggest surprise of the night was seeing Sammy Donahue on bass guitar. Not that she cared, but where the hell was Corey?

I'm in the doghouse for catting around!

Amber and Madison sang every word at the top of their lungs and went wild when the song ended.

"That was great," Joy said.

"Oh, come on. It wasn't your thing."

"No, but watching you two have so much fun was."

"You ain't seen nothing yet," Amber said, taking Madison's hand. "Follow me."

That was easier said than done, since they were fighting against the crowd flow to get to the side door next to the stage. Mighty Mack Wilburn, Gus's longtime security chief guarded the door to backstage. "Amber Halliday! Is that really you?"

She rushed into a bear hug, his beefy arms lifting her off the floor. Seeing Gus and the band onstage had stirred warm memories of her Nashville days, especially since Corey hadn't been there to remind her of the ugly way those days had ended.

"Mack, I want you to meet a couple of my friends. This is Joy and her daughter Madison, who happens to be a big-time Gus Holley fan. Did Michelle leave my name for backstage?"

Madison's blue eyes were as wide as saucers.

"Sure did." He hung backstage passes around their necks. "Y'all can go on back. They're all in the green room."

Joy and Madison stepped inside the door but Amber hung back to get the lowdown on Corey. "What's with Sammy on bass? What happened to Corey?"

"Man, that was ugly," Mack said. "He got busted in Dallas with a sixteen-year-old girl in his bed. Her old man wasn't happy. Gus fired him right out there in the hall of the hotel. Last we heard, he was picking out wedding invitations."

"You're shitting me," she said under her breath.

"It was that or go to jail for statutory rape."

Corey never could turn down an easy lay, and he wasn't smart enough to check ID. It was satisfying to know his recklessness had finally caught up with him. He probably hadn't even known the girl's name that night, but she'd be hard to forget as Mrs. Corey Dobbins.

Amber went inside and took Madison's hand again. "Are you ready to meet Gus Holley in person?"

The girl was practically frozen with excitement—glazed eyes and a toothy grin. Joy seemed nervous too, which Amber found amusing since it was a first. In the green room, they wove through all the groupies to a cluster of people that included Gus, sweaty and flushed from his performance, and his beautiful wife. Amber peered over Gus's shoulder to wave at Michelle.

"Look who's here, Gus! It's Amber Halliday."

They were the sweet, down-to-earth people they'd always been, the best of Nashville as far as she was concerned. The highlight of the whole night was watching Gus fuss over Madison, telling her what a lucky guy he was to have such a pretty fan. Joy snapped dozens of photos, and Gus signed their tickets and the CD.

The vast parking lot at the Oracle Arena was nearly empty by the time they finally made their way out. Joy took her hand as Madison skipped ahead to the Jeep. "So this is what you had up your sleeve when you asked for a special favor. Who knew you could be so sneaky?"

"I only got the email from Michelle this morning. I wanted it to be a surprise."

"It was. I think you made Madison's day…week, year, life. But you'd already solidified your place on her idol list after I told her it was your idea for her to come tonight."

"I knew she'd get a kick out of it."

"You were sweet to do it, especially after she threw you under the bus. But now that you're BFFs, does it make you think about sticking around instead of running off and joining the circus…I mean, the navy?"

"You know, what's funny is that I'm already starting to feel a change in myself. When I told all those guys from the band that I'd joined, I was so proud. Everybody congratulated me and it was the greatest feeling I've ever had. I know this probably sounds stupid—I haven't even done anything yet—but this feels so right."

They reached the Jeep, but stood outside while Madison buckled up in the backseat.

"It isn't stupid. I know exactly what you mean."

"Seriously?"

"I signed my letter of intent when I was just a senior in high school. That whole year it was like…yeah, I felt like I was in the navy already."

Even with Madison nearby, Amber couldn't resist a quick kiss as she leaned into Joy's embrace. "I'm going to do you proud."

"I have no doubt. Your head's in the right place, and I'm starting to believe you're doing this for the right reasons. I just…" She sighed and pulled Amber's head against her shoulder. "I worry you'll get out there and find a life that's better than what's waiting for you back here in Alameda. I couldn't blame you if you did…but I hope you won't."

"Joy, if I knew something like that would happen, I'd never leave. What I have with you is all I could ever want. But I can't go through life worried about *you* finding someone better. I want to be that someone."

"You will be. Heck, you already are. You've come so far in just the last few months that I can't even imagine who you'll be once you get the navy in you."

"I'll still be yours, Joy. That's all you need to know."

LIBERTY CALL

Joy inched forward in the line, wishing she'd sprung for a larger rental car than a Toyota Yaris, since her hat kept brushing against the headliner. Though she'd arrived before six a.m., there were at least fifty cars in front of her and by now more than a hundred behind. When she finally reached the gate she braced for the cold, damp wind and rolled the window down to present the DD Form 214 that proved her military service, her driver's license and the required documentation for her vehicle.

The seaman's apprentice studied her paperwork, returned them and snapped to a smart salute. "Chief Shepard."

She returned the greeting and drove toward the parking structure smiling. Her enlisted rank hadn't required a formal salute but she appreciated the courtesy, recalling one of the navy's favorite mottos: *If it moves, salute it; if it doesn't move, pick it up; if you can't pick it up, paint it.*

Never in a million years would Joy have guessed she'd find herself back at Naval Station Great Lakes. Given Madison's new fascination with the navy, there might even be another visit in the distant future.

When she entered the cavernous hall where the boot camp graduation ceremony would be held, she was taken back to a day almost fourteen years ago when she'd marched in with her division, swelling with pride to know her mother and father were upstairs in the gallery not far from where she now stood. It was exhilarating to understand the emotions that had gripped them back then.

The pomp of the drum line and flag bearers whipped up the crowd with patriotic gusto as they waited for the graduates to appear. Then the massive bay door opened to reveal the first of eight divisions marching in place, dressed in service blues with outer garments slung over their arms. One after another, they entered the hall in formation.

Joy spotted Amber in the third group, on the second row behind the seaman carrying the Battle "E" flag, which signified outstanding achievement by their division. Her curly blond hair, shorter by more than six inches, barely peeked out from the back of her cap. When her group took its position on the floor, Joy changed seats so she could snap a few photos from directly in front.

Exuberant families cheered from the bleachers, but none could have been more proud of their sailor than Joy. In a matter of months, Amber had left behind an aimless life of dependency on others to become a capable woman with purpose. By late afternoon she would be off to Texas to start coveted training as a hospital corpsman, a job dedicated to helping others that would serve her throughout her military career and beyond.

After more than an hour of marching, drumming, singing and speaking, the Pass-In-Review concluded with the announcement everyone had been waiting for: *Liberty call, liberty call!*

Joy hurried downstairs and pushed through the throng of celebrants to find Amber, who was extending congratulations to others in her division. "Hey, sailor."

Amber's face lit up in a wide smile as she dashed into Joy's arms. "I did it. I actually did it."

"I never doubted you. Once you made up your mind, I knew you would. You're too stubborn not to finish."

Joy was almost overcome with emotion, not only in her pride for Amber, but also for the fact that they could stand here entwined in front of everyone without oppression and fear of consequences. Amber could never appreciate that the way Joy did, this freedom to be with the person you loved.

"I'm so freaking proud of you, I could burst."

"You're not the only one," Amber said, her eyes clouding with tears. "This is the first time in my life I ever accomplished anything where they had a ceremony to celebrate it. And I owe every bit of it to a kind soul who picked me up on the side of the road and said this one might be worth saving. I love you with all my heart and I always will."

"You don't owe me anything for this. You're the one who made the commitment and then you came here and earned it all on your own."

"Maybe so, but it always helped me to know there was somebody out there who cared. Every time it got too hard, or when I didn't feel like studying anymore…I thought of how good it would feel to make you proud."

"You sure did." Now it was Joy's turn to fight back tears.

As jubilant families around them hammed it up for photos, Joy took one at arm's length of the two of them. Then Amber returned with her division to their "ship," the ship-like barracks where they bunked. Thirty minutes later she was at the gate, where Joy waved her over to the Toyota.

"I have to be back at two o'clock because we're flying out this afternoon. Tomorrow starts fourteen weeks of A-school. I probably won't get liberty again for at least a month."

"Working for an airline has its perks, you know. All I need is a day's notice." Joy opened the passenger door for Amber. "So we have four hours, and I happen to have a room at a sleazy motel about a half hour from here."

"What did you have in mind? My liberty rules clearly state that I must remain in uniform at all times."

Joy closed the door and walked around to her side of the car, chuckling as she got in. "I think what they meant was if you wear anything at all it has to be a uniform."

Amber fingered the crease in Joy's slacks, letting her hand dip between her legs. "As long as you have plenty of hangers. If there's one thing I won't tolerate, it's wrinkles."

Indeed, when they reached the motel room, both of them meticulously hung their uniforms in the closet before coming together in a heated embrace. As they fell onto the cool sheets of their queen-sized bed, Joy gripped Amber's shoulder. "Wow, look at these muscles. All that in just eight weeks."

"Eight weeks without a cigarette too, I might add," she answered, running her hands over Joy's hips.

"Mmm…let me see how that tastes." Joy covered her mouth and thrust her tongue gently inside. This feeling—the sensuous exchange of their bodies—was warm and familiar, an affirmation of the love she and Amber had promised would endure no matter how long they were separated.

But everything else about Amber had changed—her body, her hair, and most of all, her attitude. There was new pride and confidence in her demeanor, the kind that came from having proven herself against grueling challenges. No longer a damsel in distress, she had grown into exactly the sort of person Joy wanted alongside her when responsibility truly mattered.

"I've missed you so much," Amber murmured, guiding Joy's hand to her warm center. "I need to feel you inside me."

Joy reveled in the softness of Amber's wet heat as they slid together in a climbing tempo. Unable to resist, she lowered her face to the source and followed Amber's body signals to situate herself so they could savor one another simultaneously. Slowing the movements of her lips, she allowed herself to be brought to near-climax before shifting her focus to push Amber over the edge.

It was a full minute before Amber resumed her motions, taking advantage of her position to use both her mouth and fingers to pleasure Joy inside and out. Joy's instinct had been to tease another climax from Amber, but she was rapidly losing concentration. It took all her self-control not to cry out through the motel's thin walls when her body erupted.

"You have no idea how wonderful that feels," Amber panted.

"Oh, I think I do." She snuggled close and pulled the covers to their chins. "I had no idea how much I needed you until you left. These last eight weeks went by like a year."

"Tell me about it. I'd lie awake some nights wondering what all of you were up to. It was hard not being able to call but the worst part's over...I hope."

"You're going to love A-school, Amber. There's a ton of information coming at you all at once, but it's fascinating. Just stick with it and you'll do great. We're all standing behind you... except Pop, of course. He's sitting behind you eating Goobers." She chuckled. "Like I said, I can fly down to San Antonio on a day's notice. I'm sure they have luxurious motels just like this one near the base."

"Then what, Joy?" Her voice was tinged with anxiety. "How in the world are we going to manage to have a relationship if I'm out to sea for six months? I thought I could handle it but I'll go crazy if I don't see you for that long."

"No, you won't." Joy propped a couple of pillows and sat up, nestling Amber beneath her arm. "In the first place, you'll be so busy when you're out to sea that you won't have all that much time to miss me. And I can try to show up in port whenever you get liberty, whether that's in Hawaii, Key West or San Diego. That's the way military life is for thousands of couples, but most of the other girlfriends don't have the luxury of working for an airline. We'll manage."

"But what if I get stationed permanently on the other side of the country, like Norfolk or Jacksonville? That could be for two or three years."

"We talked about this, remember? I can put in for a transfer with StarWest. That's the navy way too. Pop will be just fine, especially now that he's spending so much time with Barbara. You just have to be sure you're ready for both Madison and me.

She can be quite a handful sometimes, but that whole incident with the gun settled her down a lot."

"She's had a tough road. I was a handful too but I turned out okay…eventually. I'm sure I'll be ready for her."

Joy believed her.

In the four weeks between the time she enlisted and when she reported to Great Lakes, Amber and Madison had grown closer, overcoming their rivalry as Amber turned her focus to qualifying for hospital corps and girding herself for boot camp. She'd been right to insist on allowing Madison to go to the Gus Holley concert, since it earned her thousands of "cool" points and strengthened their friendship. It wasn't exactly parenting, but it showed surprising wisdom and concern, enough that Joy was sure they could be happy together as a family.

"Don't worry about what's ahead, Amber. It's all going to work out. Just focus on what you have to do now and get through it. We'll be waiting for you when you're finished."

Her lips only inches from Joy's nipple, Amber planted an unexpected kiss. "Who would have thought getting tossed off a bus in Louisville, Kentucky, would turn out to be the best thing that ever happened to me?"

Joy guided Amber's mouth back to her breast and readied her body for another round of lovemaking. Only two more hours of liberty but a lifetime of moments like these. "And the best thing for me too," she said.

Dedication

I am deeply grateful to my readers who have served their country in the armed forces, and to your loved ones for their support and sacrifice. This book is for all of you.

Bella Books, Inc.

Women. Books. Even Better Together.

P.O. Box 10543
Tallahassee, FL 32302

Phone: 800-729-4992
www.bellabooks.com